THOSE HEARTLESS BOYS

SAINT CLARY'S UNIVERSITY
BOOK ONE

By

E. M. MOORE

Manufactured in the United States of America
First Edition October 2020

Edited by Heather Long

Cover by 2nd Life Designs

Huge thanks to my beta readers: Bibi, Ashton, Lisa, Jorden, Summer, Jennifer, Angie, and Julia!

Saint Clary's University

Those Heartless Boys

The Heights Crew Series

Uppercut Princess

Arm Candy Warrior

Beautiful Soldier

Knockout Queen

The Ballers of Rockport High Series

Game On

Foul Line

At the Buzzer

Rockstars of Hollywood Hill

Rock On

Spring Hill Blue Series

Free Fall

Catch Me

Her Alien Scouts Series

Kain Encounters

Kain Seduction

Rise of the Morphlings Series

Of Blood and Twisted Roots

Safe Haven Academy Series

A Sky So Dark

A Dawn So Quiet

Chronicles of Cas Series

Reawakened

Hidden

Power

Severed

Rogue

The Adams' Witch Series

Bound In Blood

Cursed In Love

Witchy Librarian Cozy Mystery Series

Wicked Witchcraft

One Wicked Sister

Wicked Cool

Wicked Wiccans

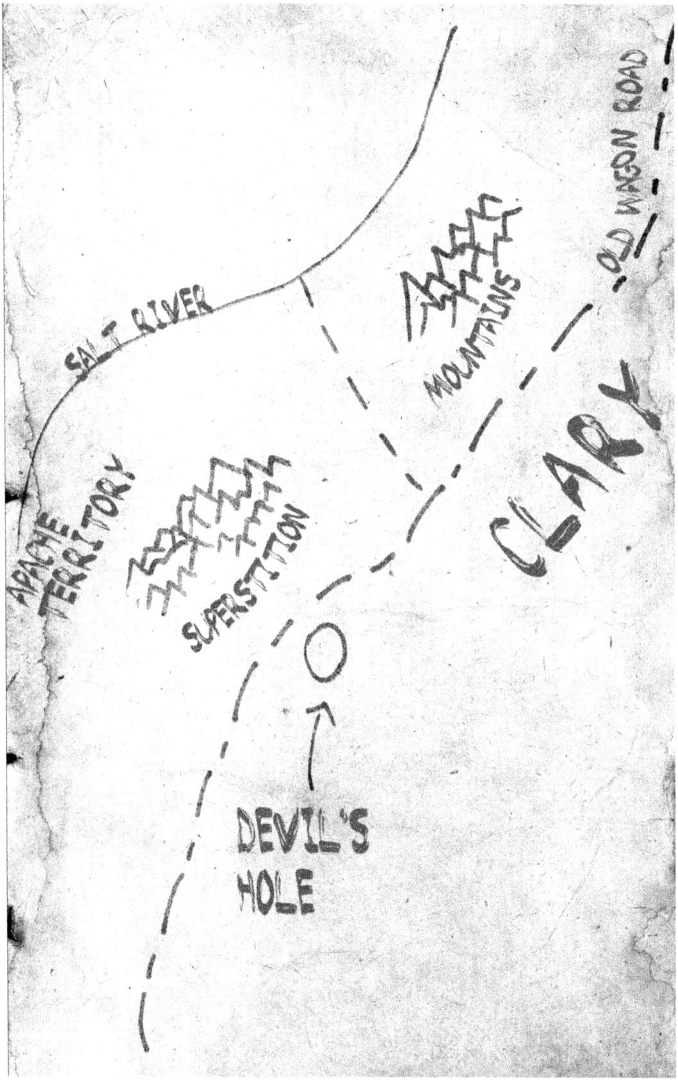
SALT RIVER
APACHE TERRITORY
SUPERSTITION
MOUNTAINS
OLD WAGON ROAD
CLARK
DEVIL'S HOLE

*P*eople say when you're drawn to the Superstitions, it's only a matter of time before something bad happens.

Volcanic activity formed the mountain range centuries ago. Comprised of layers of breccia and granite and melded together with lava, these rocks are as unforgiving as they are beautiful. It's like God made a jagged fortress out of the skyline and spray painted it in rusty reds and browns.

Most people don't venture up here. For generations, my family hasn't been *most people*. Our paths are off the beaten track. The road less traveled by. Filled with dreams, adventure, and hope. Some would call it a fool's hope, but I've never felt that.

Not until today.

"Do you understand what I'm saying, Dakota?" Lionel asks. He just happens to be Clary's Chief of Police and the head of the rescue team who've been searching these mountains for my father for the past three days.

Missing. It sounds damn near impossible. Wrong in every sense of the word. No one knows these mountains better than my father. Everything he knew, he learned from his father and his grandfather who learned it from his father and so on until he passed all that knowledge onto me. We're Wilders, after all. Searcher royalty, if there was such a thing. We're not the   go-up-into-the-mountains-and-don't-come-back type.

"Dakota?" Lionel asks, urging a response out of me.

It's funny if you think about it. My dad says Lionel is a good-for-nothing, immature novice who wouldn't know his ass from a hole in the ground, and now he's taken point on searching for my father? It's laughable, really. Though, my father's thoughts on the Chief of Police are most likely skewed on account of everyone in Clary hating us. If we saw the chief's cruiser coming up the dirt road, it was never for anything good.

I gaze up into the chief's light eyes. There are barely any crow's feet maturing his features. If wisdom is determined by the number of wrinkles on someone's face, Lionel would be a dumbass and my father would be an Einstein-level genius. "I hear what you're saying," I tell him calmly, even though my insides are roiling.

Our little tête-à-tête is hidden behind a temporary, pop-up canopy tent, ground zero for the search party that committed to finding my father after he didn't return from the mountains four days ago. Blue tarps stretch along one side and hang from ceiling to ground, shielding the interior of the tent from the sun, and right now, they're also blocking us from the prying eyes of the media waiting on the other side. Trust me, when a renowned treasure hunter goes missing, people take notice. Reporters from local TV channels and papers have been showing up for days. One guy even said he was from The Arizona Republic. We're big time if Phoenix's largest newspaper is on the trail of my father's disappearance, which also means that *this* story will be everywhere in a few hours.

"I know this is tough."

He wouldn't know anything, actually. I still don't believe it. My dad, lost in the Superstitions? Dead, possibly?

Nah. It's just not true.

I joined the search party myself, of course. I took them to the places we used to set up camp. I followed the trail I last knew he was on, volunteers fanning off, using sticks to move the sparse desert vegetation out of the way to cover every inch of space. Helicopters and their constant noise overhead were the anthem to our fight.

Nothing. Not one single find in three days. Now, Lionel wants to call off the search. *We can't look forever*, he'd just said. *At some point, someone has to make the decision that he didn't make it. If he's injured and can't move, he'll starve to death. Or, he may have met with a venomous snake or a fall he couldn't recover from.*

The truth is, there are hundreds of ways to die up in the Superstitions, and not all of them are natural.

So, yes, I get what Lionel is saying. We haven't found any trace of Dad. We didn't even find remnants of his camp. There's no evidence whatsoever that Dad was even in the mountains, except from what he told me and the fact that his ancient truck was parked at the trailhead we always parked at when we went searching.

I turn to gaze upward toward the rough terrain of the mountainside. In the distance, Weavers Needle pokes out of the landscape, a distinct spire of rock that sticks out like a beacon, always calling, calling, calling.

My stomach churns. Today, my family's legacy feels more like a curse.

"Do you—?"

"No," I say, cutting him off. I don't want to do *anything* right now, but if he's about to ask me if I want to be the one to stand in front of all of those reporters and call off the search for my dad, he's fucking crazy. I'll *never* call off the search for my dad. Not until his dead body is in my arms. Not until I see it with my own eyes.

"That's fine," Lionel says, lips pulling down on his wrinkle-free face. "I'll just go out there and give everyone the news." He hikes up his jeans with soft hands around his belt buckle, acting more important than he is. "We did all we could, Dakota. You know how dangerous those mountains are."

It doesn't seem like we did all we could. If we did all we could, we'd know where Dad is.

Except, I've seen the skeletons up in the mountains. Plenty of them. Visitors go missing every year, never to be found again. The Superstitions are dangerous. But the idea that they took out my dad? No. My mind rebels against that thought. Dad was no beginner. He's one of the most sought-after Superstition treasure hunters and trail guides around. He grew up among these rocks. He knows them better than anyone.

Lionel places his hand on my shoulder briefly and then parts the tarps to walk back into the tent. Everyone's still milling around, not just the media but the volunteer searchers, too. They're expecting the announcement that's about to come, so I don't know why it's such a shock to me. At each step of the process, I thought it couldn't get any worse. When Dad didn't come home, I went searching myself. When I couldn't find a trace, I contacted Lionel. Then, there were the volunteers and the attention and the planning and the questions. When everyone showed up to help, I thought we'd find Dad that day. I thought that every day since, too. Even today. Right up until this very moment.

I don't know why I was so short-sighted. Every day we can't find him is a nail in his coffin.

Lionel's voice booms over a sudden influx of questions, and I jump. Once I get my bearings, I walk around the edge of the tent, staying to the side and out of view. Lionel asks for silence like he's giving some sort of press conference, which I guess, in reality, he is.

Look at that, Dad. The Wilders are finally making the news. Just not in the way we wanted.

I skim the crowd, watching over the eager-eyed reporters. I can't blame them. Nothing big ever happens in Clary, and one person's pain is another's entertainment. Everyone will want to know what happened to Clark Wilder, "Superstition Mountain Treasure Hunter of Almost Forty Years."

While Lionel is giving what sounds like a well-practiced speech, the hair on my neck stands. My dad always told me to listen to my intuition. *Intuition has helped us Wilders more times than we'd like to admit* is one of his favorite sayings.

The feeling continues as I roam my gaze over the crowd, searching for the source. It takes me three passes, but eventually, my stare collides with Stone Jacobs.

My stomach bottoms out as his blue-gray eyes sear into mine. As usual, his face is impassive, unreadable, and he's flanked by his friends who might as well be his brothers. Wyatt and Lucas are so far up the Jacobs's ass, it's not funny. I was surprised when they showed up to help search. The Wilder and Jacobs families haven't gotten along in a century. Not since the Jacobs started searching for the Wilder treasure. Our mutual hatred has been ingrained ever since, and stoked like a fire every chance our two families get.

I narrow my gaze at their tiny group. No doubt those three assholes are gloating right now. The Wilders just lost their patriarch—literally—and while searching for the treasure no less. In their minds, that puts them a step above us.

Not on my fucking watch.

Two years ago, Lance, Stone's father, threatened to kill Dad for stealing his wife. No joke. Death threats, fights, and underhanded dealings are all a part of our families' mutual past. Dad couldn't help it if Marilyn preferred a Wilder, though, right? I mean, who wouldn't?

Sarcasm aside, I wish Dad wouldn't have made Stone my stepbrother. That's some disgusting shit right there. Sure, steal her away, but don't marry her. Fuck. Even now, I hate that I'm connected to him. Hate that there's more than just family feuds tying us together.

However it happened, though, Dad got the girl. Whether I hate the bitch or not, it felt damn good to have taken something from someone who has stolen so much from us. A smirk parts my lips as a memory of Lance showing up at our door comes to mind. I'd never seen someone so irate. So out of his mind with jealousy and anger. We can't compete with the Jacobs' money, but I guess money isn't everything, is it?

Stone and I still haven't looked away from each other, so I stand witness to his brows pulling in at my sudden smile. That boy doesn't miss a thing. Always watching and calculating to the point of being creepy.

He sets my teeth on edge, skin prickling under his scrutiny.

Well, he'll just have to wonder what's going on inside my head. Lord knows I'm never sure. But one thing I do know with certainty, whether Dad's here or not, things won't change on this front. The Wilders and the Jacobs are destined to be enemies, and that means I'm on my own.

I turn and walk away, leaving the media circus and the prying eyes of the Jacobs family behind me. The least I can do is tell the evil stepmother that they're calling off the search before she finds out from the news—or worse, from Stone.

I grip my hiking bag straps and take off down the trail toward the truck. The Superstitions might be behind me right now, but I'll be back. When everyone else returns to their normal lives, I'll be up on the trails.

I have two things to search for now. The treasure *and* my dad. Neither one is going to stay lost forever.

1

Two Months Later...

Finding shit in my father's house is like looking for gold in the Superstition Mountains. No wonder my family has never been able to accomplish either task.

"Paperwork, paperwork," I mumble to myself as I sift through the disarray of books and journals in his study. To think this is only a miniscule portion of his stash. The War Room is something else altogether. I glance at the ticking, old-time clock on the wall. "Shit."

Being late is nothing new for me because if it wasn't about the family business, it wasn't important. However, since Pops went missing, acclimating into the real world has been a priority, even if I have failed at it so damn epically.

I turn and run right into an open drawer. A slew of curses spit from my mouth as I rub away the pain in my hip. With more force than necessary, I slam the drawer closed, listening to the contents inside get thrown backward into the wood. If my father were still around, he'd be asking me what in the *Sam hell* I'm doing in here. Sam hell was one of his favorite phrases. To this day, I still don't know what it means. Anyway, he's not here, so I quickly shake that thought away. Dwelling on things was never a Wilder forte.

Apparently, finding receipts and work orders for my father's ancient truck isn't either. They're about as elusive as searching for treasure. I make my way out of the study, pausing in the hallway. My father's old room is to my left. The raw wood walls that make up the house quickly dig the roots of a bygone life into me, tangling around my ankles and making me just stop and think. Just for a moment.

A moment is too much.

I take a deep breath and start forward. I don't have time to search for the paperwork, not if I want to make it to my first class on time. Somehow, though, I get sucked out into the garage. Beside the camping gear and the prospecting pans, shelves of rusty tools on decaying work benches decorate the century-old building. I scan the area, all the while my head telling me I need to leave or I'll be subjected to everyone turning and looking as I make my way into my first class at Saint Clary's this semester, History 201. It's okay. The professor wouldn't know his ass from a hole in the ground. I lost all respect for him when he thought he was going to talk about the history of Clary back in 101. Please. The guy is a dumbass. I know more about Clary in my pinky finger than he does in his whole body.

My gaze gets hung up on the corners of white papers sticking out of a copper-colored toolbox. You'd think my father was a hoarder, but that's not the whole truth. He's just really passionate about a few areas of his life. Cleaning and filing important papers are not among them.

My "Shit, you're going to be really late," internal alarm goes off. Without even looking at what the papers are, I pull them out of the box, shake them off, and avoid the cloud of dust that poofs up as I run back into the house to shut and lock the front door.

My shoes kick up the dirt of the front walkway. By the time I get to my bike, it's covered in a thin layer of sand. I've lived on the outskirts of Clary, Arizona my whole life. I know about dust and heat and desert.

Trust me. I shove the paperwork into my book bag, throw it over my shoulder, and then pull my bike upright from where I left it in a heap a few feet away from the front door of my childhood home. I give the rustic exterior a quick glance before I ride back into town.

The familiar sorrow hits me, but at the same time, I know I made the right decision. I can live out in the desert as a hermit like my father—or even worse than my father because at least he had me—or I can live in the dorms at Saint Clary's and actually try to have a life other than weekend excursions into the Superstitions searching for my father and our family's legacy.

I chose the latter because...well, I'm not sure it needs any explanation. One is a life, the other isn't. Every day my father remains missing is cracking my resolve a little further. Lately, I've been wondering if I'm ever going to find him at all.

The barren roadway into town is littered with a few prickly cacti, lots and lots of brown, and the occasional rambling shed that masquerades as a home. Ahead of me, the town of Clary opens up, backdropped by the jagged, burnt copper tint of breccia that makes up the Superstitions. It's the same kind of mountain faces that are famous in the *Visit Arizona* brochures, but this isn't a tourist destination for me.

I've lived here my whole life. I've lived and breathed the dry air. I know the ranges like the back of my hand, like my family before me. The only thing I don't know also happens to be my family's greatest shame.

The wind picks up. A storm cloud rolls in from the west because of-fucking-course it would choose to rain on the first day of school when I'm late and don't have the family truck. We don't get much rain here, and because of that, whenever we do, it's never good timing.

I pedal faster. I swear I can almost see the ornate ironwork of Saint Clary's front gate as I come around the bend in the road that goes from no signs of life to life. It's like some pimpled teenager decided to put a village here in a game of Minecraft, except it isn't that at all. As with other towns near the mountains, Clary originated because of the gold rush. They needed a home base to venture out from, and soon, once the mining veins were found, they started bringing back the gold that built Clary to what it is today. Don't be fooled. It's not some thriving metropolis. In fact, it's only slightly more populated than a ghost town, but it's claim to fame is my family treasure.

You'd think that would make me popular some-how. A local celebrity, perhaps. Wrong. My family is pretty much the punchline of all Clary jokes. We're the town's outcasts. The laughingstock of generations of Clary residents.

With the wrought iron in sight, I slow my bike. Just as I'm about to make the turn onto campus, a silver Audi screeches past me, its brakes slamming to make the turn. As if by some cosmic joke, the clouds darken at the same time, turning the whole scene into a horror movie. Before the first tentative splat of a raindrop falls, a deluge of water hits me square in the chest, followed by cackling laughter.

I blink. My wet shirt clings to me, and I come to a wavering stop against the brick pillar that holds Saint Clary's gates, scraping my knee against the rough surface. I narrowly avoid the water bottle turned weapon that's tossed back at me, but the laughter that follows haunts me. The bangs on the car door sound like tribal war drums, calling out the fact that they think they're top shit and I'm nothing.

Typical Clary bullshit.

It's easy to target my family. I get it. Never any money, but dreams as big as the world. My father was a recluse at best, but he was a damn good man. Me? I'm not, nor was I ever, like the normal girls in school. I don't wear makeup or dresses. I'm more apt to show up in dusty overalls without my hair brushed. Not my fault. I have corkscrew curls. As a kid, my father gave up when mornings turned into a never-ending battle of wills, and I was winning. Now, I'm better at taming my hair, but it still seems to always look wild instead of polished.

I glare at the brake lights of the Audi as it hangs a left into the school parking lot, still driving entirely too fast. It could be anybody, so chasing after it while I'm on two wheels to give them a piece of my mind isn't happening. Plus, I'm just so fucking tired of it all. The more I fight back, the worse it gets.

As soon as I push off the brick, the fact that the bottled water got me first doesn't matter. I don't make it in time to miss the rain. For a moment, I'm barraged by raindrops, soaking straight through to my skin. I ride my bike to the rack, taking my time to lock it up because there's no use in trying to avoid getting wet now. It already looks like I've taken a shower in my clothes and headed to school afterward.

I slip the lock on and walk toward the main doors. Oddly, Saint Clary's is as gothic as this old west town gets. It's probably not even considered as true gothic architecture, but when your whole life looks like a western movie, something even a little out of the ordinary is going to stick out.

Honestly, I love the place. It's just...different. And I like different. It takes me away.

By the time I climb the stone steps to the main entrance, the rain has already stopped, and the sun is once again out in full force. My soggy, wet shoes make a slurp sound as I cross over the marble tile of the foyer. I pause a moment to look in the glass that leads into the administration offices to catch my reflection. The desert climate has never helped my curly hair, but the fact that it just got pummeled with rain is about to make it a thousand times worse.

My shoulders deflate as the frizz is already out of control. I pull the hair tie I always have on my wrist around my hair, piling the curls at the top of my head like a wild top knot. I keep moving down the hall when the Admin door opens right in front of me, and I have to skid to a stop before I faceplant right into it.

The university secretary noses her way out, looking both directions down the hallway with a frown. It isn't until I come out from around the door to step around her that she pulls back, her hand over her heart. "Miss Wilder." She breathes out a sigh. "I thought I saw you there."

I give her a smile, thinking about how she almost maimed me with the door. Well, of course I'm right here.

"This came for you in the mail." She hands a stark, white envelope to me like it's gold bars on a platter.

"We weren't sure what it was, but we thought maybe..." She trails off on purpose.

I don't even bother looking at the return address. If she thinks it's about my dad's disappearance, she's wrong. I tear it from her grip, pull my book bag around, and stuff it in the front pocket. "Thanks," I say with probably too much sarcasm.

She doesn't call me out for being rude, she just tells me to have a nice day as I make my way down the hall in wet shoes. Is there anything worse than wet shoes? I'm announcing where I am with every step I take. The back of my neck heats. At least there aren't many students in the hall right now, but as soon as I walk into History, that will change. You'd think I'd be used to being gawked at as one half of the town crazies, but it's been a whole different story since my dad went missing. Now, I'm the only crazy, and there's something very lonely about that.

Despite my father always telling me that normal is boring, normalcy sounds like icing on the cake right now. Normal people don't have to worry about the piling up of bills and the stepmother who ran away with what money there was and the—

I turn the knob to open the door into History class where a familiar figure stands at the front. His gray-blue eyes dart to me, and a wicked grin spreads his perfect, bow-tie lips. He finishes talking while holding my gaze. A few people notice where his attention is, and they turn toward me. Snickering erupts. My fellow students start making snide comments, hiding their lips with their hands as if that will stop the law of sound and somehow keep me from hearing their petty words. Even more, however, go back to staring at Stone fucking Jacobs. After all, I'll always be the weird girl, but Stone? Standing at the front of class like he's top shit, Stone is a one-percenter. One of the most drop-dead gorgeous guys I've ever laid eyes on. Too bad he's also one of the biggest jackasses I've ever had the displeasure to meet. He knows it too. So, when it comes to who the world places their attention on, it's Stone one hundred percent of the time. Not me.

It only takes a moment to figure out what the scene before me means. The book bag slung over his shoulder. The forest green polo paired with his dressy jeans. The dumbass professor standing just off to his side, smiling and nodding.

Motherfucking shit. Stone Jacobs is in my History class. He's transferred...here?

"What the fuck?"

The adoring gazes and snide remarks turn into jaw drops and unrestrained gasps. I have the whole attention of the room now as I stare at one part of my family's archenemies. He crosses his arms in front of his chest as he stares me down, but the stare isn't a normal one of mutual hatred and disrespect amongst those who dislike each other. It never was. His is one of complete distaste, like he could wipe me from this earth and not care one iota.

That's Stone Jacobs for you, and I'm completely fucked.

2

"*D*akota!" Mr. Burns chastises.

His rebuke barely registers. Stone's steady smirk and bright eyes stay on me as the titters of my classmates chirp like surround sound. He holds my gaze until he takes a seat near the front. *My* seat, to be exact. I always sit in the front. He places his bag next to him and slowly unpacks it like he has all the time in the world. A pen. A notebook. A piece of chewing gum. All the while, I can't stop staring.

"Jesus, Blue's Clues. Sit your ass down. You're embarrassing yourself."

I shift, looking straight into the eyes of Meghan Tanner. Mean girl extraordinaire, who happens to look like she doesn't belong anywhere near Clary. Maybe on Rodeo Drive in California. Or Broadway in New

York City. Not near these parts where everything looks dead, and if it's not dead, it's deadly.

Her eyes widen as she takes in my still unmoving body. She lowers her voice. "Get a clue, Dakota. You're trash." She sneers at my soaking wet outfit like she's just realized I'm standing here soaked straight through to my skin. The air conditioner kicks on behind me, and goosebumps skitter over my suddenly chilled body. It has to be the sudden appearance of Stone that I'm responding to. Out in the mountains, we're even. I like to think I top him even. In the real world, though, I might as well be the shit on the underside of Stone's shoes.

A boy behind Meghan, who's always trying to flirt with her, looks up. He does a double-take, stare plastered to my chest. "Damn, Blue's Clues, I'll take some of those nips." He sticks his tongue out, furiously flicking the air in short strokes.

Meghan slaps his arm. "Please. You'll get a disease or something."

Though he stops tonguing the air, he still ogles my chest when Meghan turns back around. I grab hold of my book bag straps and carefully maneuver my hands to hide my erect nipples. It's the fucking air conditioner's fault, dammit, but when I finally glance away, Stone catches my eye again. He's glaring at me with narrowed eyes and a chiseled chin. He holds my gaze, not looking away this time either. Everything is a contest with him. I look away first when the professor speaks from the front again, "Miss Wilder, I see you plan on disrupting the entire class. Either take a seat or see your way out."

Embarrassment rushes through me in a tidal wave of heat, and my breasts definitely stop nipping now. I turn and slop my way to the back row. Mr. Burns just stares at me incredulously, the suctioning of my wet shoes offending him until I finally plant my ass on a chair.

Class goes by in a blur. I stare at the back of Stone's perfectly coiffed blond hair, questions racing through my mind. Taking center stage is wondering why the fuck he's back in Clary. He has no reason to be here. His mom packed up and left hours before the news came that there was no trace of my father. She was already gone when I made it back to the house after the press conference, not even bothering to say goodbye. I don't know where she moved to, but she took every-thing with her. The money in the accounts—what little of it there was, anyway. She pillaged the house for valuables, even. The only thing she left me was the truck and Dad's house. And who knows if I even have that.

As I stare at Stone, my hatred for him and his whole family grows brighter and brighter until I'm a sitting inferno. I'm surprised my classmates sitting around me haven't felt my fire yet. I loathe Stone Jacobs with everything in me. I hate his father, his mother, and his entire family tree. Losing my father has only made it worse because while I'm just barely getting by, the Jacobs are thriving. They have their money and their fancy jobs and their fancy treks up into the mountain while I've been venturing out by myself week after week, searching with no luck.

At the end of class, Meghan saunters up to Stone's desk, leaning over to put her hand on his shoulder. He gazes at her with those discerning, twinkling eyes that are practically made of diamonds. I've seen diamonds in their natural state, and trust me, they match Stone Jacobs in every way. Cutting and beautiful.

Meghan turns her head to stare at me, giving me a small smirk that says she knows she's about to get something that I want. That's the fate of all Wilders, isn't it? Never getting what they truly want. I hate to break it to her though. She can have Stone Jacobs. I couldn't care less. I don't want to be within five feet of my step-brother.

Instead of stooping to her level, I give her a smile of my own, grab my bag, and try to leave the class with more dignity than when I entered, which honestly, is easy to do, considering the mess I brought in with me.

I can't believe Stone fucking Jacobs is here, I keep telling myself. I simultaneously want to confront him and pretend he's a walking case of COVID-19. Keep my fucking distance, that's what I should do. Nothing good ever came from getting too close to a member of the Jacobs family.

How dare he enroll in Saint Clary's though. He knows I go here, and last I heard, he and his friends were attending Arizona State. Even if he wanted to transfer, aren't there a lot of colleges in Phoenix that are probably ten times better than this one? Lord knows he can afford to go to a more expensive school. Saint Clary's is the cheapest college in all of Arizona. I know that for a fact because that's why I go here.

I'm so lost in my own thoughts, I don't see the towering body in front of me when I step out of the classroom. I run straight into a chest and bounce back. The first thing I see is the brim of a black cowboy hat. When he lifts his head, though, the face comes into view. In that instant, I can't fathom how this day could get even worse. "Lookie here, Lucas. It's our friend Dakota."

Cowboy wannabe and Stone's best friend, Wyatt Longhorn, slings his arm around Stone's other best friend, Lucas Govern. A cold chill runs through me as they lift their gazes over my head to greet someone behind me. My back heats, and I just know Stone is right there within touching distance. I scamper out of the way like I'm a mouse and they're feral barn cats. If Meghan is a mean girl, Stone, Wyatt, and Lucas are her counterparts in every way. They're mean boys.

Wyatt laughs, the sound dark and rich, sliding into my crevices. Lucas, as usual, says nothing, preferring to observe instead. His brown hair in disarray and with a complete look of disinterest that turns mocking sometimes. He's like a stray off the street. Always aware and skittish. Doesn't say much but knows the territory far better than anyone else.

I glance over my shoulder to find Stone introducing Meghan to the duo that make up Stone's best friends who are more like his family. She looks like she died and went to hot boy heaven. In her defense, Clary doesn't have much in the way of selection. Our high school had a total of one hundred and fifty students, which has only marginally increased at Saint Clary's. I can't blame outside people for not wanting to come here. The big cities might be relatively close by, but in the meantime, there's nothing to do here. Clary is for simple people, and I can't help but wonder why the fuck that brought Stone and his little crew here.

For the rest of the day, I simultaneously try and fail not to notice Stone, Wyatt, and Lucas wherever they go. I guess that's the curse of a small campus. I share several classes with each of them, and unfortunately, we eat in the cafeteria at the same time where I watch Meghan and all her cheerleader friends from high school get all up in the new guys' business.

I knew this would happen if the Jacobs ever made Clary their permanent residence, which was why I was always so grateful they only showed up during the summers, and even when they did, they were so focused on the treasure that they never did anything else. I knew they'd flock to him like vultures. As pretty as he is—and Wyatt and Lucas—they're going to be the talk of the town for a while now. They'll be a prick in my skin. A thorn in my side. It'll be like rubbing against a cactus every few minutes. I used to only get that pleasure during the summer, but it seems like fate has more in store for me than just taking away my father.

By the time my last class ends, I'm jonesing to leave campus. That *never* happens. Saint Clary's is a respite for me, kind of like the books I love to read. It's a place I don't have to worry about money, thanks to the full scholarship they gifted me, and a place where I can conform to the crowd as much as possible. Just another average college student supposedly living off ramen noodles and Chef Boyardee. I've talked myself into believing that, in class, we're all equal. I was just fooling myself the entire time though, blatantly looking away from the cliques that still exist from two years ago when we crossed the graduation stage. Nothing's changed.

Well, the only thing that's changed is the fact that Dad used to be the only person who got me. Now, there's no one.

The good thing about leaving Saint Clary's today though is that I'm a lot drier than when I walked in. The blazing sun coats me in heat, and the dry air makes me take in a deep breath. I make my way down to the bike rack and pause. No bikes. Not a single one. If my math is correct, there should be at least one bike parked here: mine.

My hands fall to my sides. Having my hair up all day has given me a splitting headache, and I just don't have time for this shit. A stolen bike? Who the fuck would want to steal that rusty piece of junk? I'm pretty sure it was my grandfather's and squeaks the whole time I've been riding it.

"Oh, Blue's Clues," a sickeningly sweet voice calls out from behind me.

I turn to find Meghan standing next to Stone. Her arm lies loosely around his waist, as comfortable as can be. Jealousy spits fire inside me, matching the temperature of the desert heat. If I was a dragon, I could probably roast them right now. Roast the whole damn school, including Wyatt and Lucas who hang back behind the new power couple of Saint Clary's. That can't be right, though. It's only been a couple of hours and already, Stone has something I've never been able to accomplish in Clary: Friends.

Their high school nickname for me burns like acid in my ears. My greatest enemies now know the truth. Dakota Wilder is a nobody, and she will always be a nobody. That's my family's true legacy. We may be good at one thing, but we fail at everything else.

This is not what I needed today.

"Missing something?" Meghan asks, a cruel tilt to her lips.

If I hadn't already given up on Clary residents, I'd slap the smirk right off her face. How dare she.

The thing is, she can't hide from me as much as I can't hide from her. I know the only person who really loved her, her grandma, died two years ago in the trailer they live in outside of town. Her mother's a drunk, has been ever since her husband ran off with her sister and moved to Sedona where they can be the artsy, spiritual people they claim themselves to be.

So, if you're wondering what I'm getting at, it's that I'm the better person. But that only goes so far.

Meghan takes a piece of paper from Stone's fingers, wads it up, and throws it at me. It bounces off my chest and hits the ground. She sneers at it. "If I were you, I wouldn't lose that if you want to see your bike again." The way she says bike sounds as if she has a limo waiting for her when I know damn well she's driving a shitty Ford Focus with an engine that barely starts.

I don't lower myself to pick up the paper in front of the growing crowd. I don't want them to see how weak I truly feel in this moment. Not only are Stone, Wyatt, and Lucas here, they're apparently here to make me more miserable than I already am, enlisting the help of the people who've tortured me my entire life. Awesome. If I would've known today was going to hold this, I would've stayed in my dorm room.

The crowd disperses after Wyatt gives me a wink and Lucas looks past me like I'm not even a blip on his horizon. Both reactions dig their claws into me, leaving scars behind. When the loud engines and coughing mufflers leave the parking lot, I finally bend over to retrieve the paper. I unfold it, using the metal piping of the bike rack to smooth out the wrinkles.

I glare at what's in front of me. It's a map, crudely drawn to reflect a treasure map, including a big X. I can only assume that's where my bike is, and their digs just keep getting bolder and bolder. Yes, of course the girl from the famous treasure-hunting family of Clary would need directions to her stolen bike in treasure map form. That's the thing about the Wilders though. We're big treasure hunters, we're not big treasure finders.

If my bike isn't where this X is, I swear to God... Yeah, I'll probably do nothing, but the movie playing in my head where I gouge out Meghan's eyes is good enough for me. The boys? Well, I haven't quite figured out their punishment yet, but Meghan holds her looks close to her heart. I'd definitely go for uglying her up a bit.

I trek back into the school and find the janitor. I tell him my predicament, pointing toward the map which, according to the stark lines and offensively drawn land-marks, my bike should be on the roof of the school.

The janitor tears the map away from me, tells me to stay put, and then goes in search. Five minutes later, he curses as he tries to maneuver the bike through the stairwell exit at the far end of the hall. The heavy door closes on his fingers while he holds the handlebars, and a slew of insults pollutes the air. When he emerges, I hurry from my spot, profusely thanking him as I grab the rusted-out bike and start walking out of the school.

"Take care of your stuff!" he yells after me.

Yes, of course. I'll definitely do that because I certainly asked them to steal my bike, hide it, and then leave me a map to find where it was.

The tires bang against the front stone steps as I lead it down. As soon as I hit flat cement, I throw my leg over and start to pedal when something doesn't feel right. I frown down at it, and as soon as I see the tires my shoulders sag. Bastards let the air out. My throat gets scratchy, but I haven't cried since my father went missing, so I'm not going to waste them on Stone and his cronies. I get back off the bike and point it toward Dickie's garage. Hell, I was headed there anyway. I might as well add fixing a bike to the bill I already can't pay.

When I turn the corner of the short street to head down Prospector Boulevard, the glint of silver catches my eye. By the time I turn, all I see is the back end of a silver car, rolling in the opposite direction.

---

3

*I*t takes me a lot longer than I wanted to get to Dickie's in the afternoon heat. I stop off at a tiny grocery store to sip from the fountain that I know is near the bathrooms just to cool off for a bit before heading back out into the blazing sun. By the time I make it to Dickie's Garage, literally the last building before there's nothing, I'm drenched in sweat and breathing heavy.

"Hello?" I call out. There's no telling where Dickie could be. Under a car, inside a car, in the office. Ever since he had a heart attack one day when a customer snuck up on him, I've called out to him when I first arrive. And by the way, when I say "snuck up on", I literally just mean he entered the garage like a normal person asking if his car was finished being serviced.

What can I say? Dickie's old.

He also happens to be my father's best friend and former partner.

The smell of grease and stale cigarette smoke hits me as soon as I walk in farther. The clank of metal on metal of a tool fitting around a part clinks before wheels rolling on concrete sound. "Over here," he calls out.

I walk around a white Dodge Caravan that's up on lifts and peek around a tan sedan that Dickie's just now rolled out from under. He narrows his gaze when he sees me, and as soon as he recognizes my face, he smiles. He's missing a few teeth in the front, and he's about as aged as aged can be. He's lived a hard life of manual labor and then didn't treat himself any better on top of that with the cigarettes and alcohol, even though he damn well knows he shouldn't be smoking anymore with his heart the way it is.

He stands up slowly, taking his time as his knees creak, belying his age. "Dakota, there you are." He limps over to me, brushing a stubbly kiss to the top of my head. He has grease stains across his cheeks and hands. The rag he uses to wipe it off only smears the brown-black over his skin because there's enough grease already on the ratty old piece of cloth that he could probably cover his whole body with it.

My stomach tightens. Dickie's one of the OG's of Clary. He owned the only garage in town for many years before NAPA came in twenty miles away. Like my father, Dickie spent any spare minute he could in the Superstitions with a pick axe and a dream. He and my father worked together for years until Dickie had his heart attack and couldn't actually go out searching anymore. To me, Dickie is one of the last true blue treasure hunters. When he goes, who's going to send the tourists on a wild goose chase through the unforgiving terrain?

Yeah, I know. We're fucked up around here, but someone from Clary deserves to find the gold. Not a damn outsider, and certainly not the fucking Jacobs.

I squeeze my eyes shut as soon as I recognize my father's words flit through my brain. It's harder not knowing what happened to him.

"How's my sweetheart doing?"

I groan. "My bike's fucked. I tried to find paperwork on the truck, and I'm..." I gaze up at him warily. "...hoping you have good news."

Dickie presses his lips together. His salt and pepper stubble sticks out like prickers on a cactus. His skin is about as weathered as it can get, almost like dirty leather. Creases and wrinkles dot the landscape of his face like tumbleweeds through the desert. That's what years of baking in the sun and thinking you're above sunscreen gets you. The old man clicks his tongue as he lowers himself to a grease-stained stool. He leans against a workbench and breathes in. His breath catches, bringing on a coughing fit that lasts about thirty seconds.

I go to the corner and grab a bottle of water out of a dirty fridge in the back. "Dickie," I say, trying not to sound chastising. "You know you've got to give the nicotine up."

He gives me that look that says, *Little girl, I'm about three times your age and need your life advice like I need a cactus spine up my ass.*

He doesn't say it though. He just takes the water from me, downs half of it, and then plops the bottle down on the workbench. "You should get yourself one of these, Dakota. You look like you walked yourself here from Texas."

"Ha. Ha." But I'm not about to pass up that offer. I'm thirsty as hell. I grab myself a water and then wave him out to my bike that I leaned against the side of his garage when I first got here. Outside, in the full rays of the sun, Dickie looks even worse. The shadows tend to hide a bit of weathering, but not out here under a spotlight. I'm seriously worried for him. His skin is too ashy gray.

He cocks his head, then uses his grease rag to wipe the sweat from his neck, but only manages to smear grease on the one area that didn't have any yet. He whistles. "What did you do?"

I grind my teeth together. Not at Dickie. At the assholes who thought it would be funny to hide my bike on the roof of the school and let out the air in the tires. Privileged people don't understand what a big thing having your own transportation can be, even if it is only two wheels. "Just tell me you have good news on the truck." I worry over my lip as I wait for his answer. A couple of days ago, the truck wouldn't start, so I had Dickie tow it here. I know he'll give me a fair price, but what I really don't want to hear is that my father's ancient truck can't be salvaged. There's zero chance of me affording a new ride right now.

Dickie presses his lips together again, and I know it can't be good news. I slip one of my book bag straps off and bring my bag around to the front. When I was avoiding the Stone, Wyatt, and Lucas show in the cafeteria, I finally had a chance to look at the paperwork I'd stuffed in that morning and believe it or not, I found a receipt from Dickie's that's a few years old. I don't know what I'm trying to do with it. I'm just grasping at straws.

I scan the paperwork again. "It looks like you fixed the muffler a few years back."

Dickie peeks at me. His eyes have a dull shine to them, and not a good one. Almost like I can see the cataracts taking his vision away right before my eyes. The look he gives me tells me everything I need to know. You ever just have someone older look at you like you're a little kid? That's when I know I'm being naïve, and worse, he feels bad for me because of it.

"Fuck," I sigh.

"Sorry, kid."

"What is it then?" I ask tentatively. Dickie's the best mechanic I know, but you know, maybe someone else could do something. Not that I could afford to pay them either.

"It's the engine, Dakota." He shuffles toward another bay in the garage, and I follow after him. He smacks the side of my father's old truck a few times, and I swear some of the rust falls to the garage floor like confetti. "Seeing as how it's a classic, it's gonna cost you more than it's worth."

To Dickie, every car older than this millennia is a classic. My father's truck is a 1979 Ford. Yes, it's old as shit, but it's not the kind of car you're going to see at a classic car show or anything. I have no doubt he's right though.

I lean against one of the wood beams spaced throughout the garage and sigh. What the fuck am I going to do now? Sure, riding the bike is okay, but I thought it was only temporary.

"Talk to me, Dakota. What's going on with *the bitch?*"

The bitch is none other than my stepmother, Marilyn. The one my father had to have. At times, I thought it was more about getting something a Jacobs had, and I'm probably not too far off. Normally, I'd laugh, but she ended up fucking me over, so I'm not in a laughing mood.

I shrug. "She cleaned out the accounts. Dad has a life insurance policy, but it's not worth much. The insurance company won't release the money because he's still listed as missing and not—" I can't even say the words. You ever think something is probably true, but you just can't believe it. Saying it would be believing it, and I'm not ready. "If the life insurance ever decides to pay out, I don't know if I would get it anyway. *She's* married to him, and if my father had a will, I can't find it."

"I oughtta track her down and whip that money out of her until she's spitting quarters."

Can't say I disagree with the sentiment. I can add Stone's name to his list. If he's taking hit orders, it

40

would be a shame to leave his name off. Coming to Saint Clary's feels like a direct attack. I just don't know what game he's playing. With the Wilders and the Jacobs, it's always something though.

Dickie takes his hat off, scratches his balding head, then puts it back on. "About the only thing I can do is junk it and give you the money. It won't be much, but it'll be something. I'll also put air in your bike tires and keep a look out for a cheap car."

I hold out my hand, and he puts his blistered fingers in mine. "That's more than enough," I tell him. I'm not Dickie's charity case nor would I ever want to be. His wife died many years ago, and as soon as his kids were old enough, they got the fuck out of Clary. I used to blame them, but I don't anymore. From what I can tell, Clary is a dead end where all the stragglers end up. I want more for me than that. I always have. That's where the treasure dream came in, but without my father... I have no idea if that's even a possibility anymore.

"Hear anything from Lionel?"

I kick the cracked concrete at my feet. The last I heard from the Chief of Police was at the press conference, but Dickie asks me every time he sees me in case something's changed. "Not lately," I say, almost refusing to believe that I'm truly in this search by myself. Dickie would help if he could, but he can't, and everyone else seems to have forgotten. Or never really cared in the first place.

"I knew that kid never could figure out his ass from a hole in the ground." I smile because I've heard this conversation more than a few times between my father and Dickie, and it never once changed. Lionel is a good-for-nothing.

I guess I'm just racking up the list of people Dickie's going to go ape shit on. Good. I could use someone on my side.

When Dad didn't come back, Dickie swore he was going to go out after him, but everyone told him to stay put, including me. He feels guilty because he thinks he could've found him, and he's probably right. No one knows the Superstitions like my dad and Dickie with me a few steps behind. "Can't argue with you there."

Dickie rubs his face. His tell that he's itching for a cigarette. "You know, if you need anything—"

"I know, Dickie," I say to cut him off. Asking Dickie for help would be like trying to get blood from a stone. There's just none of it to be had here.

Apparently, he's had about enough of the sentimental shit as I have. He moves away from the truck and goes back outside to grab my bike. He pulls it into a bay in front of the air compressor. It starts with a whine, and I watch as he fixes the hose to my tire. Thankfully, it starts to inflate. Dickie checks the tire pressure. "It's holding air," he calls out like we're at a rock concert instead of standing right next to each other in the confines of a garage. Even with the air compressor going, I flinch a little at how loud he is. He really is going deaf.

"That's great," I yell. I shout my response as loud as he did because otherwise, he won't know I've said anything.

That's something, I think as Dickie inflates my back tire. They could have ruined my bike altogether, but at least they just let the air out. I'm not saying those assholes deserve a humanitarian award, but I am saying they could have dropped it off the three-story roof, instead of just leaving it up there with no air.

I clench my jaw as I think about their smug as fuck faces handing over that map. Whatever they're trying to accomplish by coming to Clary, I can't let them get to me. Not now. Not ever.

4

---

*A*t least I have my bike when I make my way back into town after sharing a spaghetti dinner with Dickie. He's always been good to me, but he's definitely stepped up since Dad went missing. Even if my father couldn't find treasure, at least he found good friends. Well, one good friend. Let's not go crazy. His other relationships were an epic disaster. My mother died when I was young. Clary old-timers whisper that the desert killed her. As a woman from Minnesota, she hated the heat, she hated the barren landscape, and if you ask one of them, she hated my father, too.

I don't know. I don't put much stock in what some of these people say.

Now, what they say about Marilyn *is* true. She's a

gold-thieving bitch. Too proper for Clary. Too stuck-up for my dad. And if she didn't have a giant backhoe up her ass, I'm not sure why she always walked around straighter than a compass needle pointing north.

Instead of leaving my bike in front of the dorms like I usually do, I drag it up the wooden staircase and right inside my front door. Saint Clary's dorms are actually just an old west motel turned into college living. It's a long building, stretched out almost an entire block in length. The walkways to the exterior dorm room doors hover over a gulch that gurgles with rain water when it actually does rain. Every other day, it's just a dried-up ravine riddled with stones. Just past the hotel, there's a curve in Old Gulch Road that leads to the college.

Years ago, Saint Clary's didn't have dorms. The campus was just too small, but then the Johnsons, the owners of this old hotel, fell on hard times. They kept the motel alive for as long as they could, but once a Motel Six opened up a quarter of an hour away, no one wanted to stay at the Clary Inn, whether they were treasure hunting or not. It needed a remodel two decades ago, and the Google reviews left it with barely a single reservation throughout the summer months. A crazy occurrence considering the number of tourists we get that time of year, all of them with gold bars in their eyes. I guess the call of the new single-serve Keurig's in the Motel Six was just too much for the outsiders to turn down.

When the Johnsons put the motel up for sale, the community reached out to the college to purchase it. The last thing we needed was another building that sat unused and seeing as how Clary's higher education institution is pretty much the only business in Clary that makes money besides the gas stations and saloons, they were the only hope. Thankfully, they took pity on us and bought it, putting very little money into the building to transform it into dorm rooms. The dorms are full despite the fact that most students are locals. I don't know where the farthest commuter lives this year, but last year, it was only forty-five minutes away. We're the smallest campus of any Arizona college, but we're also the cheapest, and as my dad always said, sometimes you just can't pass up a deal.

I lean my bike against the closet door. She's safe and sound in here. I highly doubt the Jacobs' golden boys would set foot in these dingy dorms let alone stay in one of them.

And there it is again, a reminder rearing its ugly head that the one thing the Jacobs always had that we didn't was money. When you're treasure hunting, that can mean a world of difference. Treasure hunting isn't cheap. The supplies alone can get expensive, and that's not even counting the time off of work—if you're lucky enough to have a regular job. However, there's one thing that we Wilders have—an important thing—that they don't: Information. And as they say, information is king.

When I decided to go to Saint Clary's, I felt bad for taking up a room at the dorms since the commute is basically nonexistent, but I excused myself the fuck out of the house when Marilyn moved in. My dad thought it was because I wasn't used to having another woman around, but really it was because Stone's mother thought she was too good for us. Too good for the house my great-grandfather built. Too good for our surroundings. Maybe most of all, too good for my dad. I don't argue with my father, though, and Marilyn made him happy, so I took myself out of the equation.

I grab some water from the tap and settle down on the couch with my book bag, hoping I took good notes while distracted about who had shown up to ruin the only good thing in my life right now. To me, college has always been a necessity. A foundation that would lead me to being one of the only members of my family to get a real job. That didn't mean I was giving up on treasure hunting. Not at all. But I hated being the butt of jokes around town. For once, the Wilders were going to be something.

I take out my textbooks and spread them out over the rustic coffee table my dad made with two-by-fours and push my bag over the edge of the couch. When I glance down, a corner of an envelope sticks out of the front pocket. Oh shit. I'd forgotten about the letter the school secretary handed me.

I know she thinks it's about my dad. I've heard the rumors around town. People know Marilyn left me with nothing. Whether that's Dickie's doing, I'm not sure. The secretary probably thinks this is some super secret life insurance payout or something. The problem is, he'd have to be declared dead to get any sort of payout. Right now, he's not.

My vision blurs as I knock the letter onto the floor and pull my British Lit textbook onto my lap. Hopefully, the old English text of Beowulf can keep my mind occupied. I cross my legs in front of myself and settle down for a night of reading when there's a knock on my door.

I lift my gaze, eyeing the white door with the peephole and the old, slide chain lock. No one's visited me at my dorm before except for Pops. Goosebumps skitter over my skin, but then another wailing knock comes on the door, accompanied by "Dakota, open the door!"

I'd know that gruff growl anywhere. The kind that makes you feel inferior just by its tenor. I grit my jaw. *Is he fucking serious? Now he's coming to my dorm?* "Two words, asshole. Fuck off."

There's a pause on the other side. I smile triumphantly.

My smile is short-lived. A pompous laugh erupts from the other side. "Little Dakota, growing some ovaries. I like it."

I glare at the door as if I can see right through it to Stone's pretty face. If looks could kill... I'm just saying, he'd be maimed right now, and he probably wouldn't be laughing it up.

"Open up," he says again. "We need to talk."

"We need to talk like I need a hole in the head, Stone."

"Aww, come on. We're family, right?" His voice carries through the door, and I wonder how many people can hear us. We're talking about a motel that was made in the early 1900s. Soundproofing wasn't a thing. Embarrassment crawls all over me. We'd already gathered a crowd outside of the school when they hid my bike. Tomorrow, this conversation could replace that in the rumor mill.

I push all of those worries aside and laugh, my stomach twisting at the word family. I don't let the grief overtake me though. Not in front of this pompous prick. The day I show him my raw emotions is the day I'm packing it in. I don't even dignify his question with an answer.

He lowers his voice. "It's about the treasure."

I smirk. When is it not about the treasure? *Everything* is about the treasure. "Then I'm not sure why you're coming to me."

"Just open the fucking door."

I pretend like I'm thinking for a moment even though he can't see me. "Um, no. Go away before I call the police."

It's his turn to laugh. "Lionel? He wouldn't know his ass from a hole in the ground."

I roll my eyes. Is that literally everyone's damn opinion? Maybe Clary should get on that and think about replacing him.

When I don't answer, Stone knocks again. This time, the sound makes me jump, like his huge fists are testing the sturdiness of the old construction. Newsflash: It won't be good for my door. I already see it bowing under his strength.

"If you don't open up, I'll make your life a living fucking hell."

"In case you've been sleepwalking over the past few months, I'm already there. So, you can just fuck right off, Jacobs. I have nothing to say to you or your friends or your father."

A few metallic clicks sound and the door springs open. I toss my English text off my lap and jump to my feet while the threesome stride in, each one wearing heavy, dark gazes that would shrivel others. Don't get me wrong, they are equal parts menacing...and sexy. I hate to admit it, considering our families' past, but Stone is a fucking god dropped into the middle of nowhere. His gray-blue eyes are as cold as the Arctic but make me heat in places that shouldn't considering who he is.

Wyatt and Lucas flank him, each of them with their own signature sexiness. Lucas looks as if he just woke up twenty-four-seven. His hair askew, ruffled, but in that put together way that I don't understand how guys can pull off. Wyatt? He wears a cowboy hat everywhere. If you've never seen him up close, you might not understand what this does to a girl, but holy fucking shit, that low brim, just disguising his piercing blue eyes sends goosebumps skating over me, the edge like a razor blade.

I come out from around the coffee table and stand in front of them. I'm not about to let anyone with the last name Jacobs—or their friends—intimidate me. I'll just look up sexy cowboys for my spank bank later, but Wyatt won't be it. That's for sure.

"Aww, look," Wyatt says. "Little Dakota is pissed we broke into her dorm."

Stone moves closer, edging me back in my effort not to touch him. I hit the wall and his chest hovers in front of mine, his palms flattening on the wall behind my head.

Fuuuuck. This is new. I've never been this close to Stone Jacobs before. I'm used to slinging insults from a distance. Even that one time when we almost got into a fight over the perfect spot to set up camp while we were in the mountains, I didn't get this close. Dad ended up talking to the guys they hired to help them find the treasure, and we set up camp next to each other, neither one of the parties backing down.

Yeah, that's right. The Jacobs hire people to help them find the treasure. I don't even think Lance has ever been in the mountains. That's what he has Stone for, I guess. Letting him do all the dirty work while he gets to sit up in his tower in the city, demanding regular updates from behind a desk. No, Stone is more like his grandfather. His grandfather got down and dirty with the rest of us. My father didn't like him, but at least he respected him.

There's no chance of that with Lance.

"Do you rich fuckers understand the meaning of personal space?" I set my palms on his chest and shove. I briefly, very briefly, enjoy the tight muscles of his pecs before reality sinks in. Not only is Stone a dick of epic proportions, he's also still considered my stepbrother. By law, I guess, though I've never felt that way. He's no one to me.

"We do," Wyatt says. "We just don't give a fuck."

Lucas stays silent, his hands jammed into his pockets as if all this bores him. He may have a warmer eye color than Stone—a deep brown, the color of mahogany—but they're as disinterested as can be. His eyes are like a trap, ones you think you can get lost in, but once you're there, you realize you've just ridiculously fucked yourself, and now there's no getting out of the spider's web.

I turn back to Stone who's gazing at me with a smirk, his perfectly chiseled arms crossed over his chest. I look away, mentally admonishing myself for thinking anything about him is perfect. His whole family are snakes, silently slithering in the background. We've found them trailing us up the mountain countless times, trying to get on our trail.

That's where the whole feud started. The Wilders have been searching for our treasure since it went missing. The Jacobs are new, but they burst onto the scene with their money, and even though they don't know shit, their names started getting plastered all over the paper about the next big treasure hunters who weren't going to let the gold be lost forever. For some reason, that story is more palatable to the public. *A rich family who uses their resources to search for more riches.* Kind of cliché if you ask me.

I peek at Lucas who's standing next to my bike, running his hands across the handlebars. "What do you guys want?"

"You know what we want," Stone says, an edge returning to his voice. When I quirk my head toward him, he's staring daggers at Lucas.

I sigh, really not liking all these mind games. "No, I don't. I guess you're going to have to enlighten the naive, small-town girl. You can't possibly be looking for my dad because well...he's not around. Your mom, too. Haven't seen her." I sneer. "Have you? Or did she leave you, too, when she fled?"

This time when Stone gets in my face, it's not sexy at all. His face is a mask of fury, chilling me to my bones. "Don't you ever—"

I push right back. "What? Talk about your bitchy mother? Talk about how she stole from me when she left town? How she didn't even wait to find out whether we found him, she just up and left like a true Jacobs. Cowardly motherfuckers."

Stone roars in my face. With more bravado than I feel, I cross my arms, hopefully masquerading as someone who doesn't give a shit.

I used to have all the confidence in the world when our families faced each other. It's hard now that I don't have backup. Without my father here, I have to fake all of my bravado. The truth is, I have no idea what I'm doing. My mask begs to slip, but I won't let it. I'm going to find my dad, and then we're going to find the treasure. It's the Wilder destiny. The Jacobs are just flies that just won't stop circling.

"Come on, man. Let's just do what we came here to do," Lucas chastises, gripping Stone's shoulder. It feels good that I got to Stone. He's always so perfectly put together, but right now, he looks anything but.

Wyatt ambles forward with a sigh, letting us know what he thinks of all of this. He tears a white envelope out of Stone's back pocket and shoves it at me. "Lance wants to work out a deal."

I turn around, dismissing them and heading back to the couch. "Not interested."

It's not like this is the first time someone has tried to buy my family out of what we know. Just because my dad's gone doesn't mean this story is going to turn out any differently.

"It's more than generous," Stone says, finally getting himself under control. I can't help that a thrill shoots through me to know that I got under his skin.

I shrug. "I'm not for sale," I say, smiling.

Each of them give me disgusted looks. "We don't want you."

I laugh to myself. Typical reaction. I haul my Lit book back into my lap. "But let me guess, you want what the Wilders have? The legend? The stories? Hate to break it to you, but—" I pull up my book, showing it off. "It's not written down in nice, neat little journals with asterisks around what to look for." I smile broadly. "It's in me, so yes, in essence, if you want what we have, you want me, and that's never going to fucking happen."

Stone's gaze narrows, as if he's trying to figure out if I'm being serious. Oh, yes. I'm being fucking serious. Why would we ever write down something that important? If something happens to me, the clues go with me. That was done with purpose. The clues were for my family and my family only. We were the only ones who were supposed to have found the treasure, and we're keeping it that way.

"If that's the way you want it," Stone says.

Lucas is the first to leave my dorm. He leaves the door open, just begging for Wyatt and Stone to follow suit. Thankfully, Wyatt leaves shortly after, shaking his head. Stone leaves only a few seconds after that, leaving the door wide open so I have to get up and lock it myself.

Assholes.

Afterward, no matter how much I try to concentrate on my coursework, a gnawing feeling eats at me. My intuition tells me I just awakened a beast. I was afraid this might happen now that I'm alone. The assholes are going to come out thinking I'm weak and susceptible.

Just fucking let them. We'll see what happens.

5

*T*urns out I wasn't wrong.

Within an hour, the guys are back. This time, they don't knock on the door.

The stomping on the outside balcony alerts me first. I try to peer through the lacy curtains in the front room to see who the hell is making so much noise when my door flies open, catching on the chain lock that I put in place as soon as they left the last time.

From the crack between the frame and the door, a boot lands back on the ground with a hard thud.

My heart flies into my throat. *What the fuck?* I snicker outwardly though. Ha. They thought they were just going to come right in this time. Nope. Not going to—

A pair of bolt cutters sneaks into the gap, and the chain falls apart with a snip.

Fuck! I back up into the couch, my second-hand laptop falling to the floor. In steps Lance Jacobs. He's a well-dressed man my father's age, wearing a polo shirt and khakis in soft colors, almost like he just got off the golf course after playing eighteen holes. The look on his face, though, is thunderous. I've never met Lance Jacobs in person, but dollars to doughnuts, this is him. I recognize him from TV. Plus, he and Stone share the same blond hair, along with some of the other darker elements of their personalities.

"Miss Wilder, I presume?" He gazes around the room with distaste before settling his attention back on me.

I swallow. There's a solid ball of ice in my stomach about the same size that took out the Titanic. I lick my lips, my tongue darting out as I assess the situation. The boys have all entered the room, too. Lucas, looking bored as fuck, as usual. Wyatt, with his dark gaze on me. And Stone? He stands just to the left of his father, but a little back, his gray-blue eyes penetrating like liquid mercury. So fucking dangerous. I can feel it in the air, a tension thick around me, alerting me that we're not playing a normal game now.

These guys are serious.

All those thoughts I had earlier? The ones swimming to the surface that made my thighs weak? Yeah, they're definitely gone. These guys aren't the type to get mixed up with.

"I hear you won't look at my offer."

I scowl at him. "You have nothing I want," I tell him, shoving my fist into the air internally when my voice doesn't waver.

I shouldn't get too cocky though.

He tilts his head to the side, clearly telling me I'm about as full of shit as they come. "Don't think we're blind to your financial situation. You need us. Not just to find the treasure but to...I don't know, continue eating. You do want to continue eating, don't you, Miss Wilder?"

The nerve of him to break my door down and assume I'll give up my family's secrets to him of all people. That I can be bought out. I ball my hands to fists, praying I look as threatening as I feel on the inside. "I already told your son, I'm not fucking interested. Breaking down my door like you're some sort of badass—which is truly funny when I think about how much time you sit behind your desk—isn't going to win me over either."

His eyes flare, zeroing in on me. "I think you're

about to become really interested when you realize what we can do to you. Boys."

Just this one word, and my room erupts. Wyatt and Lucas spread out. Everything they touch gets smashed or ripped or broken under their heel. "Hey," I call out when Wyatt grabs my laptop off the floor. Stone's arms surround me, yanking me back to his solid chest. My half-written English paper is on that laptop. Wyatt throws it at Lance who catches it out of the air, nodding at the boy who continues to wreck my apartment.

I struggle to free myself from Stone's grip, but he's strong as fuck. I slam my foot down on his toes, and he growls in my ear, fingers digging into me. "Know your place."

Fury rises in me, making my neck and cheeks flush with an angry red hot heat. I watch a little longer as Lucas and Wyatt systematically go through my apartment. I narrow my gaze at them. They're not just trashing it for trashing sake, they're searching for something too. I laugh, the sound ruthless and harsh to my own ears. "What you're looking for isn't here."

There was a period when my grandfather was alive that everyone tried to "steal" what we knew. He had a number of break-ins and scary run-ins with people who meant him harm. I guess we're in that part of the treasure hunting process again. When no one found what they were looking for, that's when the town turned against us, calling us all kooks. Suddenly, we weren't these adventurers who were going to find a piece of missing American history, we were just crazies. Because they couldn't find it, they thought the whole treasure had been made up and followed by a bunch of ignorant nobody's.

"Your father had all the maps. The lore. He had everything he needed to find what's hidden. Now that he's dead, you have it."

I swallow, my throat about as prickly as a hundred cacti. "That's right, I do. And you're never going to get your hands on it."

"Give it to me!" Lance yells, his face akin to a devil mask on Halloween. He's furious, yes, but there's something else there, too. He's desperate. If he wasn't, he would've already pulled this shit on us

My fingers clench. "Fuck. Off."

Lance raises his hand, bringing it back to his ear like he's going to whip it forward to bitch slap me. My stomach bottoms out, but Stone swings me to the side, taking me just out of his father's reach. "Dad," he warns.

My heart catapults around in my chest. Dread slithers in with an icy fear. He was going to hit me.

This isn't just some fear tactic, he was going to take this to a whole different level until Stone called him to his senses.

Alright, that's enough.

I assess the situation, then shoot my arm forward to the weakest point of Stone's hold, the space between his fingers and thumb while they're wrapped around my arm. It doesn't hurt that he's still preoccupied with his father when I slam my elbow into his chest. He stumbles, falling onto my rustic coffee table and sliding off onto his back. He gets up with a growl, his shoulders heaving. His father laughs. "I guess she out schooled you."

The fire in Stone's eyes burns brighter at his father's comment. The destruction that's happening in my bedroom stops and out walks Wyatt and Lucas, the former fixing his cowboy hat to sit properly on his head once more. The slight shake of Lucas's head makes me certain they were looking for something, and no, they're not going to find it. I was telling them the truth before. The most important details I know about the Superstition Mountains are in my head. The rest of it is somewhere no one will ever find.

I reach out for my laptop, but Lance pulls it just out of reach. "Let's play a game. The game is called ruining the stupid girl who thinks she has options."

The amusement in his words sends a shudder through me. It's one thing to fight about the treasure, to have a competition about who's going to find it first, but this is a whole different matter altogether. I don't know why I'm surprised. The Jacobs have always been the shadows lurking. "Saint Clary's is everything to you right now. Am I right? It's the only thing you had besides the hunt and your dad, and you don't have those things anymore. I'm guessing it's even how you're eating." Lance drifts his gaze to the fridge where Lucas yanks it open, revealing its bare interior.

I swallow. The lack of food is something I've tried not to think about. There's just no money. I used what I had over the summer when I was still up in the mountains searching desperately for Dad when everyone else went home. I was relieved to go to school today because I knew I could eat. A banana sits in my bag right now that I took for dinner but didn't need to eat because Dickie fed me. "I'd have food if your whore of an ex hadn't taken off with our money."

Stone's gaze turns even more furious. He's molten heat, ready to burn everything in his path like lava.

I don't care.

Lance tsks and holds up his other hand. Lucas drops a manila folder into it that I hadn't even noticed he'd been holding. Lance feathers through the paperwork and then tosses it onto my British Lit textbook. "This is my offer. I suggest you look through it and get back to me."

"I don't need to look at it. My answer is no."

A tick in Lance's jaw starts. Stone peeks at him, then returns his gaze to me, his stare never wavering.

Lance, though, gets even more agitated. His hands turn to fists. Before I can open my mouth to tell him to get fucked again, the almost same gray-blue eyes his son has sear into me. No, actually, his aren't the same at all. They're darker. Like a living nightmare. "You think I can't make your life miserable if you don't do as I say?" He grins, composing himself. "You think your scholarship is safe at Saint Clary's?" The mirth in his eyes dances with unrestrained happiness while my life feels like it's on a high wire. "Oh no, Miss Wilder, it's not. You're looking at one of the new donors to the school. I reckon they'll do anything to keep their new funding." He nods toward the files on the coffee table. "You can be a winner. Or you can be a loser."

I let out a breath. I feel as if I've been knocked off my feet even though I'm still standing with the coffee table between me and them. It's like we've drawn sides in a war. I'm the opposition. I don't want to be on their side. I can't. It goes against everything I believe.

"If you don't do this, I'll ruin your whole life,

Dakota Wilder. Get back to me by tomorrow." He strides from the room, my prehistoric laptop dangling from his fingers. The guys follow him, but Lance tells Wyatt to hang back, winking at me. "We have to make sure our precious commodity is safe before she makes the right decision."

Wyatt closes the door behind his friends, admiring the splinters he put in the wood when he tried kicking it down. I can't hold myself up anymore, so I slide to the couch at my back. I've heard of a lot of shit that goes on with treasure hunting. Most of it is old stories. Betrayal. Greed. I know some of it from first-hand experience, but this takes the cake. The Jacobs are threatening me.

Fuck me. The only thing I have left is college and now they want to take that away?

"You look like someone kicked your puppy."

"Take this in the worst way you can possibly imagine," I say. "Fuck. Off."

I grab the manila folder and retreat to my bedroom. Slamming and locking the door behind me, I throw the contents of the folder on my bed. There's no use trying to get him to leave. It doesn't matter. He'll be as miserable as me here anyway. I run my hands over my curls. I'd taken my hair out of the hair tie after the guys left the first time to try to alleviate the pounding drums in my head, but they're back with a crescendo.

I'm almost scared to look at the contract. Even a peek is like backstabbing my family.

I stare up at the ceiling, closing my eyes tightly. "Seriously?" I say into thin air as hopelessness covers me like a shroud. Like it's not enough that my father went missing a couple of months ago, now some guy with a god complex thinks he can buy my family's legacy?

When two hundred million is on the line, people think with their pockets. My dad said that all the time. He wasn't immune to it either. He had associates who funded some of our trips up the mountain. He spent so much time researching that he didn't always have a steady paycheck, yet somehow, we always got by even if it was by a sliver. I can do the same. Pick up a job somewhere... Right. In an area that has one of the worst unemployment rates around?

I pick my way through the strewn clothes all over the floor and lie down on the newly unmade bed, propping my head up with my palm and moving the folder closer. Looking at this is siding with the devil. It might take care of my immediate problems, but it's like signing my soul away and putting it into a monster's hands.

6

———————

I dreamt of wading through inky black oil that grew thicker and thicker until it was almost sludge. Ahead of me, a full moon rose in the distance over a beautiful sandy beach. No matter how hard I tried to reach the shore, the molasses-like substance moved around me, keeping me in place until I was just spinning my wheels, drowning in sorrow and worry.

If I had balls, the Jacobs would have me by them. Lance knows it. Stone and his friends know it. Now, I know it, too. Play their game or risk my life, basically. Maybe not in the physical sense but what about everything else? You have to work for a good life. It's not just handed to you, especially for people like me. Lance knows that, and he's using it against me. It's a very real threat that I can't take lightly no matter how much I want to tell him to just go fuck himself.

After getting ready the next morning, I listen at my bedroom door for a moment to see if I can hear any signs of Wyatt before going out into the main room. I'd imagine he's still out there since Lance told him to stay and because the three boys will do anything he says. They always have.

I turn and pull the knob after silence greets me. The door opens with a slight creak. I tiptoe across the threadbare carpet, hoping I can just sneak out without Wyatt noticing. I need to meet with Dickie to see if he knows anything about Lance that I don't. Then, I need to go to school because as of right now, I still have a school to go to.

I get partway through the living room, the door in sight, when a short snore pulls my attention away from escaping. I glance over at the couch to find Wyatt lying across the cushions. He's only wearing his jeans, his black cowboy hat perched on his chest. In the early light of the morning, he doesn't look like the guy who kicked my door in yesterday and used bolt cutters to snip the lock.

Yep, still not over that invasion of space. Or the mess they left in here. Assholes.

I swallow as I glance at the dips and planes of his

abs. His naked torso peeks out from around the brim of his hat before dipping low, his jeans hiding everything south of his Adonis belt, that taper that makes women flutter their eyelashes. Heat consumes me as I wonder what it would be like to let this cowboy ride me until I remember he completely trashed my room yesterday. There's a fine line between lust and hate, and I need to remember which side I fall on.

This asshole is just going to sleep on my couch looking like he doesn't have a care in the world? No, no, no. That's not happening.

I stride toward the coffee table where a glass of tap water still sits half-full, unbelievably still there despite Stone tripping over it yesterday. I grip it in my hand, towering over Wyatt's still form. My body crackles with new energy. Vengeance, maybe. Just a little. Though, this will never make up for what they're doing to me.

I throw the tap water in his face.

He splutters awake, gasping for air. Eyes wild with an emotion that's akin to fear, he pulls himself to an almost sitting position before he narrows his gaze at me. "What the fuck, Dakota?" His eyes burn, dancing all over my body as my chest moves up and down sharply. Yes, I liked that very much. *Take that, asshole.*

I go to turn but Wyatt grabs my wrist. He gives it a

quick tug, spinning me and pulling me forward until I have no option but to fall onto him. He stealthily moves my legs to either side of his thighs, his hands on my lower back, keeping pressure there. My fingers land on his collar bone, tickling the edges of the slight indent of skin as he gazes up at me.

He licks a drop of water from his lips. "There's only one way I like to wake up wet."

My nipples peak. I've seriously just been transported into one of my fantasies. No, Wyatt isn't currently wearing his cowboy hat, but he has hat hair, you know? The kind that's flat against his head from wearing one. It's the promise of that cowboy hat that does it for me.

The water glistens on his chest, dripping from his angular jaw, down his rippled abs before wetting my shorts where we connect. If I'm not careful, I'm about to soak another article of my clothing, too. I push off him, jumping to my feet. He grins like he knows he got to me. Great. That's just what I need. My body to betray me.

I turn on my heel and go to the small kitchenette, placing the glass that's still in my hand on the countertop. Then, I get my bag together, pulling the strap out from underneath Wyatt's haphazardly placed bare feet, glowering at him the whole time for taking over my space unwanted.

He chuckles. "I would've had you pegged for a ray of sunshine in the morning. I didn't know you were prickly."

"It's the company," I bite out, trying not to look at my ruined dorm room. I don't want him to know how much what they did bothered me. I spent all night cleaning my room while thinking over the contract.

"You didn't seem to mind my company just now."

I grit my teeth. These guys know exactly the charms they have. I've seen them use it when we've crossed paths before. I've just never been on the receiving end of it because we keep our distance from each other.

When I don't lower myself to replying to his statement, Wyatt asks, "Did you look at Lance's contract?"

I barely contain a growl just thinking about it. It's evident Lance is one of those men who think they can buy their way into things. My family's centuries of research will buy me their word I can stay in school and a hefty sum of money.

The true cost of signing on the dotted line, though, is my pride and...my family's legacy. I can't forget that part.

But what does that matter when you're poor, right?

Money and college are necessities in my life right now. Without money, I won't be able to keep my family's house, or you know, eat. Without college, I can kiss my future goodbye. The decision seems inevitable even though I'm still trying to fight it.

My dad once said that the treasure was my family's Achilles heel. Maybe it's not. Maybe it's greed. If I had any self-respect, I'd walk away from Lance Jacobs' deal. I'd figure everything out on my own. Literally alone. And maybe that's why it seems like too much is on the line to refuse it.

Being poor is a stain upon your soul that if you've never been without, you couldn't possibly know how it feels.

Wyatt leans back on the couch, his glorious muscles in full view. I remember thinking it was rare to see someone his age so well-endowed, and I feel it now, too. Or maybe that's just my lack of experience and my small-town roots talking. Maybe there are guys like this everywhere else, just not in Clary.

He doesn't seem the least bit ashamed that he's sitting here in just low-slung jeans either. My cheeks flame. From an outsider's perspective, this probably looks like the morning after a one-night stand. The guy sitting there proudly while the girl is a mess of wondering what the guy thinks of her or if he'll even call her or remember her name. From the looks of the state of this room, it was some epic sex, even if that's not the case at all.

"Are you going to sign it?" he asks, eyebrows piqued.

"None of your business."

He grins. "I didn't think you'd be this feisty, Wilder. I like it." His gaze pours over me like aged wine. A confidence he shouldn't have oozes out of his every pore. My skin pricks in response. I've only had a couple of sexual experiences myself, and they were totally lacking in the sexy department. That's why I read books and have a generous imagination. After a couple of tries and fails, I figured I was better on my own. And I have been, but there's just something about Wyatt that makes me think he'd be so fucking great in bed that I wouldn't ever want to leave.

Which is exactly why I need to stay away.

I turn, heading for the door. "Where are you going?" Wyatt asks.

With my hand on the knob, I give him a smile. "Crazy."

Wyatt stands slowly, taking his time as if he's telling each muscle to move individually just to drive me insane. I turn the knob, hoping to move out of range, where the fact that he's standing shirtless in front of me doesn't matter. Hot boy immunity, that's what I need. Don't worry. His personality is doing wonders as an immunization.

He perches his hands on his muscular hips once he's in a standing position. His hat hair still flat against his scalp like it usually is. "I'd answer Lance as soon as possible if I were you. He doesn't like to be kept waiting. And whatever you think he's capable of, think ten times worse, Dakota."

A shiver of fear rattles down my spine, but I stick my chin in the air. They want to see my fear, but I'm not going to give it to them. Not now. Not ever. I whip the door open and cross over the threshold. Wyatt shouts after me, asking me where I'm going while yanking his shirt on. Getting my bike stops me momentarily since it's hard to maneuver through the narrow doorway, but I get myself and my bike out before he's even done putting his shoes on.

I start down the steps, the back tire thumping against each stair before I pull the bike out onto the road.

Wyatt runs out of my dorm after me, leaning over the wood banister that hovers over the gulch. "What the fuck, Dakota? I'm supposed to be watching you."

I ignore him as I take off, then realize I can do better than that and steer one-handed while giving him the one-finger salute. The last thing I need is to be "watched over". I've been taking care of myself from a very young age.

I shake my head, disbelief coursing through me. I pedal as hard as I can, heart thumping. I'm betting Wyatt will be hot on my heels in a minute or so. I have the advantage of knowing where I'm going, but Clary is so small, he could still find me just driving through the streets aimlessly.

The morning sun isn't as hot as the afternoon sun, but the clothes I threw on are still rimmed in sweat when Dickie's place comes into view. Relief floods me until I hear the roar of an engine behind me.

A quick glance over my shoulder, and I find Wyatt's stone-cold blue eyes focused on me as he whips around a corner, tires squealing as he fights for control through the turn. He narrows his gaze as he steps on the gas, headed straight for me. Icy fear and panic send warning bells through me. But he wouldn't hit me, would he? That's just crazy.

The closer he gets, though, I'm not so sure. The devil is in Wyatt Longhorn's eyes, and he's aimed them straight at me.

7

The faster I try to get away, the more the rickety bike starts to shake. The wheels vibrate, and if it wasn't for the roar of the engine, I'm sure I would hear the bike coming apart underneath me. I struggle to regain control over the piece of shit, but the bike slips off the pavement and into the gravel. I skid and over correct, and all of a sudden, I'm falling.

I throw my hand up to protect my face and my shoulder takes the brunt of the fall. Pebbles and sharp rocks tear my skin as I come to a grinding stop, my feet tangled up in the bike still.

I groan, kicking the bike off me. I move to my back and my eyes shutter from the sun. "Fuck," I hiss as I try to get to my feet. Pain shoots through my shoulder, and I cradle it to myself.

The squeal of brakes makes me shoot upright, my body protesting the whole time. A door slams, and Wyatt Longhorn comes out from around his truck. "Jesus, Dakota." His voice is void of any emotion.

His gaze drops to my shoulder, and it's then that I really feel it throbbing. I look and find blood trickling down my arm.

"Christ almighty," Dickie's gravelly old voice calls out.

My shoulders slump forward in relief. "Dickie."

He moves closer, his gaze widening when he's close enough to realize it's me on the ground in front of him. He has a shotgun in his hand because he's just that old school. When you're Dickie and a noise sounds that's loud enough for you to hear, you grab your gun before you investigate. It's practically law.

"What in the hell? You okay, sweetheart?"

I investigate the wound on my shoulder further. My shirt is dusty and the scrapes on my shoulder are enough to have blood dripping and pooling. I move my gaze to Wyatt who's leaning casually against his truck with his arms crossed like he had nothing to do with this.

I sigh. "I'm—"

Dickie moves his attention to Wyatt, interrupting my "I'm fine" response. "Who the hell are you?"

Wyatt steps forward, hand outstretched.

Dickie pulls his gun up to a shooting position, tucking his chin against the butt. "Where I'm from, when a girl falls on her bike, you run over to help her. Only assholes stay back. Are you an asshole, boy?"

Wyatt, who shot his hands in the air as soon as Dickie shoved the gun in his face, stares down the barrel. He swallows, but still has the gall to look almost unaffected, like he doesn't care if he lives or dies. Like staring down the length of that gun could be salvation for him instead of tragedy.

Dickie doesn't even give Wyatt a chance to respond. Not that he was going to anyway. "You know this asshole, Dakota?"

I pull myself to my feet, brushing my shorts off along with the small stones embedded in my knee. "Unfortunately, yes." I glance down at my bike. It's completely fucked now. The tire is bent. There's no just pumping air into it again to save it. I could legit cry. Between the fall, my shoulder, the bike, and not knowing what the hell Wyatt's true aim was, the ground underneath me doesn't seem as stable as it was before. I'm having my own personal earthquake. "Go away, Wyatt," I say, voice steady. I stand up straight, crossing my arms in front of myself. "You better leave before Dickie here gets trigger happy. His hands aren't as steady as they were. It might even be an accident."

"Or not," Dickie says.

For the first time since yesterday morning, I feel powerful. Wyatt shakes his head, a sneer curling his lip. "You're just delaying the inevitable."

"Fuck. Off."

"I suggest you do as she says, boy."

Wyatt mosies around the front of the truck before heaving himself inside. He glares at the two of us as the truck inches forward. I almost can't believe my eyes. A gun pulled on him, and he still acts like he has the upper hand. Just what in the world is fucking wrong with this kid? With all of them?

Dickie whistles as soon as Wyatt's vehicle is out of sight. "Kid's got balls. I'll give him that."

I take a step, testing my weight on the knee that slid over the dirt and gravel. It's sore but I don't think I did anything catastrophic to it.

Dickie looks me over. "You best come inside now. Let's get you cleaned up."

Once we're inside and Dickie puts his shotgun back in its resting place on the wall above his work-bench, I tell him what happened. I don't mention that I'm unsure if Wyatt was trying to hit me or not, but it really doesn't matter. He should've known I would freak out at him trailing me like that.

My stomach twists. Getting involved with Lance Jacobs and his little errand boys, is a terrible idea. Is it possible Wyatt *was* trying to hit me? My mind rejects the thought now that I'm not in the middle of it. Though, Lance was going to hit me yesterday. I'm sure of it. He would've if Stone hadn't stopped him, which tells me he, at least, might be okay with physical violence.

Dickie smacks his hand down on the stool next to his bench. I pull myself onto it as he hobbles over to the archaic First Aid Kit on top of the refrigerator. It's grease stained, and he has to blow the dust off before setting it down in front of me. This is not making me feel all that safe, but I trust Dickie.

His still nimble fingers open the box and rummage through what he has. He takes an alcohol pad and swipes it down my scuffs and scrapes. Next, he puts a sterile pad over the wound on my shoulder before applying some tape to hold it there. I glance over to find the tape and pad littered with smudges but I'm fairly certain the scrapes and the other side of the pad are free from dirt.

He packs up his kit. "Now that we've got that out

of the way, why don't you tell me why it looked like you were paler than Casper out there?"

I bite my lip. Dickie arches a brow at me when I don't immediately answer. I don't know how much to tell my dad's friend because I don't want him to be worried. Dickie has enough problems of his own, and I really don't want to become one more. "It's about the treasure," I finally say, trying to choose my words wisely.

Dickie immediately looks interested. He's a tried-and-true treasure believer. "How so?"

I blow out a breath. "That boy there was an associate of Lance Jacobs. They're offering me a pretty sum for my family's...information."

Dickie rubs his stubbly beard. The hairs are so coarse, they audibly scrape against his calloused palms as he muses on what I've just told him. Even Dickie doesn't know what we know. My dad and he were partners, but he never let him in on the most-trusted clues we had. That's how serious we are about it. "You know what I think about that, Dakota Wilder. No need looking to me for my opinion."

I close my eyes briefly. Dickie was always one hundred percent behind the lore that came with my family and searching for the treasure. He thinks it's a curse, and considering how things turned out, I might have to agree with him now. The only thing is, he thinks it's a curse we can win.

I'm not so sure about that.

Maybe the real curse is to have our family name ruined and impoverished and left to die with nothing to show for it. Dickie, though, likes the tales of old. He knows my family history about as well as I do, but instead of seeing a lost cause, he sees hope. He's just been waiting for me to announce that I'm going back out there looking for treasure instead of my dad because that's what Wilder's do.

He has more faith in me than I do.

"Your father never liked those Jacobs."

I nod, my mind forcing the images of Stone, Wyatt, and Lucas to the forefront. If I hand them over what I know, coupled with their thousands spent on high-tech tools, they might just find that treasure. A Jacobs. Not a Wilder. "There are a few here in town," I tell him. "They're watching me until I decide what to do." I busy myself by looking at the bandage on my shoulder. "I don't think they're going to give up. They don't seem the type."

"I don't need to tell you my thoughts," Dickie reiterates again. "If it weren't for my eyesight, I'd be out there looking for the gold myself."

It's more than just his eyesight that's off. It's his

balance, his old limbs, and his health. There's no way he'd be able to cross the rough terrain anymore. Plus, there's the liability factor. What if he had a heart attack up in the mountains? It could be a days' hike back. Or a helicopter ride, if you were in a place that could accommodate one. No, Dickie's treasure hunting days are long over. "I just don't know," I say.

"I know that your Pops wanted to find that treasure more than anything."

His words aren't meant to hurt, but they do all the same. There were too many times when I felt those words to be a simple fact. *...more than anything.* Meaning more important than me. More than his sanity. More than our well-being. Don't get me wrong, I loved my father, but obsessed is an understatement. It's lonely living with a recluse with a one-track mind. "Yeah, he sure did," I say on a sigh.

"The terms?"

"Generous," I admit, but leave out the gut-wrenching feeling that I'm giving up a lot. Sure, I'd be securing my future with college and a sum of money that means I won't have to worry about anything that comes up but putting myself in league with the Jacobs' just seems wrong...and possibly extremely dangerous.

"You know what it's like out there," Dickie says,

turning toward the opening of his bay garage. From where we are, you can just see the peak of one of the mountains. Even though I doubt Dickie can actually see it, his eyes glaze over like he can, like he's staring at a long-lost love just returned. "Sponsors hand money over like water just for a slice of the pie. We're the real winners. The adventurists. The researchers. The hunters. The boots on the ground to get shit done while they sit in their city high rises demanding updates. Cooped up in their steel cages, wishing they were like us."

I try to picture Lance Jacobs back in Phoenix, and that picture is so easy. The only thing I can't picture is the cage part. Nor the part where he actually cares that we're the ones putting our lives on the line to find the treasure. Guys like Lance Jacobs think they're entitled to the treasure because they can throw money at it. They don't understand the blood, sweat, and tears my family has put into finding it over generations. They think cash solves problems. And maybe it does. I've heard countless stories about backers and hunters actually finding their sought-after horde, both parting ways happily, living their lives like kings.

"Why did Pops think he was close?" I ask Dickie. I'm ashamed I don't know the answer to this question.

Marilyn created a gap between us a mile wide. I didn't make time to listen to Dad go on and on about the treasure because... Well, because I'm a shitty daughter. I scuff my feet against the footrests of the stool. I threw myself into schoolwork instead.

Dickie cocks his head at me. "You don't know?"

I shake my head.

His gaze narrows to beady slits, but then he turns toward the Superstitions again. "I guess that information is lost with your father then. He didn't tell ol' Dickie. I know that."

Surprise shoots through me. He tells Dickie practically everything. Not our secrets, but everything else, he would've shared. My skin pricks. If he didn't tell Dickie, maybe he really was onto something.

I could tell Dad was excited during his last treks into the mountains. He hinted toward finding another clue and asked me to meet him a number of times. I'm too stubborn for my own good because look what that got me. We may never know where Dad was and why, and how close he got.

And there comes the real travesty about what happened. If I'd just asked Dad about the treasure, met with him one time, I might've been able to answer the questions about where Dad was headed when he walked up the trail to the Superstitions on the west side of the mountain that day. Instead, all I could do was shrug and rely on old information.

The guilt of that will follow me around forever because my father paid the price.

---

8

*L*ike a moth to a flame, the new students on campus attract everyone. Wyatt, Stone, and Lucas are everywhere. It's like Saint Clary's has three new shiny toys and everyone wants their chance to play with them.

No matter how much I wish it wasn't true, jealousy rears its ugly head. It's not only that they just got here and already have more friends than me. Yes, that part really isn't fair, but it's also watching the girls paw all over them like they're a drink of ice water in this heat.

Life isn't fair though. If a Wilder knows anything, we know that.

Thankfully, Dickie gave me a ride to campus since my bike is fucked now. He said he'd look at it, but I don't have hope that it's salvageable, or if it is, if it's even worth saving. I guess with the money I get for scrapping the truck, I can buy a new bike. I'll have to think on that when I walk back to the dorms later. My dad always said walking was the best exercise. Bodies and minds aren't meant to be idle, and walking takes care of that. Then again, my dad said a lot of things, and I'm wondering if the majority of them were to make up for the fact that we were going without. Sure, you can walk. But if you have a vehicle to actually take you places, isn't that automatically better?

After lunch in Saint Clary's cafeteria where the displays of curiosity about Stone, Wyatt, and Lucas come to a head, I try making my way to class only to have the three new hotshots at the school surround me. Wyatt, if I'm not mistaken, is more reserved than earlier. If I look closer, he may even have shadows under his eyes, like he didn't get enough sleep on my terrible, hand-me-down sofa. I smile at that. Maybe they'll let me sleep in my dorm alone now.

As usual, Stone moves closer than needed. "Do you have an answer for us, Dakota?" His gray-blue eyes are sharp today, like the crackling of the air before a big storm.

No thanks to them, I haven't been able to concentrate the whole day. At least one of them is in every single one of my classes, glaring at me, watching me.

My mind has been filled with what to do about Lance Jacobs' offer but knowing what I'm going to do and saying it out loud are two very different things. Maybe I'm actually holding out hope that I won't have to say yes. That I can stick with the plan I had after my father went missing.

"Why do you want to find the treasure?" I ask Stone, narrowing my gaze. "Is it all about the money?"

Stone's gray-blue eyes sear a brand into my flesh. Before he can say anything, Wyatt answers, "Of course it's all about the money. What else would it be?"

I try to scrape away the hard surface of Stone's skin to see what's underneath. The hidden stuff is always the most important, and he's teeming with secrets. Wyatt and Lucas are the same. The three of them are like science experiments, ones that could go very, very wrong.

Lucas runs his hands through his hair, looking every bit the part of alley cat. I heard him talk earlier. It was nothing really. A simple exchange. He dropped his pen and the girl sitting next to him picked it up. When he said thank you, the girl who picked it up promptly turned to her friend and fanned her face. She wasn't wrong. His voice is rich and deep. I guess there's a good reason why my father kept me away from these guys.

"We have our reasons." He reaches out to grab one

of my curls, giving it a quick tug in his hand to straighten the strands of hair and then letting them bounce back. It reminds me of what the boys used to do to me in elementary school. "What I never understood is why the Wilders think their reasons are more important. Like you're somehow better than us." His voice bleeds through me, leaving an aftertaste of tang.

"We just don't like the way you go about things. Obviously," I say, pulling my shoulders back. "You guys are blackmailing me for my family's stuff."

The guys laugh, sending a shiver through me. They don't have a care in the world about me or my family or what they do to get the treasure, do they? My family does, though. At least we still have morals, even if we are single-minded.

I wish I could slap the grins right off their faces. I smirk at Lucas. "Did Wyatt tell you what happened this morning?"

Their humor dies in an instant.

My lips curl up. "He met my friend Dickie...and his gun."

I don't really know what I'm trying to say to shut them up. I don't know that Dickie would've actually shot him. I mean, maybe. Or maybe I'm trying to tell them getting me on board won't be so easy. I do have *some* friends. Well, *a* friend. A friend who doesn't mind aiming guns at people to protect me. It's a reminder that they're not the ones who have all the power.

Stone licks his lips. "You're too cute. He told us about your one and only ally being an old man with a vision problem. Maybe you'd like to see what my father is capable of before you start bringing other people into the line of fire. I'm sure you'd be upset if something happened to Dickie."

A rush of cold air swamps me, tingling the tips of my extremities. It's a douse of reality that I'm way out of my league with these guys. Before I can think twice, I reach out and slap Stone Jacobs. "Don't you dare—"

Wyatt and Lucas grab my arms, dragging me down a barely used hallway. My feet slide over the tile, trying to gain purchase, but they're holding me just high enough so I can't plant my feet. My bruised shoulder pings painfully, but I grit my jaw. No way will I show them a weakness.

Stone stalks after us, a smile on his face with a blooming splotch of red on his cheek. They move me around an ornate stone stairwell. In the shadows, they hover around me while my heart ricochets against my rib cage. To my left is a small window with a hole-riddled screen over it, kind of like the divider that separates the sinner from the priest while making confession. A quick check of the area, and I'm fully aware the guys are blocking the only way out. Not that I could struggle out of their strong grips anyway, but I would give them a damn good fight if there was a shot.

"What do you want?" I growl, still trying to yank free. Regardless of whether I think I can escape or not, I'm not going to be their little puppet either.

"Shh," Stone says, then lifts his gaze to the window.

Shadows move in front of it, blocking most of the light coming through. I don't know where the window leads, but voices filter through clearly, as if we're in some sort of tunnel.

The first voice that speaks I recognize as belonging to Dean Smith. "Mr. Jacobs! Wonderful to see you. I'm thrilled to have your son and his friends on campus." His voice oozes that sort of sugary sweetness of someone who needs to keep their companion happy.

I guess money buys you dogs who will pant at your feet.

Lance speaks next, and his chilling voice freezes me in place. "Thanks, Rob. That means a lot. I've actually come to discuss another student with you though. Dakota Wilder." He lets my name hang in the air, and I wonder if he knows I'm listening. Waiting here with my heart beating a crazy rhythm to see what he's going to do next. The wait is terrifying. "I'm just not sure she's Saint Clary's material. My son says he's already had a couple of run-ins with her. I'm not sure you're aware, but her family has always had some sort of perceived rivalry with mine, and it looks like she's taking it out on Stone."

"Oh," Dean Smith says, clearly shocked. "I'm... I don't know what to say."

Stone takes my chin and moves my head until I'm looking straight into his eyes. "Do you see how easy it would be, Dakota? A few words to the dean and your scholarship is pulled. Say goodbye to that other life you dream of."

I can still hear the voices of Lance and the dean in conversation, but it doesn't matter what they're saying anymore. Stone is right. They have all the power. "You're despicable, and your father is even worse."

"No, he's a businessman. He makes decisions based on the good of all. You're either an ally or you're not."

He skims his hand up my arms, past the patch Dickie placed on my shoulder after this morning's "accident". He lets his fingers roam all the way around the square pad. His light touches send goosebumps skittering over my skin, and I hate myself for it.

Stone's lips part as he watches the invisible trail he

makes, almost as if he can tell he's marking me. "Meet us at Devil's Hole tonight to give us your answer."

Wyatt and Lucas release their hold on me, and the three of them turn to walk away. Lucas looks back at the last minute before they disappear around the corner. His brown eyes the color of caramel catch mine before looking away again.

Once they're out of sight, I take in a deep breath. I move to the window, careful not to make any noise to see if Jacobs and Dean Smith are still talking, but I no longer hear their voices. It's over. Just like that, whatever they decided is out of my control.

I rest my forehead against the stone underneath the weird screen, lifting my palms to place near my head. Why is this happening? First, my father. Now, my life is being infiltrated by the Jacobs.

I slap the stone with my open palm and stand straight again. It's time for my next class and dwelling on how fucked my life has gotten isn't helping at all.

I walk out of the secluded corner and immediately run into Dean Smith himself. My mouth drops when I see him, and instead of walking right by, he stops me. "Miss Wilder, I was just about to pull you out of class." He gives me a look, knowing full well I should be in class right now on the other side of the building.

"I um…" I clear my throat. "I felt sick," I say immediately. "I was just headed that way."

"Come with me first." I follow Dean Smith all the way to his office. He closes a huge wooden door and then instead of going over to the other side of his desk, he leans against it, facing me with a furrow in his brow. "Mr. Jacobs came to see me a little while ago. I've been informed you're well acquainted with the family."

I wouldn't call it well acquainted, but that's neither here nor there. I don't think many people would understand the depths of distrust and hatred between the Wilders and the Jacobs. I swallow. Bowing my head, a grate catches my attention. The hole pattern matches the window I stood underneath. Well, at least I know where they met now. The not-so-private office of the dean.

"He's made some serious claims against you. I want you to know that Saint Clary's doesn't allow bullying of any kind." Dean Smith opens his hands. "I'm not going to pretend that I don't know your situation, Dakota. Everyone who lives in Clary knows what happened to your dad, and I'm sure you're struggling because of it, but bullying behavior is unacceptable." He leans forward, hands on his knees. "Now, Mr. Jacobs says he's been made aware of an incident that doesn't hold you in the best light. He wasn't specific but let me lend you some advice. If I were you, I'd make things right with him and his son. You've seen what it's like to live your whole life in this town, and you have far greater potential than that, and not just because your last name is Wilder. Do you understand what I'm saying?"

I blink. My mind shorted out when he said Mr. Jacobs is aware of an *incident* that doesn't put me in the best light. "Did he say what the incident was?"

Dean Smith rubs his forehead. "He didn't come right out and say it, but he hinted that it had to do with your stepbrother, Stone." Dean Smith straightens, giving me a small smile. "Mr. Jacobs is a generous, well-esteemed man. I am sure you can rectify this so no action will have to be taken."

Well, this is just rich. Lance and Stone have everyone fooled, and this is all about money. Dean Smith doesn't care that no evidence of this "incident" even exists, yet he warns me anyway. Just the thought that Jacobs might pull his funding from Saint Clary's is enough for the dean to lecture me.

Honestly, I shouldn't be surprised. This is just another power play. Another push to get me to see that siding with them is ultimately the best choice. I stand abruptly, and Dean Smith reels back, blinking. I hold out my hand. "Thank you for bringing this to my attention," I say, a lump forming in my throat. "I'll make sure to deal with it."

After we shake hands, I start for the door, but Dean Smith's voice pulls me up short. "And Dakota, I hope whatever incident Mr. Jacobs is referring to doesn't get out. We know about the gossip that goes around Clary, don't we? I think the Wilders have had their fair share. You don't need another reason to have the town talking."

I don't even dignify his statement with an answer. Because, of course, why not send me off with one more warning?

Lance Jacobs must be a great businessman because he sure as hell knows how to play the blackmail game.

9

*I*t isn't until I get home from school that I remember where Stone told me to meet them. The Devil's Hole. The place isn't unknown to me even though I've never been there to party. It's the typical high school hangout where all the cool kids get drunk and whatever else it is that they do at these things. Apparently, that's moved to college now, too.

The good thing about telling them I'll meet them later is that I get the rest of the day to myself. They act like I'm invisible. Wyatt doesn't follow me in his truck at school's end. They even leave with Meghan and a couple of other girls while I take to the sidewalk to walk the couple of blocks back to the dorms.

When I get there, my door is unlocked. That'll be

the first thing I fix as soon as I get money. I continue to rack my brain, trying to think of any way I can make a decent amount of cash without accepting Lance's offer, but I know if I don't, I'm fucked anyway. My reputation, what good of it there is, will be gone. College—everything—it'll all be over.

I lie to myself about what I'm going to do when I get to Devil's Hole tonight, but I already know. What a fitting place to surrender my pride. Devil's Hole is rooted in Apache legend. They say the very hole to hell is there. It may seem inconspicuous. A slight depression of the earth surrounded by a circle of rocks, but it's known in the area as a place to avoid. Through the years, stories emerged about terrible things that happened there, only strengthening the validity of the legend. The occurrences sound paranormal—like the majority of the tales that come out of the Superstitions —but mostly it's just dumb teenagers getting drunk and doing stupid shit. They can blame it all they want on the devil coming out of that hole, but that's not it at all. It's immaturity and thinking you're invincible.

The Apaches have their own ritual to keep the devil underground. Once a year, they hold a tribal meeting to secure the gate. Then, the teenagers move back in and open it right back up. The thing is, Devil's

Hole isn't on Apache land, it's on state land, and as far as the teenagers are concerned, it's free rein, whether or not the Apaches are trying to save us.

I get ready for the party with a dead weight in my stomach. I know what I have to do. They've put me in a corner with no other way out. But I also wish I could find a different path. In fact, I wish my dad had never left that day. He'd know what to do.

Instead of doing my hair, I throw it up in a ponytail and make my way back over to the contract on my bed. My heart hurts just looking at it. I, in no way, want to hand over all of my ancestor's hard-earned work. It's not happening. I'll have to think of something else.

I stand in front of the mirror, tugging on my shirt. It's just shy of a crop top, flirting with the tops of my jean shorts. Since this will be my first time in Devil's Hole, I should at least try to make it worthwhile. No one's ever invited me to school parties before because I'm one half of the town crazies.

Not that I think I was actually invited to this party either. Not really. They only asked me, so I could give them a decision and they just happen to be going there tonight.

I'm still pulling my shirt on when I head into the living room. I start picking up the mess the guys made.

I don't have a lot of things, but what I do have is in the middle of the floor in tatters. I quickly gather everything up and throw it onto the coffee table. On my way to the couch, I spot a white envelope off to the side. I pick it up and stand. Shit. I'd forgotten the school secretary gave this to me.

I let myself fall backward onto the couch. A hint of cologne plumes around me. I breathe in deep, recognizing Wyatt's scent. He smells like the earth after a rainstorm. All country, like a breath of fresh air. Despite being a douche, he smells good.

I run my finger under the flap of the envelope. I hadn't noticed before but there's no return address, only my name written in black ink. Boxy letters stare back at me as I pull out the sheet of paper inside.

My heart glitches for a second as I read the note. **FIND THE TREASURE AND YOU FIND YOUR DAD.**

Just that. Nothing else. It's not signed. The note was written by hand, but by someone who painstakingly took the time to make the individual letters look generic. Each line of every letter is straight and squared off. There's no personality. No discerning features. There's nothing. Maybe that's why my heart wrenches a little. The impersonal nature of it all.

Dozens of questions spill into my mind with a roar.

Who would send me this? Is my dad alive? Do they know where he is?

Most of all, I wonder if someone from Jacobs' team sent this. Another way to get me to fall in line. Dangle my father over my head. If that's the case, their cruelty knows no bounds.

I carefully place the letter back into the envelope and retreat to my room. I open the closet door and move to my tiptoes to place the letter on the top shelf above where some of my more formal clothes hang. My cheeks flush with angry resolve. I'm even more determined than ever to figure out what the hell is going on and why now when the Jacobs have decided to drop into town.

I walk straight through my apartment, pulling the front door closed behind me and hoping no one decides they want to get into my place while I'm gone. Not that there's anything worth stealing. Lance Jacobs confiscated my laptop, and I picked up a little, but it's still a mess in there. That alone should deter any intruders. Textbooks are about the only thing of value I have. Other than that, it's pretty sparse.

I turn to stare out over the walkway balcony, watching the sun slowly disappear behind the mountaintop while the orange blaze over the sky starts. A whistle sounds from behind me, the appreciative kind you hear in movies when construction workers are demeaning women. I turn my head to find Todd from history class. His eyebrows shoot up in his hair. "Whoa, Blue's Clues. I didn't know you lived here."

I almost roll my eyes. I've only lived in the same building with him for a year now. Dumbass.

He looks me up and down. "You heading out to Devil's Hole tonight?"

I nod, glancing at the keys in his hand. I really don't want to walk all the way out there. "Can you give me a ride?" I ask.

He winks. "You read my mind."

I follow Todd down the steps toward the parking lot situated to the east of the building. He opens the passenger side door of his truck for me, and I jump in. He walks in front, blowing his breath into his palms and then smelling it. Ugh, God. I wince. I hope he doesn't think I'm going to kiss him for giving me a ride because that is so not happening. Is that the payment for rides nowadays? What happened to being a good person?

When he gets in, he shoots me a wide grin as if he thinks he was invisible and I never saw him check the smell of his breath. My own smile is tight, but he is giving me a ride, so I try to be as polite as possible.

He pulls out onto East Gulch Road. "I don't think

I've ever seen you out at the Hole before, Blue's Clues."

I gaze over at him, disbelieving. "Really? You do know that name's an insult, right?"

"What? Blue's Clues?"

I nod, wondering how the hell this guy is even getting through his classes at Saint Clary's. He's a total moron.

"Yeah, but we've always called you that." He shrugs like that's enough of an explanation. Now, I'm not even going to feel bad if he tries to kiss me and I tell him to get fucked.

He jabbers on for the rest of the ride, not really talking about much of consequence until we turn off the highway and start down a dusty back road flanked by cacti and dirt. A quarter of a mile down the road, he pulls off and parks next to several other cars. When I glance behind us toward the road, I can't even see it from here. Devil's Hole is secluded, which is probably exactly why they like to party here.

I jump down from the truck and shut the door before Todd meets me in front of the car. We take a trail downward until smoke from a fire appears, wafting toward the night sky. Voices rise. Music plays. By the time we get there, it's exactly like parties I've read about in books, but it's being held in a place of legends. "I hope you're not scared," Todd teases.

I scoff. "Of fairy tales. Hell no."

He looks at me appreciatively, but I glance away and look right into a solid chest. Lucas stands in front of me. His hair is going every which way, and he has a beer bottle hanging from his fingers. The bored look he usually carries is replaced by fire and a drunk-like haze. It's obvious Lucas pre-gamed unless they've been here since school ended, which could very well be. I know nothing about partying at Devil's Hole.

"Well, I'm here," I say to Lucas, shrugging.

Todd looks at me. "You came here to meet *him*?"

"No," I say at the same time Lucas says, "Yes."

Todd sneers at me. "Used for a ride, and not the kind of ride I wanted."

"Fuck off," Lucas says. "Meghan's around the corner. You've been sniffing around her, so have at it."

Todd narrows his gaze. "You're a dick, you know that?"

Lucas laughs at Todd's attempt to get under his skin. I have a feeling not much does. When he's out of earshot, Lucas nods toward a different trail and then starts down it. I walk behind him until he asks, "You ever been here before?"

I snort a laugh. "Yeah, right. I think the cat's out of

the bag. My family isn't the most popular in Clary, so no, I don't get invited to parties."

Lucas glances over his shoulder. If I'm not mistaken, his lips are pulled down in a frown, but he quickly places them on his beer bottle and takes a few swallows.

It turns out, the trail we took just deposits us on the other side of Devil's Hole. Big boulders dot the landscape, light from the fire playing off them. I gaze into the sky, almost smiling at how beautiful it is here. The locals say my mom hated it here, but if she did, my love for the place makes up for it. I'm not talking about the small town or the dead-end jobs, I'm talking about the scenery. The rustic, natural landscape. It's almost otherworldly, as if I could transport myself into another place and time just by being here.

"It's my first time, too," Lucas says.

Jeez. I would hope so. I'd hate to think that the moment he'd gotten into town he was already invited to the primo party spot while I've waited for years to party it up in a secluded, sparse, somewhat dangerous place.

"What do they call it again?"

"Devil's Hole," I tell him.

He snickers, and I can tell from the alcohol

coursing through his veins right now that he isn't himself. This is the most I've heard him talk.

I lean against the rock with him. "It's actually kind of cool," I say, glancing over at the ring of stones that are just to the west of where everyone else is enjoying themselves. Someone turns the radio up, and a rap song splits the air that's so at odds with where we are, but still, it can't take away from the view. Stars sparkle in the sky, highlighted by different colors. It's almost as if I could reach up and pull the Milky Way right out of the universe.

"How so?" Lucas asks.

I blink, returning down to earth. "Well, the Apaches think this is the gate to hell." I point out the stone circle to him. "They hold rituals here to keep the devil down there and us up here. They think removing the barrier could be a very bad thing."

Lucas's gaze turns sharp. "That's not hell," he says abruptly. He nods toward the depression. The reflection of the fire in his eyes darkens as he casts a curious glance over it. "I've seen hell, and that's not it."

He flicks his bottlecap, snapping his two fingers in front of him, and it lands in the dirt in front of us. Hopefully, we're not too far away from the fire that the snakes and scorpions stay where they are and don't come out. If you're from here, those things aren't *that* big of a deal, but if you're an out-of-towner, you might just pee your pants a little at your first sighting.

"Are you going to sign Lance's contract?" Lucas asks after taking another drink from his beer.

The note about my father burns in my brain. It has to be from Jacobs. There's only one group worried about the treasure right now. "I don't really have a choice," I say sharply.

Lucas sighs and takes another swig of his beer. "I was afraid you were going to say that."

He doesn't sound pissed. Just resigned. Not that he has any right to sound anything. I almost completely forgot who I was having a chat with. His purring voice, his inebriated openness pulled me in. None of Jacobs' guys are my friends. I turn toward him. "You know, Dean Smith had a chat with me today." The noises of the party heighten as more people arrive. "College is the only thing I have left, and you assholes are trying to take it from me," I tell Lucas, fixing him with a look that I hope says I mean business.

A guttural growl comes from the back of Lucas's throat. "You don't know—."

"I know enough."

"You don't know anything. That's the sad part, Dakota." He lifts his hand, skirting around the bandage on my shoulder, then up to the curve of my neck. He tightens his fingers there, holding me in place. "You *really* don't know anything."

Nerves skate through my body on fine edges of discomfort and pleasure. I should be scared, but the way Lucas looks at me doesn't give me any vibes other than dampening my panties. I shake my head, but his hold on me only tightens. I grab for his hands. As a warning or something else I'm not entirely sure about.

My breath heaves in front of me, my nipples rubbing against his chest with every intake of air. They turn to stone, peaking to the point of pain. It should be illegal for Lucas to have this effect on me. He pulls back, creating a space of mere inches. I want to kiss him. I want him to kiss me. His gaze mirrors the sentiment, casting me in a heady glow.

But no, I'm too damn proud for that. Also, I'm not an idiot. He runs with the Jacobs, not the Wilders.

I slam my hands against his chest and push him. "Get away from me."

Lucas smirks once he regains his balance. "I hope you know you're only making this more fun for us. It's about the hunt, right? Not the actual find."

I swallow. He just took words my dad said only a few thousand times in his lifetime and made them dirty. Confusion pricks at me. I push past him, skirting around the edge of the crowd with my mind and my core still at odds. Since they're determined to play this game, I have to be smart about things. It doesn't matter what comes out of their mouths, I'm not the small-town girl who'll drop her panties at their whims. What's frustrating is that they'll stoop to any level to get me to sign that damn contract.

10

*L*ucas follows me, but I don't acknowledge his presence. The partygoers sit in a horseshoe-shaped ring around a bonfire, no one situated with their backs to the Hole. I guess some legends just can't be shaken.

A few stand in groups, others are sitting on rocks or large pieces of wood that have been dragged out here from who knows where because logs sure as hell aren't derivative from this area. Most everyone has a beer in hand, and I follow the tracks of two girls who are just now getting to the party back to a cluster of guys. That's where I spot the coolers, so I head that way. I didn't come all the way out here just for the guys. No, I finally got invited to my first Clary party, so I'm going to make the most of it, whether I'm the odd one out or not.

My father never shied away from giving me a taste of alcohol here and there. He liked his hard liquor, sipped from a tin cup. If I asked for some, he'd let me have a small swallow. The burning liquid would scorch down my throat and warm my belly. I never sat and got drunk with him. Not that I wanted to. That would be the ultimate depressing thought. Father and daughter, drowning their sorrows together. We weren't *that* type of family. Plus, alcohol was a luxury in our house.

Skirting around the guys, I pull a beer out of the cooler, wiping the water still clinging to the glass off on my jeans. One of the guys holds his bottle opener out and pops the top for me. I take a long swig.

Dear God. This stuff is disgusting. I choke it down. Must be my tastes run finer than this shit. I glance at the bottle, but I have no idea if it's a cheap beer or an expensive one. Judging by the fact that we're all students, I'd bet cheap. I shrug it off because whatever works. If that's what they're drinking, that's what I'm drinking.

I scan the crowd, recognizing most of the people here from either high school or college...or obviously, both. There's a whole big sky out here, mirroring what a huge world we live in, and I wonder if I'm ever going to have a bigger circle than this right here. The sad part is that I'm not even part of this circle. I'm like a drifter, only pretending that I actually fit in.

A giggle to my right interrupts my thoughts that are just way too deep for my current company and piss-tasting beer. I roll my eyes when I spot Meghan sitting next to Stone on top of a tall boulder. She's cuddled into his side, even though he's not paying any attention to her. Lucas has just joined them and the three have their heads together. Meghan doesn't notice she's being ignored though. Her sharp eyes have focused on me. "I never thought I'd see the day," she slurs. "Blue's Clues at Devil's Hole." She laughs loud as if she's said a hilarious joke. "That's definitely a juxtaposition."

Not to sound too bitchy, but I'm surprised she even knows the meaning of that word.

When no one pays her any attention, her voice pitches higher. "Maybe you should get a clue and leave because no one wants you here."

Of course, the song happens to end at that moment, and everyone twists their heads toward us to find out what's going on. Meghan seems almost stunned by the attention, but she doesn't dare lose it either. She's thrived on people fawning over her her whole life.

She slides off the rock, landing in the hard-packed

clay with a thin layer of dirt. She saunters toward me, but I don't fix my gaze on her. I look over her head to the guys who are watching with interest.

"Actually," I say, knowing full well this could blow up in my face. It more than likely will, but I can't stand to see her preening like a peacock. "Stone invited me."

Meghan barks out a laugh. She turns toward Stone as if she needs clarification. Or because she's trying to get him to sound off on what a ludicrous thing I've just said. I can tell by the lilt of her shoulders that she's not quite sure. He is new, after all. He might as well be a big question mark in her world, but I understand her concern. She's not used to being second-guessed. Especially not by me.

"Now, if you'll excuse me," I say, running into her with my shoulder. "I have things to discuss with them."

"What?" she screeches, and I swear high school was two years ago, but you'd think we were smack dab in the middle of those suffocating halls. I guess old habits die hard.

I burn the trio with my gaze, daring them to say they didn't invite me here. The heat from the fire makes me sweat, but so is waiting for them to decide what they're going to do next. "Ready?" I ask as soon as I get to them, my heart in my throat.

Stone jumps down from the rock, landing just in

front of me. He towers over me, especially with the slight incline leading to the rock, but I'm not going to let him intimidate me. He smirks. "Let's do it."

Stone throws his arm around my shoulder, and a shocked gasp comes from Meghan. The noise quickly fades into the background. In its place is feeling *him* next to me. It's hard not to feel the pull, even if my mind rejects it.

Wyatt leads the way back to the parking lot where he lowers the gate on his truck. He jumps in then holds his hand back to me. I grab it, and he heaves me up into the bed. I find a place to sit, my feet resting on top of the wheel well as the others climb up and find a spot, too.

Once we're all sitting in the back of the truck, the area behind my eyes heat, but I swallow the emotion down. Only Dickie seems to realize what the loss of my father has done to me. I take a deep breath and let it out, addressing the guys. "I had a chance to look over the contract."

Stone nods. "My father is eager to hear your decision."

"I bet he is."

His lips thin, but he doesn't bite.

I tap my finger against the bottle and take another swig. It doesn't taste nearly as bad as it did in the first swallow. I guess this is the kind of shit that grows on you. What doesn't grow on you is being blackmailed to betray your family. Generations of work. Generations of blood, sweat, and tears. Hopes that are at my fingertips. I can't just hand them over, and definitely not to the Jacobs. "Before I answer, I want to know why now. Why ask me about my family's stuff now? Why not when Dad was alive?" I have a suspicion that I know the answer, and if I'm right, they can all go fuck off.

"Jesus, Dakota. Really? It's a simple business decision," Stone says. "You either give up the stuff or you don't."

Anger flares inside me. "You've made it a terrible decision. It's not easy at all. I either give up what my family has worked so hard for, or I give up my life. Yeah, super easy."

Stone grits his teeth. His perfect face is on edge, but there's a wariness about him, too. Why do I feel like I'm more like these guys than not? Caught between a curse and a need so deep. The treasure runs through my veins. I may not have been born with it, but it's taught in Wilder blood from birth. This is how you rock climb. This is how you spend the night in the mountains without dying. This is how you make sure a scorpion doesn't sting you. I could go on and on and on. I know more about the treasure than I know about any other single thing in this world.

I pause at that thought. It's kind of sad when you think about it. It's always just been Dad and me for as long as I can remember. I didn't just get to do things like this, even if I'd wanted to. There wasn't time for it. It was always research, search, treasure, treasure, treasure.

Stone snaps his fingers in front of my face. I bat his hand away, and he snarls.

"Give her a second, man."

All three of us turn toward Lucas. He stares at me, those brown eyes awash with conflict. I feel his stare all the way down to my toes.

No, no. This isn't good.

For so long, these three were like the forbidden fruit. It's surreal to even be talking to them. They're every bit the entitled assholes I thought they were, and that's fine. Lucas just can't go being human on me now. They are not allies.

Stone glares at him then moves his stare back to me. He clenches his hands to fists, and it's apparent he's trying to keep himself under control while they wait to hear what I have to say.

Lucas chugs his beer and stands, throwing the bottle. It flips end over end until it moves out of sight. It doesn't make a sound when it lands, which is unnerving, but my guess is it hit a patch of sand. He shrugs. "This fucking treasure, man." His laugh is empty and indecipherable, almost mocking. "It's ruining our fucking—"

"Hey," Stone says, interrupting him. I wish I could see enough to decipher the look he's giving Lucas right now. "Dude, get your fucking shit together."

I pick at the label of the beer bottle with my fingernail, ignoring the boys' stare off. My mind keeps going back to the letter. I can't let it go, and I certainly won't help them if...what? I don't even know. My mind is giving me a thousand possibilities. "Tell me one thing," I say finally. "Do you know where my dad is?"

Stone leans forward until the moonlight washes over his face. I peek up at him, expecting the same raw hatred he's shown me tonight, but what's there is much more welcoming. "Why would you ask us that? Your dad went up into the mountains and never came back. We helped search for him."

My hands tighten around the bottle. It would be so easy if they knew what happened to him, right? Maybe that's why my mind went there, but Stone actually looks sincere for once.

Lucas prowls toward me, moving into my line of

sight. He bends, squatting in front of me while he fixes me in place with a glare. "Why did you ask us that?"

I stand, shoving him out of the way and shake my head. None of this is making sense. "I know." I spin toward Stone. The feelings that letter conjured threaten to spill out. "Your dad sent it then. Why?"

Stone stands now, too. "Sent what?"

"Please," I say, holding onto the thread of hope I have. A glimmer that I might actually know what's going on.

Lucas gets in between Stone and I again. He actually reaches for my hands, squeezing my fingers in his sure grip. "This is important, Dakota. Please tell us what someone sent you."

Lucas's plea sends me reeling, but his touch holds me firmly in place. I search his eyes for the thread of truth to his words. I find it. It's there, but just because he doesn't know about the letter doesn't mean Lance didn't send it.

Lucas reaches up to cup my face. "Please."

Jesus. Being touched like this feels good. It's like the universe has stopped spinning off course. Stone and Wyatt may as well not even be here because I'm transfixed in place. "A l-letter," I say finally. "I got it yesterday right before I walked into history class and found Stone standing at the front of the room."

I glance toward Stone, and Lucas follows my gaze. Stone just continues to stand there, his knuckles turning white.

"Who gave it to you?" Wyatt asks, voice like thunder in a storm.

I pull away from Lucas and breathe out. Being in his vortex is suffocating, choking every sane thought I have out of me. I shake my head. "It doesn't matter. I'm ready to give you a decision now."

"But—"

Stone shushes Lucas.

I close my eyes. My mind has been working on a solution, and I think I have one. It's only half a betrayal of my family, but if it means finding my father, I'm all for it. I take the last swallow of my beer and toss the bottle to Lucas. He catches it out of thin air like he hasn't had a shitload already to drink. Both he and Wyatt watch the standoff between us, gazes flicking back and forth. "My answer is…" The air seems to settle, draping over my shoulders like a weight. The only thing you can hear between the four of us is our collective breaths and the insects chirping just outside the perimeter of the truck. "I told you before that if you wanted what my family had then you needed me." I can't even open my eyes while I say this. If my dad's dead and watching from above, I can imagine the pain he'll feel in about two seconds. But if he's alive...and I have the chance to find him, I have to take it. It's a fine thread, but I have to keep pulling at it and pulling at it until I find the truth. "You guys can't have my father's papers, but you can have me." I swallow. "I'll help you search for the treasure."

Stone takes a deep breath, letting it out between us like an exorcism. An expulsion of what? I don't know. Eventually, he says, "Fine."

"No," Lucas blurts.

I turn my head to face him. I guess I wasn't seeing through all his exterior bullshit. He is his exterior bullshit.

"Stone..." he says in warning, panicked eyes meeting his.

There's so much going on here that I don't understand, but I'm still getting my thoughts in check. I just agreed to partner up with our rivals. The fucking Jacobs. "Your father backs off of me. He leaves my college status alone. And if he sent that letter, I'll kick his fucking ass."

Stone shrugs. "We'll start tom—"

"We'll start when *I* say," I demand, cutting him right the fuck off. "You're not running the show. No one knows more about the treasure and those mountains than me, so we work on my schedule and my timeline. You understand?"

It's Stone's turn to look pissy. "Maybe you don't understand what a partnership means."

"Listen here," Wyatt says, jamming his hands into his pockets. "There's something you don't know."

I glance over only to find the brim of his cowboy hat. I swear he wears that thing on purpose. Not that it doesn't look sexy on him, but he also gets to keep his expressions guarded.

"Shut up," Stone growls.

"She has a right to know." Lucas chucks my beer bottle wherever he threw his. For the first time, I hear the slur in his voice. "And you know it."

Stone's eyes shutter closed for a moment. In the light of the moon, they appear way darker than they do in the sun. I guess that's only fitting since we're not having the happiest of conversations right now. Stone straightens his shoulders, his hard gaze on mine. "There's someone else looking for the treasure," he says simply.

I scoff. "There are always people looking for the treasure."

"Yeah, well, we have reason to believe that these people might be a tad bit dangerous," Wyatt says, speaking up.

I smirk. What? Do these guys think I'm new? "Do you know how many skeletons are populating the Superstitions right now? There are always people searching for the treasure and about half of them you wouldn't want to meet in a dark alley. The other half are split between worse than that, and families who want to take home pictures of their *adventurous vacation*." I make finger quotes in the air. "First rule of treasure hunting with me, boys, is that you realize I'm not the girl everyone at Saint Clary's thinks I am. I don't roll over. I don't play dead. And I'm sure as fuck not scared of a little competition."

I walk to the edge of the truck and jump down. I smile into the moonlit landscape, my limbs afire. I'm closer to my dad. I'm closer to feeling more me than I have in a long time. Just talking about the treasure reminds me of who I really am.

"I told you I liked her spunky," Wyatt says, his voice pitched low.

I smirk at his words. Not only did commanding those assholes feel awesome, but I also can't ignore the excitement threading through me at the idea of heading up into the mountains to search for treasure again. The treasure runs in my blood. There's no use fighting it.

11

I make my way back to the bonfire and go straight for the cooler again. Despite the feeling like I might have lost a little bit of my soul, I'm at peace with this decision. I didn't just crumble at their feet, I gave them a win-win scenario. They had to strong arm me into it, but maybe it will all turn out for the best. A mutually beneficial arrangement where we all get what we want.

I have the cooler in my sights when a body blocks my view. Let's see, ample cleavage even though she claims to be all innocent and a pair of pouty lips. Yep, it's the devil incarnate. Meghan tosses her hair over her shoulder as she eyes me up and down. "What was that all about?"

I peek at her, laugh, and attempt to move around

her. She's so desperate it's funny. At least I never threw myself at people. I knew where I stood. Maybe I should give her a heads up that sometimes it's better to sit back and keep your mouth shut.

"What's so funny?"

I bend over to grab a beer out of the cooler. The same guy who popped the cap for me before does it again, and I take a long swig before I turn toward her. "You," I say simply.

Her glare turns murderous.

I don't know what it is about today. Maybe it's striking the deal with the three devils or the fact that we're outside in *my* territory, but her very existence is pissing me off. "Why do you care, Meghan? I'm no one, right? You've treated me that way my whole life. If you want to know what that was about, ask them."

A hand drops on my shoulder, and I nearly come out of my skin. I turn to find Stone standing beside me, a cocky grin on his face. "Ask us what?"

Meghan's eyes round, and mine almost do the same. Why does he keep touching me now? Heat radiates from the spot where we connect. I may be a social outsider, but I do know I shouldn't be having that kind of reaction when my stepbrother touches me.

I slip out from under his arm, and Meghan looks justified. She moves forward, slipping in next to Stone in the spot I just vacated. "I was just wondering what you were doing with her."

"You know she's my stepsister, right?" Stone says, confidence seeping through his very being as he gives me a look that says way more than stepbrother-stepsister. In an instant, the look vanishes though. "We had things to discuss."

"She's not your stepsister now though." She tiptoes her fingers up his chest, and I want to throw up. "Her dad's dead."

"You bitch," I snarl. Lucas comes around me, grabbing me by the hips to steer me away.

Meghan is all smiles until Stone grabs her wrist, tearing her fingers away from him. "That was rude."

"Well, it's true," she says, still using her teasing voice like this is all a part of her mating ritual. Flirting and insults. It's disgusting.

"Come on," Lucas says in my ear until I stop fighting him. If Stone is attracted to that kind of trash, he can have at it. Meghan turns, glaring at Lucas's hands on me, but all I can feel is the heat from his flesh on mine, his fingers gripping my hips where my shirt doesn't cover. "You can deal with that," Lucas says to Stone, giving him and Meghan a mocking salute.

I let Lucas steer me away to where the radio is. Couples dance, swaying to the music like the stars above have put them in a trance. He lets me go in the thick of things and twists me around. "What are you doing?" I ask, placing my hands on his, which are still curving around my hips. The only thing is, I don't shove them away. My fingers just stay there, like I'm holding him to me. His brown eyes capture mine. The bored look I've seen since he started school at Saint Clary's is gone. In its place is a tumultuous hold on the present. He always has this way of simultaneously looking like a stray cat, but also with a sly gaze that says he knows too much. I heat under his inspection. "Stop touching me," I say, my voice coming out too breathy.

"You like it when I touch you, Dakota. You might as well admit it." He yanks me closer, and we start an easy rhythm of sashaying to the Imagine Dragons song that just started. My neck pricks as people watch us. I try to break free, but his hold only tightens, his hips firmly against mine as he pins me against him. Not to the point of pain, but to the point of captivity, caught between two steel arms. It's not just his arms either. It's his stare. His brown eyes shimmer with the reflection of the bonfire flames.

"What are you doing?" I ask. I'm used to flying under the radar, but this definitely isn't that. It's my book heroines who get dragged onto a dance floor with the sexy guy who says something to them that they're not used to hearing. Do I like it when Lucas touches me? In two words, fuck yes. But that's my body talking, not my mind.

"What am I doing?" he asks playfully. "Holding you. I thought that part was obvious."

Despite trying not to dance, I get carried away. His hips move against mine, and if I didn't move with him, it would just look awkward as fuck. "Why? You came here because of Lance. That's it. You've done nothing but treat me like shit."

A small smile parts his lips. "That was when you were working against us. You just said that we can have you, and I mean to take you up on that."

"I meant as partners. Partners in treasure hunting, Lucas." I manage to make enough of a gap between us, so he can read my face clearly. "Nothing more."

He lets go, his face pulling taut. "I guess you can head back over there and let Meghan pick you apart then. Would you rather that?"

"Meghan?" I scoff. "Please. She's tried her best since Kindergarten, but I'm still standing. Her idea of winning is pointing out how she's the best while tearing everyone else down. She's a coward, and if I felt the inclination, I'd kick her ass. Instead, I find her sad and petty. I don't give a fuck what she thinks, nor anyone in Clary for that matter."

A slow grin tracks over his face. "There you are."

I narrow my gaze.

He takes a curl that came loose from my topknot and holds it between two fingers. "I was surprised to see you here, like this." His stare eats me alive. It's simultaneously sexy and dangerous. "For years, I thought you were shy, a little meek. But you're also funny, adventurous..." He drags his gaze down me again. "...sexy."

I bite down on my lip, wishing his words away. "That's where you're wrong. In Clary, I'm an outcast. You've been here a few days, so I'm sure you've heard the stories. The rumors. The whole town thinks the Wilders are a bunch of freaks."

"You know what I think?" Lucas asks. He cups my face. "I think—"

A booming voice interrupts us. "What the hell are you doing?" Wyatt asks.

I jump, immediately moving away from Lucas after getting caught in his stare again. Somewhere in our conversation, I'd completely forgotten the stay away from the archenemies rule. His hand was on my cheek, and the way he stared at me... It almost looked like he was going to kiss me.

"Fuck off, Longhorn," Lucas spits, his voice thick with alcohol.

Wyatt grabs a hold of Lucas's upper arm and drags him off to the side. They stand and argue. I can't hear what they're saying, but their shoulders are tense. I hug myself, close my eyes, and try to talk some sense into my brain. I can't get caught up in them. This is a business transaction, nothing more. In fact, I'm using them to find my father.

"Hey, are you okay?"

I peek up to find Stone. He's looking over my head at Wyatt and Lucas arguing, but then he moves his gaze to meet mine. I cock my head. "Are you serious?"

"Dead serious."

Anger rolls through me. These guys just can't strong arm me into working with them and then pretend like they give a shit about what's going on. "What do you care?" I force out.

Stone's jaw tightens. He grabs my arm and moves me behind a boulder, out of view from the rest of the party. "Come on, Dakota." His smile turns devilish. "We're partners now."

I laugh because that's just rich. "You blackmailed me. We're partners under duress. Just admit it, Stone, you don't give a shit about me or my family. This is all because you saw me as prey and you know you need me to find the treasure because you were never going to find it by your damn selves."

"Technically, I am your family. I'm your step-brother, remember?" His eyes flash greedily, raking me over. He grins as my body heats all over. "You still can't keep your needy eyes off me, watching me with every move I make. Practically eye fucking me from moment one. And now, you decide to grow a spine because you're jealous over some made-up Barbie doll."

I suck in a breath. His words are so wrong. That's not what's happening at all. "If you weren't watching me, how would you know I was watching you?"

"I'm not the one lying to myself. You bet I was watching you." He drags his gaze down my body. Heat creeps up my neck until my face is flaming. His mouth parts as he takes me in. He trails his fingers just below the hem of my crop top. "Why in the hell would you hide this all these years?"

My muscles jump underneath his touch. It's been so long since I've gotten laid, and the few times I had sex weren't anything special. A quick lay in a tent with a boy on vacation. As a way of getting money, my dad used to take families up into the mountains on "trea-sure hunting tours". The kid was my age, and I was curious. No one in Clary ever looked at me, but he did. We kept in touch for a little while, but it was obvious what we wanted from each other, a casual exploring of our bodies.

Stone Jacobs though? There's nothing casual about him. I can already tell there would be no fumbling our realigning or soft apologies in the dark. It would be so much more than that.

But also so, so wrong.

I stick my chin in the air. "I've never hid from you."

He grabs my hips. "Your dad kept you locked away like I was the big, bad wolf."

I breathe out. "Aren't you?"

We are enemies, anyway. When two people want the same thing that only one person can have, that makes them competition. When the competition goes deeper than sport, that makes them at odds. It becomes personal. Feelings get involved, and despite the fact that I'm going to be working with him, I don't have to like it.

"Why do I have a feeling you'd like me that way?" Stone purrs. He grabs me under my thighs, hoists me up, and presses me against the rock, leaning between my legs.

I let out a cry as soon as he nestles against me, his cock erect under his pants and rubbing against my core.

Fuck, fuck. I close my eyes, trying not to focus on the needy pulse between my legs. This can't happen. Not with any of the three of them but definitely not with Stone Jacobs. My ancestors would turn over in their graves, and that's not to mention that we're actually related. Technically.

Stone doesn't seem to care right now though. His hips move ever so slightly. "I know that feels good, Dakota. Don't hide it from me." After a moment, he stops. "I have a stipulation to our agreement."

I arch my hips, letting myself revel in the growing need pumping through me. It's hard to even think straight while he's pressed up against me. My mind is telling me to get the fuck out of there as quick as I can, but my body is singing a much different tune. Technicalities be damned. Stone fucking me against this boulder sounds like the best way to scratch this itch.

He hums a low growl in the back of his throat. "Open your eyes, Dakota."

I shake my head. As soon as I see his penetrating gaze, I won't trust myself.

He leans forward, his breath teasing my ear. "Look at me."

His command curls my toes until I blink my eyes open.

He gives me a nod of encouragement, yanking me toward him again until my panties are on fire. "You said you were ours," he starts, echoing Lucas's words from earlier. "Then, you're ours. No one touches this body while we're partners. Understand?" He pulls away to stare those captivating eyes right into my soul.

I don't even know what to say. Part of me wants to tell him to go fuck himself. How dare he? But the other part of me is here for it in the dirtiest way. "You might not have noticed, *Partner*, but no one wants me. I'm a freak," I say, echoing Meghan's words.

He pushes forward and growls into my ear. I suck in a breath as his cock grinds into me. "No one touches you. No one bullies you. No one so much as whispers your name unless it's mixed with ours."

I'm breathless, holding onto his shoulders for dear life. Abruptly, he sets me on my feet, and I palm the rock behind me to keep from falling on my face.

He grips my chin. "Are we clear, Dakota Wilder?"

I will not submit. Not to a Jacobs. Not to anyone, but definitely not to a member of his family. This is just him trying to regain the upper hand because they know they need me. If they don't have me, they don't have what my family knows. "Not nearly," I say. "Don't mistake this for anything more than a business partnership, Stone. You want what I have, and I want to find my father."

His brow creases. "Dakota..."

I hold my hand up, wanting to slap myself for that coming out. "If we happen to find the treasure, that'll just make my father's homecoming that much more special." I turn away from the look on his face. It's akin to pity, and that's not flying with me. I prefer him to be a prick, pressing me against this rock.

I turn, take a few steps, and am immediately blocked by Wyatt and Lucas. "Looks like we missed the real party," Wyatt says, taking in my wild hair, and I'm sure even in the moonlight he can see my flushed cheeks.

I meet Lucas's gaze, and he immediately looks away. Wonderful. This tentative partnership isn't going well at all.

"I'll make sure you get home," Stone says.

Wyatt steps in front of Stone after letting me by. "I think we need to stay back and discuss some things. How are you doing, Lucas? You good?"

"Drunk as fuck," he says, but the earlier good-naturedness is gone. In its place is a cold, disinterested voice. Whatever he and Wyatt fought about must have been big.

"Great," Wyatt spits.

"Here," Stone says. A flash of silver shines in the air. I hold my hands out, and by some miracle, I catch a set of keys. I glance into my palm and see the truck keychain. "You owe me," Stone says. "Not only did I have to pay that old mechanic for the truck, but I also

136

paid him to fix the engine. I knew a guy who could find me one, and we had it overnighted to your pal Dickie's shop."

I want to jump up and down. My dad's truck! I can't believe I'm holding the keys again. I thought I had to say goodbye to it forever. Stone's words keep me grounded though. He tries so much to control everything, and that's not going to work for me. "Let's get one thing straight, Stone. I don't owe you anything. We'll call it even. You're not getting everything you wanted with the contract and I don't want your money anyway, so let's say our partnership costs you this truck. Oh, and my laptop. Deal?"

Stone narrows his gaze at me. I'm a good people reader, but I've never figured out Stone. I've always just thought it was because there were too many differences in our upbringing. I can't even fathom what it would be like to be rich, and he can't understand what it's like to be me. I don't even want to try to figure him out anymore. I'm not sure I need to go down that winding path.

"Deal," he says. "Though that laptop's a piece of shit. It broke when my father's assistant tried searching through it."

He holds my gaze as I grind my teeth together. "I have a paper on that laptop that's due next week."

"Not anymore you don't. It's in the trash."

Asshole. I open my mouth to tell him where he can shove my trashed laptop, but Wyatt interrupts me. "Lucas, go back with Dakota. Sober up and be on the lookout."

"Sure thing," Lucas says, voice bored again, like the effects of the alcohol are wearing off. He's so different from the guy who danced with me out there in the middle of the party.

I don't argue with Wyatt because apparently Lucas has had enough to drink, and he doesn't need to stay and drink anymore.

Stone points at the keys in my hand. "She's parked a few down from Wyatt's." He nods toward Lucas who's already heading that way. Lowering his voice, he says, "Make sure he's okay."

"I didn't know pairing up with you guys made me a babysitter."

He gets that fierce look on his face again. "Oh, it makes you so much more than that, Wilder. You can deny it all you want, but you're ours however we see fit."

Wyatt snickers. "Oh, I bet she loved that conversation."

"I'm pretty sure it made her all hot and bothered, actually."

"Think again," I call back, waving over my shoulder at them as I follow Lucas up the trail.

Wyatt's dark laugh carries with me as I head toward the parking lot. Just as Stone promised, my dad's truck is here, so close to Wyatt's that I'm not sure how I missed it when we were solidifying our partnership in the back of Wyatt's truck. When I get in and it turns over, I place my head on the steering wheel and smile. It's such a dumb thing to equate a possession with a person, but I can't help it. This truck is my dad personified, and I'm thrilled to have it back in my life again.

I'd be more appreciative, but all Stone had to do was throw his money around to get me this, and it probably wasn't even a drop in the bucket for him. I don't care what my body says around him or the others, the line of men in my life who've warned me off the Jacobs can't be wrong.

The Jacobs—and any of their friends—can't be trusted.

*L*ucas sprawls out in the passenger seat of the truck like he owns it, hands resting on his thighs. He's quiet as we make our way back into Clary. Even though we don't talk, I'm attuned to him. Every steady breath he takes makes my nerves ratchet higher. I can't get over the things he said while we danced. The claim he made on me. It was easier to be mortal enemies with these guys from far away with a history between us a mile wide and stories told around a campfire buzzing in my ears. Now that they're here, they seem dangerous but in a different way. Not like they want to take the treasure from my family, but like they want to take something from me instead.

"A picture lasts longer. You're going to break your neck if you keep looking over at me, Wild Girl."

I choke on my next breath. "Wild Girl?" I ask, my face flaming. "You clearly don't know me."

He smirks when I peek over at him again. "I think I do." He lifts his hands to wrap around the seat back. The way he's lying there so casually, yet domineering, plays with my emotions. He can find a comfortable spot almost anywhere. Maybe that's why I get that stray cat feeling when I watch him. "I think there's a caged tiger in there just begging to be set free."

I bear down on my jaw, trying not to let his words get to me. They shouldn't hit so close to home, but they do. Being an outcast has always kept me in the background. The only place I've ever felt alive was in the mountains, and even then, it was the Jacobs who got all the attention.

"You think so, too, or else you never would've worn that outfit."

Jesus Christ. That's the second time someone mentioned this outfit. I've had it for years. Literally years. The only reason why the shirt fits me like a crop top is because it was one of mine from almost a decade ago. That's what happens when you're poor. You don't get new clothes on whims. You have to make do. "I have clothes like this, you know?"

"So, why do you dress like a farmer at school?"

"You've been in my school for two days. You can't possibly know how I dress."

He chuckles. "That's where you're wrong. When you're me, it's easy to spot who people really are. If you weren't comfortable in the clothes you wore to school, I'd be able to tell. But what you're not comfortable in are the clothes you wore to the party. You keep pulling the shirt down despite the fact that you have nothing to be embarrassed about. You should have zero self-esteem issues on that front. Unless you were lying and you actually do let Meghan get to you."

I glare at him as we hit the city limits. "Sounds like you fancy yourself a therapist, Lucas. I got a question for you then. What's up with you and Stone claiming me like some sort of possession?"

His lips pull up, and he immediately turns toward the window to hide it. It takes him a while to answer, and when he does, he only psychoanalyzes his friend, not himself. "Stone likes pretty things and puzzles. I guess that puts you at the top of the list at Saint Clary's."

"And Meghan?" I ask. I can't fucking help myself even though I feel petty for even bringing her up. She was all over him for the past two days, but things turned after I jumped off that truck bed with them.

He turns heated eyes toward me. "Meghan? She's basic," he says, mimicking a girly voice. "He can see through her ten miles away. She's not strong enough to keep his attention. Someone like you though…"

I turn into the dorm parking lot, marveling at the quiet engine and obsessively trying not to disseminate all the information Lucas just gave me. The last time I pulled into this parking lot with Dad's truck, I swear everyone within a five-block radius could hear me.

Lucas jumps out once I'm parked. He stretches his hands above his head, revealing a toned set of abs. I gaze away before he catches me looking and chastise myself. Lucas is just as off-limits as Stone is.

I push the truck door open, and he's right there, pulling the open door wider for me so I can jump down. He keeps doing the opposite of what I expect him to do. It's unnerving to say the least. I'm used to being by myself. Even when my dad was there, he wasn't really there.

"You know you don't have to stay with me," I tell him, half hoping he'll take me up on this offer. "I'm locked into this now." My attention turns to the letter that's currently sitting at the top of my closet. If I find the treasure, I'll find my dad. There's no going back now because no matter what, I have to find out what happened to him. I owe him at least that, and despite my feelings toward Stone and his friends, I can't let that derail me from getting what I want.

As much as it sucks to admit this, Stone, Wyatt, and Lucas will be helpful up in the mountains. I mean, if I can't have ol' Dickie, then they come in second place. It's a far back second place, don't get me wrong, but they're second place, nonetheless.

"We take care of our own," Lucas says, that purr back in his voice like he's trying to trap me. If it wasn't for the meaning behind his words, I would probably fall right to the ground in a pile of mush. The tenor in his voice strikes a chord in me. A drawn out note that turns something on inside me with the ferocity of a lightning bolt.

"And here I thought I was taking care of you. Stone told me to make sure you were safe."

The grin Lucas gives is straight from Lucifer himself. If I didn't know any better, I'd drive right back to the Devil's Hole and try to force him back underground where he belongs. "That's Stone trying to make you feel important. He has a way with people."

My lips thin. "You know, you're kind of a dick."

"Oddly not the first person who's said that to me." He steps in closer. "But I've also been told other things..."

His voice trails off, letting the innuendo hang in

the air between us. "If they said you have a sparkling personality, they were lying."

The corner of his mouth tips up. "Told you. Caged tiger. Your daddy was right to keep you locked away in that house when you weren't up in those mountains."

I push past him. I don't mind verbally sparring with the asshole, but let's not bring my dad into it.

"Aww, come on, Dakota," he says from behind me. His sneakers kick up the small pebbles in the stone parking lot. I suppose I could give him a pass because he's probably on the drunk side, but no. That's not my style. Since he thinks he knows me so well, he should know that. I march up the steps that lead to the second floor. Lucas's footfalls sound behind me. Compared to my soft thuds, his are like anvils being dropped on each step. I groan inwardly. Does this fucker have no respect for people? It's got to be past midnight and people are probably sleeping.

Or maybe that would just be me if I hadn't actually been invited out to the party that I'm never invited to.

I get to my door first and push it open, silently planning to close it in his face, but then I remember I have no real lock on the door and my stomach sinks again. If they're so keen on letting me be one of them, maybe the first thing they can do is buy me a lock for the door they ruined. I go to flick the light on, but nothing comes on once I do. "Oh, for fuck's sake," I growl. I start inside, trying to remember where I put that flashlight I brought from home, but Lucas's arms come around me again, pulling me back to him. I try to struggle free, but he only holds me tighter.

"What?" I demand, definitely not in the mood for any of this shit.

"Shh," he chastises, and just the way he says it pulls me back into reality. His chest thumps against my back.

I hold still, nothing sounding but the beating of my heart in my temples. My eyes scan the dark interior, picking up shadows, but discarding them when they don't move.

"Look at the other dorms," Lucas whispers. "Their lights are on."

I look up and down the wooden walkway. It's true. Beyond the front curtains, hazy glows of interior light can be seen. "I must've blown a fuse, maybe?"

Lucas's hand tracks down and squeezes my own. He moves in front of me. At my doorway, he squats and removes something from his shoe. It's only when he brings himself to full height again that I realize he's holding a knife.

My heart thumps wildly. I hold on to the railing behind me as Lucas moves into the dorm. He doesn't bother with a flashlight as he prowls like a stray on the hunt.

Waiting outside feels like it's taking forever. Any other day, I wouldn't be freaked out. I'd sigh in annoyance and charge right in like I attempted to do at first. Lucas is taking this seriously though, so fear dances up my spine, settling with a tension right in the base of my neck.

A few minutes later, Lucas reappears. He's on his phone. I only catch some of the conversation but it's enough to set me on edge. "Yeah, we can't stay here. Compromised."

"Compromised?" I ask. What are we, in a James Bond movie?

Lucas ignores me, pulling my dorm room door closed. He moves to the balcony, propping one foot up on the lower ledge as he listens to whatever is being said on the other side of the phone call. Eventually, he says, "Yeah. Sounds good."

I roll my eyes and push off from the railing to head into the dorm myself. If it is *compromised*—whatever that means—it's because those assholes broke my fucking lock.

"Dakota," Lucas calls after me. "God dammit."

I head for the kitchen and pull out the small flashlight from the junk drawer. I shine it around the dorm.

It's in an even bigger mess than the guys left it. I gasp when I see that not only are the cushions pulled off the couch, but they've been torn up, tufts of stuffing litter the floors in white, puffy clouds. All the cupboard doors in the kitchen are hanging open. The refrigerator, too.

I close that door and then march into my bedroom, pulling up short. I hold the light on my perfectly made bed and blink a couple of times.

"Dakota, come on," Lucas says. He seems to have sobered up in the last few minutes. "We can't stay here."

I clamp down on my jaw as I read the bright red message on my bed. *Good girl.* I walk forward, fingering the G in girl only to find it slightly damp. Red spray paint. The edges of some of the letters end in fading red dots instead of thick, straight lines. However, it matches the same block lettering as the letter that's in the top of my closet.

I swing the flashlight to the closet and find all of my clothes on the floor. There are even a few holes inside that look like the drywall has been hammered through. Chunks of the wall decorate the heap of clothes at my feet.

"Come on, Dakota," Lucas urges. "We have to go."

"Go? Go where?" I ask, spinning around to shine the light in his eyes.

He brings his hand up to block it, squinting against the light.

My voice is desperate and lost. "This is where I live, Lucas." I want to cry at the mess. At the intrusion into my life. Who would come in here and write that? What makes me even more pissed is that it has to be Lance Jacobs. I know Wyatt, Lucas, and Stone couldn't have done it because they were with me, but Lance was the last person in here making a mess, but I'm supposed to believe someone else did it this time?

"You can stay with us."

"Fuck that," I growl. I agreed to be their partner, not to give up my freedom. Lucas's and Stone's voices are ringing in my ears. They want me for their own. Maybe they had someone come here and tear this place apart while we were gone, just so they couldn't get blamed for it.

I move to the closet and run my hand across the top shelf. I make a noise of pure frustration when the letter isn't there. The one I was sent two days ago? It's just fucking gone.

I march past Lucas and head right through my living room, eyeing the fucking broken lock with a snarl. These assholes managed to uproot my life in only two days. Fucking bastards. Twice my dorm room has been ransacked. I'm getting creepy letters and messages.

It's so dark inside my dorm that when I head outside, I still can't see anything, and I run right into a body. "Whoa," a slurred voice says.

I peer up at Todd who's clearly just getting home from the party. He stops to smile at me, but then almost falls over.

Jesus. I hope he didn't drive himself home. I right him, holding the top of his arms until he can get his feet under him again. He narrows his eyes, and they sparkle over a cloudy haze. "Blue's Clues. You're killing me." His gaze rakes down my body, but I shrug it off. He clenches his shirt right over his heart. Well, it would be over his heart if he had the right hand up. "You hurt me today. Straight up wounded me."

I start to walk away, but Lucas's footsteps in the living room sound, reminding me I have nowhere to go. I put on a placating smile even though I doubt he can even see me clearly. "Hey, do you need help to your place?"

He grins, and it's kind of cute in a sloppy kind of way. "You might be making my night—"

"Dakota," I supply for him before he can even think to call me by that stupid name. Fucking Meghan,

I swear to God. It felt good to pull one over on her today. Come to think of it, I didn't even see her after Stone had a talk with her. Good. Bitch. I hope she left the party alone and feeling miserable.

"Da-kota," he says, testing it on his tongue, and it doesn't sound nearly as sexy as when Lucas says it. Or Stone for that matter. That's neither here nor there though.

Speaking of... Lucas finally emerges and steps out onto the balcony. "Dakota, what are you doing?"

I look back over my shoulder. My arm is around Todd's waist. He towers over me by at least a good foot. "Helping Todd back to his place."

"Wait..." Todd says, putting two and two together. "Is this the dick?"

Lucas snarls. "Get your hands off her."

Todd, whose hands weren't even on me before, slides them around my waist. He must've grown some balls with all the alcohol. "This way, pretty girl."

I turn away from Lucas, leaving him right where he is as we move the few doors down to Todd's room. He tries to go one too many, and I have to convince him that the door we're in front of is actually his room. I take his keys from him and actually place them in the lock to fully convince him, to which he says, "You really are a treasure hunter."

The awe in his voice is too funny. I can't help but laugh because his comparison is just outrageous.

As soon as I swing the door open, Todd trips into the room. At least, I think it's a trip at first until a strong arm pulls the door closed in front of me. I gaze to my left to find Stone Jacobs standing there, a mask of fury on his face. "What did I tell you about other guys?"

"Blue's Clues? Where are you?" Todd calls out from the other side of the door.

Stone moves my back to the door, crowding into my space like he did at the party. He sniffs the air, and his demeanor turns even more sour. "You smell like cheap beer now."

I try to push him off, but he doesn't budge. "Get away from me."

"Mmm, nice try. You're finally ours, and I'm not backing away." The handle on the door tries to turn, and a guttural noise comes from the back of Stone's throat. "If you open this door, I won't just maim you, I'll kick your ass for thinking you can put your hands on what's mine. Do you understand me, fuck boy?"

"Fuck boy..." It takes a moment but then a laugh erupts on the other side of the door. Todd is well and truly obliterated.

I glance behind Stone to find Lucas and Wyatt

standing there. It's Wyatt's turn to look bored, but Lucas is frowning.

Stone moves my chin, so I look him in the face again. "You were going to get down with that?"

This time, I really do shove him off. "Fuck you," I growl. "In case you didn't hear, I don't have a place to stay now because of you three fuckers. I wasn't going to fuck him. I was going to ask if I could spend the night."

Stone tightens his grip. "Do you know what 'spend the night' is code for in fuck boys like Todd's eyes? It means you're down to fuck. He's drunk as shit. He outweighs you by seventy-five pounds or more, do you really think you want to go down that route, Wilder? All he has to say is that you said yes."

My throat burns. Embarrassment creeps to my cheeks in a wildfire of scorching shame and fury. I don't know if it's because I didn't think of that first or if I'm pissed because he thinks I can't handle my own shit.

"You're too innocent," Stone says. His words are nice, but he says it like a curse.

Indignation clogs my throat. Stone doesn't know me at all. I'd wager no one does. "Not that innocent," I bite out, pushing past him.

A growl rips from his throat as the meaning is one-hundred percent clear between the three of us. "After I get through with you, you're going to eat those words."

I ignore him and head past Lucas to get my truck. I can always stay with Dickie. I didn't want to wake him in the middle of the night because of the surprise factor, but I'm desperate. Here's to hoping he doesn't have another heart attack when he hears me knocking on his door well past midnight.

Lucas jogs ahead of me and leans against my truck door with his arms crossed. "Sorry, Wild Girl. You're coming with us tonight." His gaze turns serious as I approach him, and he lowers his voice. "It's not safe for you here. Plus, there's an extra bed and everything. You won't have to sleep on the couch or on the floor. Also, I promise there are locks. Exterior and interior."

I look around. Todd's probably passed out, Dickie's house was always a last resort, and an extra bed with locks sounds too tempting. It's obviously my best bet, not that they're going to let me get away with staying anywhere else. But, if I decide now, then they're not making me, and I can still keep some of my dignity. "Fine," I say. "But tomorrow, one of you assholes is fixing the lock on my door. Got it?"

Lucas is already sharing a look with Wyatt and Stone well before I get the demand out. There's something about it that unnerves me. They warned me about someone else looking for the treasure. Maybe they were right. Or maybe this is just some elaborate plan they concocted to make sure I follow through on my word.

Whatever the case is, I'm still on my own and the plan hasn't changed.

13

I follow Wyatt's truck out of town. The blazing red taillights cut through the dark night as Lucas sits stiffly beside me on the bench. He's acting differently than when we made our way to the dorms after the party. I'm itching to ask him what he thought about my room being fucked with, but I can't quite make myself say the words. I'm still debating on whether I think they had something to do with it even though my intuition is telling me otherwise. For once, I think it might be wrong.

Wyatt puts his signal on and turns down a drive-way. I don't ever come this way out of town because it's in the opposite way of the mountains, so I have no idea what's in store for me until the house looms into view when we're halfway down the driveway. It's set back from the road about a half-mile, and I almost choke as it comes into full view. It's legitimately the nicest thing in all of Clary.

I'm astounded, and a trickle of unease courses through me in the next moment. I'm so out of my league. I grew up in a rustic cabin without my own bedroom. Sometimes, we didn't even have running water. My dorm is a five-star hotel to me. This may as well be a palace.

"Nothing but the best for the Jacobs," Lucas says, sighing like he can already read my mind.

"You're staying *here*?" I ask.

A tick flutters in his jaw. "Lance had it built because he knew we were going to transfer to Saint Clary's."

"Why did you transfer anyway?" I ask. I park behind a garage bay while Wyatt pulls his truck into it.

"Why do we do anything?" Lucas says cryptically.

His words hang in mystery, and I just can't stop myself. I take the bait, if that's what it is. "Why do you do anything?"

He flicks his gaze to me, then gives me a small smile before pushing the door to my dad's truck open and jumping out. He's definitely sobered throughout this whole ordeal. With his sobriety brings more guarded behavior. Ridiculously, I liked the Lucas that opened up to me more. Even when he was saying shit that pissed me off, at least it wasn't this Lucas who's retreated back inside himself.

My truck door swings open with a loud creak. I cringe at the sound of the rusty parts moving together when we're in such opulence. Stone doesn't seem to mind though. He offers me his hand like I need help getting out of the truck I've spent my whole life jumping down from.

I roll my eyes and lower my feet to the ground on my own, making him move back just a little. It's a small win. Like regaining some of my territory that I've lost throughout this. The Jacobs seem to know how to infiltrate someone's life.

Wyatt is nowhere to be seen, but the garage door lowers as Stone gestures toward the main walk of the house which Lucas is striding up now. On either side, flowery plants dot the landscaping. Every little detail on the outside of the house has been thought of, even ones I doubt the guys have looked twice at.

"Come on," Stone says. "It's just a house."

I fight the urge to snap at him. Not that he doesn't deserve it but I'm worried that if I do, he'll see right through me and realize the discomfort I'm feeling from just being next to a house like this, let alone inside it. Seeing something this nice makes me think about everything I didn't—and don't—have. I don't like feeling this way because I know my father did what he could. At least, he did what he could while also fixating on the treasure. My father was a brilliant man who could have made something of himself. He just had one priority above all else, and that never panned out the way it was supposed to.

"Why do you even want the treasure if you're already rich?" I ask.

As soon as I say it, I want to take it back. It doesn't show my discomfort, but it does scream jealousy. Not a good look on anyone.

"It's not about the gold, Dakota," Stone says, somehow sounding demeaning and scolding at the same time. "You know that."

Well, I do. Sort of. The gold would be nice though. When you're Stone Jacobs, you don't have to worry about that. You can think about what else the treasure means. Finding a missing piece of history. Getting your names written down in the history books.

Lucas pulls the front door open and looks over his shoulder at us. The look he gives me spurs my feet into gear. I didn't just drive all the way out here to be too intimidated to walk into a nice house. I know that. As soon as he sees that I'm moving again, he disappears inside, leaving me with Stone, which somehow seems like the greater of two evils.

As I make my way up the stone walkway that's flecked in colors that reflect the porch light, I try to look at the Jacobs objectively, removing any preconceived notions I might have of them. No matter how hard I try, I still keep coming up with the word assholes. It's branded in my brain.

If I thought the outside of the house was nice, I wasn't ready for the inside. It's a one-level ranch house with everything meticulously decorated right down to the curtain rods. The Spanish-style design boasts white stucco walls. I can't keep myself from gazing up at the high ceilings and the modern furniture that's so different from the couch from the 50s that I called my bed back home. If ever there were two homes that were opposite, it's this one and the house I grew up in.

"I'll show you around really quick," Stone says. The door shuts behind me, and beeps sound. I glance over my shoulder to find Stone punching numbers into a keypad. When he turns to find me watching, he shrugs. "Can't be too safe."

"Apparently," I say, lifting my brows. From then on, when he takes me through each room, I spot security cameras in the corners. There's one in almost every room. It should make me feel safe, but it also sends warning shivers through me too. Who could possibly need this much security?

The kitchen looks like it's straight out of a spread from a magazine. Stainless steel appliances, white cupboards with a sparkly black countertop. The bathroom just off the hallway is decorated the same. He leads me further into the house where the hall opens up to a room that spans the length of the back wall. Glass walls encase the space that looks out onto a huge pool complete with deck chairs, a hammock, a grill. It's like Lowe's threw up on the patio, but even better than that is the backdrop of the same rugged terrain I grew up in overlooking it all. In this light, the mountains couldn't be more beautiful.

The less-than-picturesque view from my house is out a small window that needs a good scrub to actually be clean. Once I look past the decaying, rusty mailbox, we have partially the same view, but it's nothing like seeing it like this. These windows bring everything outside in. It's being one with nature instead of separating us from it.

"Beautiful, isn't it?"

I swallow down the emotion clogging my throat. My first thought is that I wish Dad could see the mountains like this. But I also know he wouldn't set foot in a Jacobs' house. Not even if his life depended on it.

I push past the guilt. "It's...nice," I say, even though I'm bursting to say more. If Stone was anyone else, I'd gush about how awesome this house is. How beautiful the scenery, and just how crazy it is that the house actually adds to the landscape. It's not just some metal box that doesn't go with the terrain. No, the roof is a burnt copper terracotta, matching the color of the mountains in every way.

Stone grits his jaw, a muscle ticking. I almost smile. So, it pisses him off when people don't gush over his opulence? Good. Now I know.

Wyatt moves past us. He pulls open a square in the glass, revealing that they're doors. They open like an accordion, bringing the outside in and the inside out. He turns, a mischievous smile on his face, as he drinks from a beer clutched in his hands.

"Come on," Stone urges.

I bite my lip as I follow them out onto the pool patio. The pool is sunken in, and before my eyes, Wyatt flips a switch that makes pool lights blaze, showing off colors that slowly fade from turquoise to red to green to purple. Other bursts of color light up the surrounding fence every so many feet. He dims them using a remote, the lights turning soft, allowing us to see the mountain landscape again.

Christ, this is the most beautiful house I've ever seen.

I'm smiling, and when Stone walks past me, he smirks, so I know he's seen my delight. Fuck. I school my face into a frown. I can't give him an inch because I have a feeling he'd keep taking and taking until there's absolutely nothing left of me.

Stone sits in a patio chair while Wyatt shucks his cowboy hat, jeans, and shirt off and jumps into the pool. Stone groans. "How many times do I have to tell you that boxers aren't acceptable swimwear?"

"A lot," Wyatt says as he breaks the surface. He knocks on his skull. "Thick head, remember?"

Stone just smiles and shakes his head. Behind me, a sound makes me jump, but when I turn, it's just Lucas joining the party. He takes a seat on a half-moon type bed that has a wicker sunshade overhanging half of it. He lies right down, taking up all the space just like he did in my car. He winks at me. "Have a seat, Wild Girl."

"Wild Girl?" Stone scoffs. Then, he scrunches up his face as if he's thinking it over. "I like it."

"Too bad. Get another name," Lucas says. "That one's taken."

I decide that Blue's Clues is much more condescending, so if he wants to call me Wild Girl, I guess he can, even if I don't measure up to that moniker.

"You should have a seat," Stone says. "We need to talk about what happened."

I eye a seat next to him and pull it over the concrete, giving us a good few feet of distance between us before I sit in it. Stone's jaw tightens, and Lucas pretends not to smile behind his hand that just so happens to be wiping over his mouth at the right time. "Good," I say. "I have—"

"First," Stone says, interrupting. He glowers at me. "I thought I made it quite clear that you weren't to have anyone else touch you but us."

My mouth drops, hanging open like I want to catch some flies. I snap it shut. "I thought we were going to talk about the state Lucas and I found my dorm room in. The whole reason why I'm here."

"The reason why you're here is because you didn't listen to simple instruction," Stone explains. His voice is so haughty and proper. There's no twang or velvety tenor like Lucas's. He's city all the way, and yet, he's not at the same time. He knows what he's doing up in the mountains even though the attitude he puts off would say otherwise. "Todd is a grunt, nothing more." Anger lances Stone's face, and he bares his teeth. "That he even thought he could touch you."

His words hang in the air. I keep waiting for someone to explain the big deal to me, but no one does. "Oh, okay," I say, letting how puzzled I am about all this seep through. "You're serious about this. So, for starters, fuck you. I'll touch who I want."

Lucas chuckles in the corner, but it's drowned out by Wyatt's laugh and splashing in the pool as he kicks away from the opposite side to glide across the water and heave himself out of it. "Ah, look. Stone looks confused."

"Fuck off, Longhorn."

Wyatt doesn't heed his warning. He goes to the side of the patio, rummages in a cement shelf and pulls out a towel. He rubs it over his face and then through his hair. It's the first time I've seen him without his hat or without the hat hair he's usually sporting. It's— Who am I kidding? It doesn't matter what Wyatt wears—or doesn't wear—my body instinctively wants to climb him like a tree.

I catch something Stone says as I tear my gaze away from Wyatt's abs. His voice is filled with disdain. "...you don't need to stoop to their level."

"Wait. Whose level?"

"Fuck boy Todd," Lucas helpfully supplies.

"Todd isn't—" But then I shake my head. Why does everything they say make me want to argue against it? "Yes, he's a fuck boy, but I wasn't going to sleep with him. Not that anyone I sleep with is any of your business." Jesus. Just because he's some sort of local celebrity doesn't mean he gets to tell me what to do.

Stone's gray-blue eyes capture mine. He's always intense, no matter what he's doing. I wonder how the cogs in his brain do so much overtime. It must be exhausting to be him. To want things just the way he likes but thwarted at every turn because there are mere mortals in the world who can't easily oblige him. "It is, actually, my business," Stone says. He puts up a hand when I start to argue with him. "Because we have a real problem on our hands, Dakota. We don't actually know exactly where it's coming from, so we have to be careful about who we talk to."

"You mean *you* guys have a problem," I say. "Not me."

"The condition you found your room in would say otherwise."

I groan. "Then you brought the heat on me."

Wyatt chuckles as he moves to one of the chairs beside Stone, drying off his chiseled chest in the process. This isn't the first time I've seen it glistening with water, and it's really nice. Both times. "The heat?" he questions with amusement.

"Shut up," I say for lack of a better comeback.

"It was only a matter of time before they came to you," Stone says.

"Who?"

"I told you. We don't know." He runs his fingers through his hair, pulling the ends for a moment before he maneuvers it back into place. It falls perfectly, and I suddenly hate him even more. He has no idea how I've struggled with my hair for ages. Ages, I tell you. I tug my hair out of its elastic because the weight of it on my head is adding to the headache the guys are giving me. I tame it down my shoulders as best I can and then blink when I realize I have the attention of all three of the guys. They're staring at me intently as if I'm an animal in a zoo exhibit.

I calm my beating heart for a moment, schooling it back to beat out an even rhythm with a deep breath. "But Todd? I've gone to school with Todd since middle school. He's harmless."

"It only takes a wise man to arm someone."

I narrow my gaze at Stone, but he stares back with the same even stare that looks like it belongs in boardrooms and not the untamed nature around us. Despite the fact that his statement sounded more like it came from a fortune cookie than a twenty-something year old, I suppose he's not wrong.

At that thought, the wind picks up, tossing my hair around my face. I quickly tuck it behind my ear.

"You're lucky we got to you in time," Stone says.

I laugh at that. "Are you kidding? Quit acting like I'm some sort of naïve little princess who lives in a castle at the top of a hill surrounded by an alligator-ridden moat."

"That was oddly specific," Lucas says.

Okay. I've had like years of daydreaming and book reading to come up with lots of shit, but they don't need to know that. "I don't need your help, Stone Jacobs. I don't need any of you."

To prove my point, I stand from my chair and stride through the house. If there's one thing I can't fucking stand it's superiority complexes. Stone and his friends have one a mile wide. They sit in their fucking castle and throw stones at people like me. Sure, I didn't grow up in a life like his, but that doesn't make me weaker. It makes me much stronger than him.

I pass the living room and yank open the front door. As soon as I do, a blaring alarm sounds. I shield my ears with the palms of my hands until a body moves to the keypad near the door, quickly shutting the horrendous sound off. "You were saying?" Stone asks. He turns toward me, arms crossed. "That is an alarm that keeps bad people out and good people in. Wherever you think you're going right now, do they have this? Hate me or not, beautiful, but you can be rest assured that when you're in my presence, you're safe. Is that really something that you want to risk right now?"

I close my eyes, breathing in deeply until I can form better thoughts. While I'm just standing there, Stone shuts the door and reengages the alarm. He walks back down the hall, leaving me to myself.

I really hate that he's fucking right.

14

*W*hen I wake the next morning, I'm pretty sure I slept on clouds. Heavenly clouds sewed by the angels themselves. I lift my head off the soft white pillow only to place it right back down again. I've never slept in a bed so nice. Hell, I only got a bed when I moved into the dorms. I guess being rich definitely has its perks.

I finally find the willpower to turn over, the heat of the sun calling me. I borrowed one of Stone's muscle shirts to sleep in. It's entirely too big, but that was the last thing on my mind when I slipped my tired ass into bed last night wearing just the shirt and my panties.

This morning, though, I'm rethinking that decision. Especially since all the bedrooms are off the glass hallway that looks out onto the pool deck. They, too, have one glass wall that lets in the light, and right now, Wyatt passes by. He smirks, and I'm pretty sure I'm slipping a tit. God dammit. I should've used the remote to lower the blinds like Stone showed me last night, but it was so peaceful looking out at the stars before I went to sleep. It was like camping but better because of the bed.

This. Fucking. Bed.

I fall back down onto it, making sure the muscle shirt is covering the goods in case one of the other guys decides to walk by. With the blazing rays of the sun streaming in, it's hard to tell what time it is, but if I had to guess, it's probably almost mid-afternoon. Or at least late morning. I haven't slept this long in ages. On Saturdays past, my father and I would already be up the mountain, sharing breakfast on the hike through the rocky terrain. College Saturdays have me doing homework until I gather my poor excuse for a hiking pack up and go in search of my father again. Though, I haven't been able to do that for a couple of weeks since the truck has been broken. No wheels meant no ride to go searching.

Finally, I have my truck back though. It's ridiculous how much freedom comes with having a vehicle. It's like I'm an eagle soaring through the sky.

I pull myself out from under the luxurious sheets

and head toward the en suite. When I readied for bed, my eyes were blurry with sleep. I don't think I even turned the bathroom light on, but this morning, it's bright as can be in the interior. I move my gaze up and am rewarded with a view of the Arizona sky. The bathroom has a fucking glass ceiling. Holy shit. A bird flies overhead, spreading its wings and gliding on a breeze.

I keep staring as I do my morning business and then move into the huge shower stall. A rainfall showerhead greets me. It dances along my skin in the perfect thrumming of water. I could get used to niceties like this. Who couldn't? I bet even if you're the Dalai Lama you like nice things.

After showering, I grab a soft bath towel and wrap it around myself. Believe it or not, there's a toothbrush in an unopened plastic wrapper in the drawer of the vanity along with a hairbrush, toothpaste, and both men's and women's deodorant. It's as if this place is set up for unknown and unexpected guests.

I make use of the toiletries and then walk back out into the bedroom. This time, I use the remote to lower the blinds that slide down through two panes of glass. I'm prepared to wear the clothes I'd chosen for the party, but in a bag on the floor, I find a few sets of clothes from my closet along with my textbooks. One of them must've gone to my dorm this morning to get some things for me. I suppose this means they're expecting me to stay awhile.

It doesn't matter. I dress in the clean clothes, of which I'm grateful for. What I realize, though, is that the clothes were painstakingly picked out. There are only one pair of overalls, and hardly any of my regular t-shirts. If I had to guess, this is Stone's controlling ways coming out to play. He went out of his way to point out my different attire yesterday, and today, he brings me only my most fashionable clothes, if they could even be called that.

I throw the clothes on, and as soon as I'm dressed, I raise the blinds again, letting that beautiful sunlight back into the room. I press on the door to open it. It releases via a small magnet. Or magic. I'm not sure which.

As soon as the door opens, the smell of bacon calls to me. Bacon was a rarity in the Wilder household, and weekends were tough back in the dorms. The school is so small that the cafeteria closes on Saturdays and Sundays. If I hadn't saved enough food from the cafeteria over the week and I couldn't think of a good enough excuse to see Dickie, there were times when I went to bed with a growling stomach. It was never that bad when my father was alive. We always had at least a little something to eat, even if I didn't always like it.

Shockingly, when I round into the kitchen, Wyatt is in front of the stove. He has a piece of bacon hanging from his mouth as he flips omelets, cowboy hat and all. "Mornin', Tits. I thought I saw you waking up in there."

He gives me a wink, but if he thinks he's going to make me blush about that, he can go fly a kite. He didn't *have* to look into my room.

"Tits?" a voice questions behind me.

I turn to find Lucas striding into the room. His hair is a mess. More than it usually is, anyway. He yawns, running his hands through his brown locks, only to tousle it even further.

"Yep," Wyatt says. "I got an unexpected surprise when I walked down the hallway this morning. I think I'll get used to having a girl living here real quick."

"You know the blinds lower, right?" Lucas asks, shooting me a look that's half jealousy, half heat. Is that what his problem is? Even yesterday, he got moody when Stone—Well, I really don't know what Stone was trying to get at. Maybe he wanted to rile his friend up.

I stick my chin in the air. "I was just waking up. It's not as if I was standing there with my tits out."

"If you do, make sure you let me know," Wyatt says. "The only thing I've been seeing lately is a whole lot of cock."

"Stop looking and you won't get an eyeful," Stone says as he saunters into the room. "And please, Dakota, remember to use the blinds. Wyatt is the biggest perv around."

Wyatt shrugs as if he has no need to claim his innocence. "Women are—"

"We know," Lucas says, cutting him off with a stern look.

"Keep that up, and I won't be feeding your asses," Wyatt says. He spins back to the stove, grabs a plate from the cupboards, then turns back around with a plateful of omelets. "Follow me if you want to eat," he says, mimicking Arnold Schwarzenegger's voice.

I chuckle and do as he says. I'm pretty sure I'd flash him for a strip of that delicious smelling bacon if that's what he wanted. He leads us outside, a plate full of omelets in one hand and the bacon in the other. When he sets the platters down, an alarm goes off on his phone. "That would be my cinnamon rolls."

"Cinnamon rolls?"

No one answers as Wyatt holds onto his hat while he walk-runs back into the house. Stone retreats to the side patio where Wyatt pulled a pool towel out of just yesterday and returns with silverware. Lucas and I sit while Stone goes back, returning with a tray of glasses and a glass pitcher of orange juice.

Jesus. I think I died and went to food heaven.

I bite my lip, telling myself to get a hold of the emotions threatening to crawl out of me. The food at school is nothing compared to this. Plus, I'm only ever eating half of it because I try to save as much as I can for when I'm not in school. The omelet platter itself is piled high, enough for three or four for each of us if we want it. That's not to mention the bacon and fucking cinnamon rolls.

Cinnamon rolls!

"Go ahead and start," Lucas says, moving the omelet platter toward me. "I hope you like meat and cheese because Wyatt refuses to put vegetables in practically anything."

I snicker. "I'm with Wyatt. Vegetables don't belong in omelets."

I take a plate from Stone and use my fork to slide one of the omelets onto it. I add a few strips of bacon, trying not to horde it like I want to. I'm just biting into the bacon, letting a "Mmm" pass from my lips in appreciation for the pork goodness, when Wyatt returns with the cinnamon rolls.

"That good, Tits?"

"You can't call her Tits," Stone says, voice firm as well...stone. Apt, of course, as everything Stone Jacobs does is ruled, measured, and well thought out.

"Why not? Lucas gets to call her Wild Girl."

"Tits is so demeaning," Stone says nonchalantly like we're discussing the weather.

"Mmm," Wyatt says, setting the cinnamon rolls down within reaching distance. I grab one just as he says, "You think that because you haven't seen them yet."

"Ever," I say around a mouthful of omelet. "Won't see them ever." I can't seem to stop shoving things into my mouth, which probably isn't good while around three sexy as hell men. My cheeks flame. I definitely shouldn't have thought that. Nope. Not ever. "You can call me Tits," I say to Wyatt, trying to take their attention away from my red cheeks.

The guys settle into their seats around the stone patio table. I barely notice any of them are there as I dig into my meal. I only look up when I'm grabbing my third omelet from the tray and stuffing the last of my second cinnamon roll into my mouth. When I do, they're all staring at me, but they quickly look away.

I cringe, telling myself to slow the fuck down. These assholes must eat like this all the time, so it's not that big of a deal to them. I don't need to stuff myself for days. My stomach clenches, and I decide I really do need to slow down. I eat my last omelet slowly. Then, I take one more cinnamon roll, picking it apart piece by piece while the rest of the guys finish their breakfasts. I finish the roll off with the remainder of my orange juice, sighing when I feel how full I am. It's been a long time since that's happened.

"Want more?" Stone asks. He lifts the orange juice pitcher, and I nod. He tops me off. When he settles back into his seat, he says, "We should probably talk about how we're going to move forward."

I eye the guys suspiciously. They've been alarmingly civil this morning, and I'm just waiting for the shoe to drop. There's no talk of owning me or making sure I stay away from other people. In fact, it's been *almost* nice. "Thanks for letting me sleep here last night," I say tentatively. I was raised with fucking manners, and if someone lets you stay at their house because some weirdo walked into your dorm and left you a creepy message, you say thanks. Regardless of your feelings about said person. Or whether you trust them fully.

"That about killed you, didn't it?" Stone asks.

I let out a breath. "Damn near. I think I feel a stroke coming on."

"You know, our families don't have to hate each other." He pins me with a look that I know is just a trap waiting to spring.

"We're just wired that way," I tell him, shrugging

like I can't stop it, just like I couldn't stop the world from turning if I wanted to.

"I've always thought it was dumb."

"I've always thought it necessary," I counter.

He narrows his gaze, and I find I actually do like talking to people. Who knew?

"Now that we're working together, I hope you'll open your mind a little more."

I wipe my face with a napkin. "We'll see," I say. I stare around at the mess that's left. We wiped out the omelets and the bacon. There are two cinnamon rolls left, and I have to tell myself that I don't need to stuff them in my bag. I stand, taking my empty plate and starting to gather theirs as well.

"What are you doing?" Stone asks.

Lucas chuckles. "She's cleaning up after herself."

"Oh," Stone says, a line forming between his eyes. "You can stop that."

"Um, what?" The perplexed look on his face is, dare I say, adorable.

"We have a housekeeper who comes in every day."

I drop my plate back to the stone table, and it rattles. "Of course, you do."

"I told you it's weird," Wyatt says, sniping at his friend.

"We were ten," Stone groans.

Wyatt turns toward me. "This guy has never cleaned up after himself in his life. He's lucky he can afford to keep the help. Otherwise, he'd be fucking screwed."

I glare at Stone. "Not ever?"

"I can," he says defensively.

"But you just don't?"

Crimson rushes to Stone's cheeks. "I can pick up after myself. I do it on occasion," he says, glaring at his friend. "I was brought up with the idea that everyone has their jobs to do."

"And yours is to watch the help clean up after you?" Anger laces my voice. I just can't help it. How fucking ridiculous? How is that teaching anybody anything?

"No," Stone growls. "My family is run like a business. Our jobs were to work on more complex problems. It's why you see people hiring housekeepers or gardeners or mechanics," he says. "We could all, theoretically, do the work ourselves, but that would take away from the time needed for more important things. If my father cleaned the house or did the dishes, do you think he'd be as well off as he is right now? Think about how many hours you waste doing things you *need* to do rather than focusing on school. Or when you get older, a job. Doing those things only takes away a precious, limited commodity: Time."

"But you might also learn something really important," I say, disbelieving that he was really brought up like that. "How to be humble."

"That's where you're wrong, Dakota." For the first time today, his voice gets that haughty edge to it again. It's cold and lacking emotion. "You should only be humble to those who deserve it. Once you start acting that way, people see you as weak. A target."

I swallow. I can tell he believes every single thing that is coming out of his mouth. "What a shitty world you must have grown up in."

"As compared to yours? When's the last time you had a decent meal, Dakota?"

Fury surges through me like the crack of a whip. Embarrassment surges in quickly after. I push back from the table and ignore my name on his lips as he yells for me to stop.

Just when I think they might be okay, I'm reminded of why us Wilders have sworn off the Jacobs.

Pompous fucking assholes.

15

"God, you're a fucking prick, you know that?" It's Lucas's sure voice that calls Stone out as I make my way back to the bedroom I was given. Sticking up for me, his voice is that kind of chocolate-dipped caramel dessert that calls to me. Stone responds, but I can't decipher what he says.

I go into the room, closing the door and keeping the blinds lowered, so I don't have to see their faces or the fancy shit I'm surrounded in. At least in this room, I can just pretend I'm in a box. A well-furnished box, but a box just the same.

I should've been more careful. I should've guarded myself more. Maybe I should ask Lucas how he does it. It's like he can pick and choose what facets of himself he wants the world to see. With my dad, it was the exact opposite. He always told me to feel my feelings, unless they were about him, of course. I never went there.

This house—this life of theirs—made me too comfortable. I've only been here less than twenty-four hours, but it's true. I can see how your bones can ease in a place like this. Relax into a world where every-thing is done for you, and you truly don't have to worry about anything. Hell, with their fancy security system, they don't even have to worry about whoever this so-called other treasure hunter is. If that's what's actually happening.

And who just might it be anyway? It makes no sense. This person would've tried for my father's stash a long time ago. Everyone knows. Well, at least everyone *knew* we had the secret before the Jacobs showed up to the game. They twisted everything. They became the center spotlight. Taking the media's atten-tion, getting sponsors. I don't think for one second that they use their own money to search for the treasure. Not that they don't have plenty of it to spare.

I will say that about Lance Jacobs. He took his family's empire to a whole other level. I'm wondering if it's the lack of morals that got him there. If that's the case, I don't want anything to do with that kind of money. Even if I find the treasure, I still want to be a good person.

"Dakota?"

It's Lucas. I lie down on the bed and stare at the ceiling. I'm feeling particularly raw right now. Exposed. Like I just showed my weakest link to my sworn enemy, and he did just exactly what they do in books—they eat you alive because of it.

"Can you let me in?"

I still don't say anything. Lucas has his moments where he's a decent guy, but he's still associated with that asshole. I should say *those assholes*. I saw the way Wyatt looked at me too.

I realized there was a difference between me and other kids when I went to school. The rest of the time, I could pretend I was just like everyone else, but not there. Not with their fancy lunch boxes and clothes and seemingly always knowing the right thing to say. My young mind thought it was because they all had moms and I didn't. That might have been some of it, but as I grew older, I realized it was much more than that.

We were fucking poor.

The door opens, and I swing my gaze toward it as a

body comes into view. Lucas gives me a small smile. "Funny thing about this house. No locks on the glass doors."

"I would've thought my silence said enough."

Lucas sits at the edge of the bed, and I move my feet, curling them up toward me as I bring myself to a sitting position.

He just stares at me, and I grow tired. "I'm about to start homework, so if you wouldn't mind—"

"Fucking off?" he asks.

I smile tightly. "You got it."

"The thing is, I don't want to fuck off, Dakota." He takes a deep breath and lets it out. "You look like you need a friend, and well, I'm here." He cringes. "Jesus. Is this the Dr. Phil show? Is he even on TV anymore?"

I give him a dead stare.

"I'm just saying," he says almost in exasperation. "None of us knew how bad it was. If we had, we would've—"

"We would've what?" I snap. "I'm not your responsibility. I'm not anyone's responsibility. I don't need to be taken care of, and I certainly don't want to be treated like a porcelain doll."

"I think you just scared us down there, that's all."

"Scared you?" I laugh. It's caustic and bitter, and I

know it makes me sound about as desperate as I feel, which I hate. "Just leave, Lucas."

He moves, but he doesn't leave. He pulls himself back to the wall, leaning against it with his feet outstretched over the foot of the bed. Crossing his arms over his chest, he just lazes there, staring ahead. "I remember when I first saw you," he says eventually. "You were dressed like a boy. I swear if it weren't for your messy pigtails, I might have actually thought you were one."

He grins, and I happen to peek in time to enjoy it. It's boyish and throws Lucas into a whole different time of life. One where there's no weight on his shoulders or worries over his head. I hadn't realized how much he was holding in until I saw his innocence.

"We weren't allowed to talk to you, of course, but when I asked about you, Stone told me who you were. We were at some Clary field days or something. It had something to do with treasure, I remember that. You had your hand wrapped around your daddy's so tightly. Your eyes were big and round, staring at all the people, like you'd never seen that many in your life. Like you never even knew that many existed." Lucas swallows and looks at me. "So, no, Dakota, I'm not going to leave. Because you need to know that people exist. That not everyone out there thinks you and your dad are crazy. We don't all despise you. We don't all think you're scum or want to torment you because you grew up differently. Hell, if you stick around long enough. You might even realize that we *all* grew up differently."

I suck in a breath at the raw honesty of his words. I don't remember seeing him, but I remember the Gold Festival Clary used to put on. It was one of the only times I was allowed to go into town with Dad, so I can surmise that what he's saying is true. I remember feeling lost in a sea of people. Honestly, crowds still get me sometimes. I bite the inside of my cheek as a happier memory churns just under the surface. "My dad was always really bad at doing my hair."

Lucas grins, and it's absolutely stunning in a way because he's not trying. Stone walks around like he knows he's gorgeous. Wyatt, too, has that whole cowboy thing going for him, but Lucas? He's a sleeper. But when you really see him, you fall down the rabbit hole of his good looks, wanting to sink deeper and deeper.

We just sit there for quite some time, neither of us saying anything. We're both wrapped in different worlds, an eye to the past. A few times, I peek at him to wonder what's plaguing him. When I was little and saw people, I used to make up their life stories. With Lucas, it seems wrong to do that. I don't want to mess with whatever his true story is because I bet it's far different than anything I could even imagine.

Eventually, I pull out my Lit textbook to do some reading. Lucas leaves for a couple of minutes and comes back with his own books. We sit there quietly, each doing our own schoolwork until he receives a text. I'm so engrossed in the story, reading past where I'm supposed to have read that the buzzing of Lucas's phone makes me jump. "Sorry," he says. He pulls it out and glowers down at the screen. "For fuck's sake."

He pushes his textbooks off him and stands, heading for the door. He leaves without looking back, and I can't not follow him with that type of exit. I close my textbook and jump to my feet. Using the remote, I raise the blinds. The sun hits me, and I have to shield my eyes like a vampire. I lost track of time while we were studying, but I bet Lucas and I were in this room for hours. Probably the most amount of time I spent with anyone outside of Dad and Dickie.

How sad is that?

I move down the hall to find Wyatt and Lucas standing on either side of the front door. They're staring at the floor, but that's not what's caught their attention. It's what's happening outside the front door that has. Through the sheer curtains, I see a row of TV vans lining the driveway along with dozens and dozens of cameramen.

Wyatt reaches out and pulls me next to him and Lucas, using the front door to shield us. Outside, though, the reporters talk over each other until the cold voice of Lance Jacobs drones over all of them. My body chills.

"Calm down, calm down," he says, chuckling. "I know everyone wants to hear treasure news but just breathe."

I roll my eyes. My father and I would watch the news with his face plastered all over it when anything regarding the treasure came up. My father would sit in his ripped armchair and seethe, his fingers curling into the dusty, dirty, outdated material while Lance Jacobs smiled into a camera with a suit on. Even at a young age, I could tell the difference between them. I could see the way my father reacted to him, and since my world revolved around him, the hate grew in me, too.

"What news do you have for us about the treasure? Did you find it?" an eager reporter asks.

"Not fucking likely," I grumble under my breath, unable to help myself. The idea is preposterous to me. First, he'd have to actually search to find the treasure, and the only reason Lance makes his way up here is for photo and media opportunities just like this.

"Not yet," he says, oblivious to the words that spewed from my mouth. He's oozing with charm now, and it makes me want to vomit. "I've been waiting a long time to bring you this news, and I'm happy to say that I can finally announce it."

It's a whole different experience listening to Lance talk to the press in person. It makes it much more real than watching him through an old, flickering TV screen. It's harder. It makes me angrier because it's happening right under my nose.

"Well?" the same eager reporter asks, and I wonder if she has more important places to be. Don't we all? I can think of a hundred different things I'd rather be doing than listening to Lance.

"As of today, the Jacobs and Wilder families are joining forces to search for the elusive Clary treasure."

"What?" I exclaim, the question bursting from my mouth in surprise.

Lucas grabs for my hand, squeezing it as Lance keeps talking. "I have no doubt with our combined resources that the Clary treasure is within our grasp. The legend won't be a legend for long, my friends."

I heave in a breath of air. Several, actually. I can barely hear him talking through the buzzing in my brain. I knew what teaming up with them meant, but I didn't think it would be a big deal. I didn't think he'd tell the world. Dear God, if my father is somewhere where he can hear this, he'll hate me.

"The Wilders?" someone asks. "The feud between your families is well-publicized. How did this come about?"

Another reporter asks. "Isn't that a risky business decision, Mr. Jacobs? The Wilder family has a less-than-stellar reputation."

I squeeze Lucas's hand so hard that he turns toward me. More questions and insults are being thrown at my family while Lucas moves to stand in front of me. He tips my chin toward him. "Dakota," he whispers. "Focus on me."

Tears gather in the corners of my eyes as I stare into Lucas's soft brown irises. I made a huge mistake. I want to throw the door open and tell them all it's not real, but I'll just be playing into their hands if I do. After all, they already think my dad is crazy. Now I will be, too.

Another voice splits through them all. It's not Lance's, but it's as confident as his. It's teeming with sense and savvy. It cuts through all the others with a definitive tenor. "The Wilders are treasure hunting legends," Stone says. "We're happy to be working with them. Now, if you'll excuse my father and I, we have a tremendous amount of planning to do."

The door opens a crack, and the erratic voices of the reporters aren't so muffled anymore. They're still yelling out questions as Lucas moves us away from the door, and the two Jacobs step inside, shutting the prying voices out, effectively shutting them up.

"You, dick," I growl as soon as the door is closed. I free myself of Lucas's hand and make a fist.

Lance brushes off imaginary dust from his suit jacket. "We are working together, aren't we?"

I pull my hand back and let it loose. It flies toward Lance's face. He doesn't notice until the last moment, but it doesn't connect. Wyatt catches my hand, squeezing it in his palm.

Lance's face switches from fear to snark. "I see you take after your father's hotheadedness."

I growl in frustration. I'd love to feel the crack of my knuckles against his skin. Just once. Just for being his pious, self-centered self. "How's this then? We're done. Take away college, I don't give a fuck. There's something more important than that. Something you couldn't possibly understand."

"Enlighten me, girl."

"Staying true to your family."

I nudge him out of the way as I go for the door. My

truck keys are hanging on a hook over a table near the exit, and I grab for them.

Strong arms wrap around me from behind. I relax at first, but then I realize they're not Lucas's, they're Stone's. His words about my family only marginally made up for this stunt. "Stop fighting me," he growls. "You can't go out there right now. The press will eat you alive."

"I'd rather them than you."

"Ugh," Lance says in disgust. "Has this little infatuation with her only gotten worse? Just fuck her and be done with it. You know it can never be anything more."

I still in Stone's arms. Without him holding me, I'd have probably fallen over.

Stone pushes me away from him. "I assure you that's not it," Stone growls, fixing his polo shirt so that it lays evenly across his shoulders. "She only responds to physical measures."

Is this family for real? I gaze over at Lucas who's wearing a hard frown, but he keeps his lips pressed together. I guess our truce only goes so far.

Turning, I meet them all stare for stare. It feels like David versus Goliath at this point. However, as much as I'd love to just find my way out of their hair forever, I'm stuck. Not only did he just announce our partnership, they're the only hope I have of finding out what happened to Dad.

In his absence, there's one thing I learned above all else. One person does not make a team. In fact, it's pretty fucking lonely being by yourself. And if I ever want to not be lonely again, I need to find my dad.

I spend the rest of the weekend in my room at Jacobs Manor, as I've come to think of it in my head. I imagine myself behind bars, secluded, locked away, but honestly, this is the nicest room I've ever been in. The view is spectacular as long as one of the assholes isn't walking in front of the glass wall. The furnishings are pristine, and Wyatt brings me food on a rotation, leaving it just outside my door. So, if this is jail, it's a nice one.

I've even met Stone's cleaning lady. I almost gave her a heart attack when she came into the room. She no doubt expected it to still be empty. I tried to tell her she didn't have to clean the space, but she wouldn't hear of it. She told me to continue doing my coursework while she worked around me, chatting cheerfully as she scrubbed down the bathroom and used a fancy mop on the floors.

Her cleaning prowess wasn't the craziest part about meeting her though. The crazy part was how well she spoke of Stone Jacobs. I had to ask her twice who she was talking about before it finally dawned on me that she was talking about the same person who I've been cursing for over twenty-four hours.

On Monday morning, despite my cohabitants, I wake up cheery. I'm not hungry. I've done all of my homework—except for that damn English paper—and even moved onto the next assignments according to the course syllabi. While standing in front of the bathroom mirror, I realize I'm not stressed either. I know my truck is out front. I know if I walk out of this room right now, I can find food in the cupboards. I also know that I'm surrounded by people. They may not be the people I would've chosen, but even I can admit that seeing them walk down the hall at various times over the last couple of days made me feel less alone.

Which makes me about the saddest person alive. I'm glad to have my enemies near. Jesus. What is my life coming to?

I dress and head toward the kitchen with my bag in tow. I'm relieved to see that Lance is gone. I don't even know how long he stayed on Saturday, only that I'm glad I didn't stick around to hear any more bullshit come from his mouth.

"Good morning," Wyatt says in an even tone. He's dressed in a dark blue t-shirt, sleeves stretching over carved muscles. He has a perfectly tapered waist, jeans hitting him just right. And like a typical cowboy, he has a belt on with the t-shirt tucked into the front. The only difference with Wyatt is that his belt buckle isn't flashy like you see some cowboys wear on TV. It's a normal belt with a tame, silver buckle.

And the hat. Jesus. There's just something about this guy in his hat. "Morning," I say, almost forgetting that he greeted me.

He sips a glass of orange juice, perched on a bar stool at the island. "Mornings during the week are low-key. It's a fend-for-yourself kind of venture," he says, nodding toward the kitchen itself. "The cupboards are completely stocked. Cereal. Toast. Bagels. Oatmeal. I'm sure whatever you like to eat, we have it."

Honestly, I... Wow. Fuck. I've never had a choice before. I always just ate what my dad bought or what was on the menu at school. Shame crashes into me. I've had oatmeal before. That must've been relatively cheap. Cereal? I've had that before, too, but not like those brands that are on TV. I've never had Lucky Charms or Frosted Flakes. Whatever we ate was off-brand and typically pretty bland, kind of like eating the desert floor. Oh, and no milk. We ate it with water.

For a moment, I just stand there, gazing at their huge kitchen. It may as well be a labyrinth to me. A puzzle made up to confuse people.

Wyatt's gaze narrows. "You did hear me, right?"

I nod slowly and swallow. "Yeah, I heard you."

I peek at him as he runs his hand across his chin. "Can I ask you a question, Dakota?"

I shrug. It's not as if I can stop him, and even if he asks it, that doesn't mean I have to answer. "Sure."

"Do you like chocolate or fruit?"

It's my turn to look at him strangely. He gets off his stool and goes into the kitchen. He starts pulling things out of the cupboard. A plate, a measuring cup, and some sort of cooking appliance.

He gazes over his shoulder when I don't answer. "I know. You probably like both."

"I do..." I say, letting myself trail off. Admittedly, my experiences with both are limited. I didn't get treats or snacks when I was a kid. Or ever, actually.

Wyatt smiles. "I'm going to make you something that will blow your mind, Dakota Wilder."

I lift my brows. "Yeah?"

He returns to cooking, chuckling softly to himself. I watch him work from where I'm standing, but then move closer. He whips up a batter that I realize is going into a waffle machine—the appliance he pulled out of the cupboards. Then, he grabs some fruit and Nutella. He chops up the fruit and when the waffle machine beeps. He places the waffle onto a plate, layers Nutella over it and then drops a sprinkling of strawberries and blueberries over the top.

"Hell yes!" a voice exclaims. "Hurry up, Stone! Wyatt's cooking!"

I jump at the intrusion. I'd been salivating over the waffle and hadn't even heard Lucas come in. I'm also not used to so much noise. My father was a quiet man when he was doing anything except for discussing treasure.

"Not for you two fuckwits." Wyatt hands me the plate, and I take it with a smile.

I pass by Lucas to the barstools surrounding the island. He frowns as he looks at my plate. "What?"

"Nothing's changed," Wyatt says. "I cook on the weekends. What happened to you guys cooking a little during the week, huh?"

Lucas gazes at the waffle machine like it's a UFO. I'm right there with him. I'd never seen one in use until just now. After watching Wyatt, I think I might be able to make one though.

Wyatt hands me a fork. I cut off a piece, spear it,

and put it into my mouth. The chocolate hazelnut flavor mixed with the sweetness of the waffle melts in my mouth. "Mmmmmm," I moan. "Oh my God."

Wyatt winks at me. "I knew you'd like it."

My next bite, I grab one of the blueberries piled in the center and eat it with the waffle and Nutella. My lids flutter closed. I keep going until I realize everything around me has stopped. When I glance up, Wyatt, Lucas, and now Stone are staring at me. I lick the fork, grabbing as much of the chocolate as I can, not wanting any of it to go to waste. They watch my every move, and heat creeps up my neck then blossoms on my cheeks.

They look away, Stone clearing his throat. "Um, waffles then?"

"Have at it," Wyatt says, nodding toward the waffle maker. He takes another look at me and then retreats from the room, lines wrinkling his forehead as he goes.

"Fuck it. I'm going to try it," Lucas says. Stone, however, opts for cereal, pouring himself a bowl and sitting two seats away from me at the bar.

We eat in silence while Lucas curses over the waffle maker. The batter doesn't turn out to be the same consistency as when Wyatt made it, and when he shuts the top on the maker, it spills down the sides. Steam rises all the way to the ceiling and reaches out like tendrils. He cleans up as best he can, but when the machine beeps, announcing it's done, it's burnt.

"Seriously?" he growls.

Stone chuckles. "And that's why I didn't even attempt it."

Lucas pries the burnt waffle out of the maker onto a paper plate and then throws the whole thing away. He grabs a bagel instead after Stone remarks about the time.

After I'm finished, I take my plate to the sink, rinsing it off. Once it's clean, I start to head toward the front door when Stone stops me. "I'm sorry about Saturday, by the way."

I come to a stop, my brain still two seconds behind trying to make sure I heard Stone correctly. I peer over my shoulder at him.

He clears his throat. "I didn't know my father was going to hold that press conference, or I would've warned you."

I had a lot of time to think about what happened while I stayed in my room over the weekend. I'm definitely not over it, but what's done is done. It helps to hear Stone apologize. I want to hold a grudge. My mind tells me I need to. Maybe it's because I'm satiated and calm that I feel like being the better person though. "If we're going to be working together, I would appreciate updates on everything," I tell him. "Everything. Especially things that have to do with my family. I wasn't aware that by agreeing to help you that it would be widespread news. I'm not used to working like that," I admit.

Stone drops his spoon into his bowl and lifts his head to meet my gaze. "I'm sorry."

The contrite look in his blue-gray eyes is sincere. I nod, refusing to say that it's okay because it's not.

When I start to walk away again, he says, "I'd prefer it if we all rode to school together. It's safer that way." My hands ball to fists, but before I can object, he cuts me off. "I know you don't like being told what to do, but we're better off. If you don't trust me, ask one of the others."

"Like I trust one of the others," I snap.

"Ouch," Lucas says.

"And here I thought we were bonding over food, Tits," Wyatt says as he breezes past me. "Come on, assholes. I've got a date with a nice boo-ty this morning." He pinches the air in a crude gesture.

Stone shoves away from his place at the bar. "Please make it clear with this one up front that you're not looking for anything more than a quick fuck. Your last girl was horrendous."

Wyatt shudders then composes himself. "I assure

you," he says, mocking Stone's professional tone. "They always know. I'm just that good."

I roll my eyes, and the four of us start for the front door with bags in tow. Instead of using mine or Wyatt's truck, we head toward the second bay in the garage. Stone presses something on his phone and the door opens, revealing a Silver Audi.

My mouth drops open. It's the same Silver Audi that threw water at me the first day of school. "You assholes."

Wyatt smirks. "Oh, come on. My hand slipped." He winks at me again, and I don't find it charming at all.

I do have the sudden urge to stab them though. "On second thought," I say. "I'll be giving myself a ride to school." I turn on my heel and walk the other way, thrusting my middle finger into the air as I put distance between us.

"I'll come with you," Lucas calls out.

"The fuck you will." I grab my truck keys from my bag as I approach the truck and then heave myself into the cab. Lucas still strides toward me, but I lock both doors before he can get to the passenger side.

I turn the car over with a saucy smile, but nothing happens. No sound. Anything. I try again. The pretty purr that it had just a couple of days ago is gone. It acts like it's dead for good. It may as well be a toy. I bang my hands against the steering wheel, cursing the metal beast.

When I look up, Stone has his arms crossed. Just the way he's looking at me, I know he's done something. I throw the car door open and lean out, coming to a stand with my arm draped over the door. "What the fuck did you do?"

"Your truck is perfectly fine, but I had a feeling you'd try something like this, so I took a precaution. You'll get the part back when you can be trusted."

"Trusted? Are you serious? You want to talk about trust?" I hop out of the truck, slam the door, and step toward him. "How about you guys stop acting like assholes and then I won't want to be by myself. Would you step into a vehicle with someone who's treated you the way you've treated me? I highly fucking doubt it. You're Stone Jacobs. No one gets to say a bad word about you."

He ignores everything I've just shouted at him. Instead, he answers with, "The previous incident was before we teamed up."

"And you're still controlling everything," I growl, pointing back to my poor, useless truck.

"It's for your own good," he says, checking his watch. No doubt the proper rich kid is worried about being late to his first class. He would've hated growing up with my dad.

"You're...insufferable," I stammer out.

He raises his eyebrows, and I just glare at him. I first read that word in *Pride and Prejudice*, and it totally suits this douche. I highly doubt Stone Jacobs is going to turn out anything like Fitzwilliam Darcy, though. He'd have to rearrange every thought in his pea-sized brain.

"We can argue about this later," Stone says curtly, "but we need to leave for Saint Clary's now."

"Why? Your fan club awaits?"

His eyes flash. "As a matter of fact, yes."

The jealousy that tears through me makes me furious. Has he been talking to Meghan the whole weekend while I've been in my room? Logically, I want to drill a hole in my brain right now to empty all those thoughts. I should not be thinking that way about Stone. My stepbrother. My nemesis.

Lucas sighs. "Give me the keys to your truck, Wyatt."

Wyatt cocks his head. "What?"

"Just give them to me. I'll take Dakota to school, and you two can go in the Audi." Wyatt sends Lucas a warning look. "I'll be careful," he promises.

Wyatt fishes in his pockets and throws the truck

keys in Lucas's direction. I'm not keen on riding with Lucas either, but it's the lesser of two evils, so I follow him into the other garage and get into the passenger seat of Wyatt's enormous truck. The one that almost plowed me over. Since that incident was also before we teamed up, I suppose Stone wants me to forget it ever happened, too.

I grit my teeth as I gaze around the interior. Wyatt's truck is nothing like mine. It's brand new with all the technology mine lacks. Hell, mine doesn't even have a working radio, while this has satellite radio along with a GPS. It starts with a barely restrained growl.

Stone floors it out of the garage, kicking up little stones in his wake. His engine thrums like a tiger, and I hiss "Asshole" under my breath.

"You bring out the worst in him," Lucas says, shaking his head to himself.

"By breathing?"

He backs the truck out of the garage carefully and hits a button on the ceiling that lowers the garage door. "Nothing gets under his skin more than you."

I'm reminded of what his father said on Saturday. Stone's "infatuation" with me. Surely, he's not using infatuation for the usual meaning. He must mean his infatuation with being a prick toward me. Or his goal of trying to ruin my life. Either could work.

"I understand what you see when you look at him. I used to see it too. The rich, pompous kid. He's not like that though. Yeah, he has more money than he knows what to do with, but despite all that, you guys are more alike than you think."

"I highly fucking doubt that." I glare at Lucas like he doesn't even know me at all, which he doesn't. Of course. Sure, he saw me when I was a kid. We go to school together now. We've had glimpses of each other over the years, but that doesn't mean that any of these fuckers actually know me.

Sometimes, I'm not even sure I know myself, to be honest. What I do know is, I am the furthest thing from being Stone Jacobs, pretentious asshat extraordinaire.

Fuck that notion.

17

Stone is in most of my morning classes, and we manage to ignore each other. His fan club hovers around him. Most of them ask about teaming up with my family... Well, just me, I guess. More than a few girls giggle snort like teaming up with my family is the worst thing his could've ever done. Stone, though, unlike the other days, doesn't seem to be in the mood. It's not just me he's ignoring. It's everyone.

During lunch, I stand in line to get food when a body hovers behind me. I know who it is, but I don't acknowledge him until that rich voice of his sends a blast of heat through me. "Hey," Lucas says.

I turn my head, and he offers me a tray. I take it with a small smile. "Hey."

"I thought maybe we could take our food outside."

"You want to eat with me?"

The smile on his face grows. "Don't sound so surprised. I would've bothered you more over the weekend if I hadn't thought you needed time to process things yourself after the press conference."

I groan and turn back to the cafeteria line, telling the food servers what I want. At the end of the line, I hold my student ID up, so they can take the meal off my plan. Lucas is right behind me as I turn to find a seat.

"Come on," he says when I go to sit at a vacant table. He motions toward the doors at the far end of the cafeteria that lead to a sitting area. "Let's sit outside."

Lucas is an enigma to me. I've read so many books in my short years of life. Books that have every type of person you can imagine, yet I can't quite make him out. He's the quiet one, but not really. He can be an asshole. He's pulled the "You're mine" bullshit just like Stone did, but from him, it didn't sound as bad as when Stone said it. It seemed like something else entirely.

"Well, I—"

A girl bumps into my shoulder and the pizza on my plate slides. I try to save it, but she hits me again, "Oh, sorry." The plate and the tray hit the floor, clattering over the tile, silencing the room for a second before the closest table bursts out laughing. Lo and behold, Meghan is front and center, giggling into her friend's shoulder.

"I didn't see you there," the girl says. She bats her eyes at the seething hunk next to me. "I couldn't keep my eyes off Lucas here."

Lucas rolls his eyes, and the girl smirks like this is all a part of a mating ritual. She trails her fingers up and over his shoulder while Meghan watches, sticking her chin in the air and glaring at me. The girl, who is one of Meghan's cheerleader friends from high school, flicks her gaze over to the table, and it erupts again. It doesn't take a rocket scientist to figure out this was all pre-planned.

"Wow. You went to school with these bitches?" Lucas asks.

The girl, Lucille, rears back. She fights for control over her astonished smile. "Bitches? I think you may have mistaken me for someone else."

"No, what you're mistaken about is that you think I have the temperament to sit here and watch you fawn all over me."

Behind the girl, Wyatt strides toward our group. My cheeks blaze. We already have the attention of the entire room, but Wyatt's appearance only makes it worse. I bend over to pick up the mess on the floor since it certainly isn't any of the cafeteria workers' responsibility. Plus, it'll hide my flaming cheeks.

"Maybe you can find a clue somewhere down there," Lucille mocks. She kicks my silverware back toward me.

"Stand. Up." Lucas growls the words like he's having a hard time restraining himself.

When I glance up, Wyatt's wearing a huge smile. He places his hands on Lucille's shoulders. When she jumps and looks back at him, she automatically melts into his touch like he's just made her whole day. See? The guys in Clary are severely limited. I don't fault her reaction to them, but I loathe that they belittle me to get their attention. "Hey," she says, batting her eyelashes again.

His smile thins, and her mouth drops into a pout. He moves around her, gesturing toward the floor. "I see you dropped your tray."

"It's not mine," she says. "It's Blue's Clues'."

Lucas steps up to her. With their height difference, she has to tip her head back. "Say that again." His voice is a warning if I've ever heard one. A skitter crawls up my spine.

She smiles. "You guys are fucking with me, right?" She looks around, her gaze landing on all of us, even her table of cronies.

Lucas grabs my hand and pulls me to a standing position while Wyatt places his hands on his hips, tipping his head down low, so he can give her his cowboy stare. "Did no one ever teach you that it's the worst kind of shame to be someone's bitch?" he asks, tipping his head in Meghan's direction.

Meghan stands. She wobbles on the short heels she has on and then takes short little steps to greet us. She has on a short, jean skirt, her makeup meticulously done. "What's going on here?"

"What's going on here," Lucas says, "Is that you're so transparent, you're practically glass. If you even want Stone to look at you again, I suggest you tell your little friend here to pick up Dakota's tray and walk her little ass over to the line to get her another one."

I start to slink away, but Lucas holds my hand tightly. Meghan's jaw ticks. "Listen," she says, lowering her voice. "I know you guys are new, but—"

"What a mess," a cold voice says from behind me. Stone's presence pricks my skin. "Care to tell me what I've missed?"

Meghan puts her manicured hand on her hip, tossing her hair over her shoulders. "Blue's Clues walked into my friend."

Stone smirks. He comes up on the other side of me

before placing his hand on my shoulder. "Dakota, are you okay?"

Everyone in the lunchroom looks on. They would be looking anyway because of Wyatt, Stone, and Lucas, but right now, there's a line being drawn. Meghan and her high school bitches on one side, and the most significant thing to happen to Clary for a long time on the other.

With the way Meghan and Lucille stare at the guys, they think they have this in the bag. They think the hot guys will just realize how stupid they're being and suddenly remember I'm the social pariah here, not them.

Stone moves in front of me. He has the same hard face as this morning when he told me he disabled my truck. I don't trust him. Not at all. If it weren't for Lucas's steady hand in mine, I probably would've shriveled away by now.

"I'm fine," I say, putting more confidence in my voice than I usually do. "Lucille was just going to replace my food that she knocked over. An accident, of course."

Stone's gaze twinkles. He clearly loves this shit. He's in control, and he has the spotlight. It's a Jacobs's wet dream.

"The fuck I am," Lucille says, scoffing at what I've just said.

Lucas squeezes my hand again. I take a deep breath, and with everyone watching, I drop his hand and step forward. "I think you will, Lucille," I say, giving her a broad smile. My heart is pumping a mile a minute. I'm so scared I think I might throw up, but at the same time, there are three assholes behind me, and those three assholes don't mind being that way to anyone. Not just to me. I reach my hand up and pat Lucille's head. "Go ahead. Be a good little pet and do as you're told."

She growls and steps forward, her shoulder knocking into mine again.

Wyatt steps between us, and I'm thankful my feet don't move. My limbs tingle. I've kept my responses to their bullying inside my head my whole life. My snappy comebacks were held in, reserved for just me, myself, and I. My father was always inside my head saying, "Just be a good girl." Or "Those dumbasses don't matter." And he's right, they don't. Not in the grand scheme of things, but in the halls of high school and college, they matter. They've been walking over me my entire life because I felt like I could never stand up for myself.

Not anymore.

"Lucille doesn't have to," Meghan says, keeping all the bravado. She's grinning, but I can see the fear underneath her mascara. Her gaze keeps darting between the guys as if any moment now, they'll wake up and realize what they're doing.

Stone steps up to her. He places his finger under her chin and tips her face up to his. My breathing halts. I'm transfixed. Jealousy burns through me because I clearly have some issues when it comes to Stone Jacobs. I hate him. I really fucking do. But the thought of him kissing Meghan right here in front of everyone burns my ass. Stepbrother be damned.

Like me, it looks like Meghan is having a hard time breathing too. I get it. Stone is drool worthy. If it weren't for the natural contraception of his personality, I'd be putting him in my spank bank every fucking day. My skin turns to fire. Just the thought of him has liquid lava singing through my veins.

Stone hovers over her lips. Meghan moves onto her tiptoes. There's barely any distance between them. I want to look away. I need to look away. The whole cafeteria is waiting to see what will happen though.

"Tell your little dog to do as Dakota says."

Meghan blinks. "Lucille," she says. Her voice is almost angelic. She's caught in Stone's gravitational pull. "Do as Stone says."

"Meghan..."

She turns her head. "I said fucking do it," she snaps. Lucille still hesitates, so Meghan bites out. "Do it or I'll tell everyone what you thought you did with tampons."

Lucille's jaw snaps shut, and the whole cafeteria erupts into laughter. I have to hand it to Lucille. She pulls her shoulders back and crouches to pick up the tray. She crosses the cafeteria, discards the trash, places the tray back in the return window, and then gets in line.

"You had a chocolate milk, right?" Wyatt asks.

I shake my head.

"Get her a chocolate milk!" Wyatt calls out, ignoring me. "There were also two slices of pizza on that tray. Napkins, silverware, and one of those chocolate cupcakes."

Lucille shakes her head and tips her chin in the air some more, but she does as he says. I barely restrain a laugh, but when I gaze over at Stone and Meghan, they're still transfixed with each other. My stomach curdles. I can't believe he sees something in her. He sure as hell is eating her up right now.

Meghan is someone Lance might approve of. No one in Clary is rich, but her family fakes it the best. That's how she got to be the queen bee. Isn't that always the way it goes? I mean, I only have books and *Mean Girls* to compare to real life, but I'm fairly sure that's how it works more often than not.

"Here," Lucille says as she walks back up to us. She thrusts the tray at me, and I start to take it, but Stone interrupts.

"One more thing," he says. He leaves Meghan there, still dazed as if she's two seconds away from falling into a hot boy coma. He spins away from her and grabs my hand, pulling me to him. Our chests collide. His hand roams over my hip, gripping me as his other hand fists in my hair, elongating my neck. Showing it off like it's a precious metal. "Dakota is ours. She's no longer your punching bag." His hot breath filters over my skin. Fear turns to lust. Arousal awakens my body, starting from the curl of my toes all the way to my core. It continues in a sweep that hardens my nipples while Stone holds me against him. He leans over, grazing his lips across my cheek. I close my eyes, suddenly fully aware of how Meghan felt a second ago. His lips trail up the line of my cheek to my ear. "You..." he whispers. "...are so much better than them."

He releases me, and I fall back to my feet. I blink. Stone's already ten strides away, heading toward the exit of the cafeteria. Meghan looks like she wants to murder me, and the cafeteria is about as quiet as a church. I grab my new tray from Lucille while she's still shocked and turn away from all of them. Wyatt's laughter cackles through the room.

I don't fight Lucas on wanting to eat outside now. In fact, I lead the way. We head toward a circular table that's away from everyone else, and I sit, setting my tray down, but ignoring the food all together. Fuck me. I wanted Stone to kiss me. Me—my body—practically everything down to the cellular level, wanted him to do it. To just kiss me right there in front of the whole cafeteria.

My face burns. I'm sure what I looked like to everyone else. A dazed sex toy puppet, perhaps?

Lucas sits, which catapults me back to reality. He ignores his food, too. Instead, he runs his hands through his disheveled hair and levels me with a stare.

"What?" I ask, my voice coming out hollow. I'm astonished, turned on, and confused. It's an interesting mix.

"I don't think you understand how fucking sexy that just was."

"What?" I ask again, though this time my voice is pitched much higher because he's fucking crazy. No one has ever put me and sexy in the same sentence.

"You," he says. "That pink in your cheeks. That

stare." He stands briefly, lips pressing together, and if I'm not mistaken, I'm pretty sure he rearranges himself. "Fuck," he groans, breathing in deeply. "Do you know how much longer you might hate me for? Because I certainly don't hate you."

I sigh. "Lucas, don't."

"No, I'm serious," he says. He pushes his tray aside and slides over to my small bench. He straddles it, and it's impossible not to see the pitch in his shorts. My body reacts to his in turn. Suddenly, I'm all too aware of him. Shallow breaths make my breathing falter. He reaches his hand up to cup my cheek. "Jesus, Dakota. You're—"

"Am I interrupting anything?" Wyatt drops his tray to the table, and it clatters.

I jump, breaking the connection between Lucas and me. "Yes," Lucas says, eyeing his friend like he'd love to stab him with the cafeteria-issued butter knife.

"Oh." Wyatt shrugs with a huge grin. "Well, I actually don't care. I was just trying to be nice."

He plops his ass on the seat across from us. Sighing, Lucas pulls his tray over, and we all bite into our food like it's the only thing we want to be doing right now. For me, it's only a distraction about what's just happened in the past ten minutes.

It isn't until I've polished off both slices of pizza

that I understand the buzzing coursing through me is just the high of finally sticking up for myself. I'm living every dorky girl's dream right now. The bitches actually got what was coming to them.

I smile as I sip my Lucille-bought chocolate milk. Can I get an amen for dorks everywhere?

he last class of the day, I share with Lucas. I get to the room first, but when he comes in, he sits next to me, pulling his desk close to mine, ignoring when the teacher tells him to move it back into his row. Miraculously, the professor doesn't push it. She rolls her eyes like she has more important things to do than tell a twenty-something year old where to put his desk. Which, let's face it, she probably does.

However, despite her airs, she plays a video during class. It's a mythology class, so I guess that makes sense. Five minutes into it, though, it's apparent that Lucas is either bored or has no apparent interest in a three-headed beast.

Slyly, he moves his desk even closer to mine. "Don't ignore me, Dakota," he whispers.

I glance over at him as if I'm bored when I'm far from it. Ever since he cupped my face earlier, staring into me with those deep brown eyes, I haven't been able to get him out of my head. Actually, I haven't been able to get Stone out of my head either. The two of them have taken up space in my brain and won't leave.

I tell myself it's an easy fix. I'm just fucking horny, so a little alone time with myself with the blinds drawn in my room tonight is definitely in order. In high school, I started to have feelings that just wouldn't go away. I refused to relieve them, but then one day in the computer lab, I looked up a scientific article about self-stimulation. It turns out it's perfectly normal and healthy to masturbate, and I've been doing it ever since. That particular research incident, however, did earn me an embarrassing conversation with the librarian who told me that there was school-appropriate research and there was home-appropriate research. Yeah, like we had the internet. No way. If Dad needed to look something up, he went to the public library, and even then, he'd tell me it was the slowest connection he'd ever had the displeasure to wait for. I never minded when he went, though, because he would bring me home books. So. Many. Books.

"You're doing it again," Lucas teases.

I point toward the screen. "I'm watching this."

"No one's watching this," he scoffs.

I take a quick look around. Literally no one was actually watching it. A few students were blatantly on their phones while others were doing assignments from other courses.

Jesus hell.

He leans closer to me, and I swear I can smell mint on his breath. "We thought we might talk treasure tonight." He watches for my reaction, waiting.

Talking treasure with them is something I've been putting off, but I also know it needs to happen. It's not just about the treasure for me though. It's about finding my dad, too, and we won't be able to do that unless we go up into the mountains.

The note said, "Find the treasure and find your dad." If these people aren't fucking with me, then that's exactly what I need to do. It's Stone who's holding me back. I still have a mental barrier the size of the Titanic when it comes to him, and it certainly doesn't help when he's a gigantic asshole.

"I promise Stone will be on his best behavior."

"I don't doubt that," I tell him with a sigh. "Because he wants to know everything I know, and if he thinks I'm going to give it to him, he'll be a stand-up guy for point seven seconds."

"Meh. Maybe point five."

I smirk at Lucas. "How'd you get mixed up with him anyway? All of you," I tack on. I've always wondered how their friendship started. First, it was just Lance and Stone all over the news. Then, we started to see Lucas next, followed shortly after by Wyatt. I never dared pose the question to my father. If I seemed at all interested in the Jacobs, I would've had to endure an hours long lecture about how evil they were.

Lucas's brown eyes darken over like storm clouds rolling across the desert. He runs his hands through his unkempt hair that manages to look sexy as hell. If only my curls could pull off that look, I'd be one happy girl.

"That kind of information will cost you," he teases.

"Cost me?"

"A date."

"A date?" I say it so loud that the professor shushes me and glares at Lucas again. Lucas and I school our features, pretending to watch the movie until the curious onlookers turn back around.

When they do, Lucas grins at me. "Ever been on one of those?" he whispers.

His tone, even now, sets my skin afire, leaving a burning in its wake. "Maybe I have," pretending to be coy, even though I'm sure I'm not fooling anyone. Least of all him.

I think back to the guy who took my V-card that summer. We *kind of* dated. If sneaking off to fool around means dating, then we definitely did that. But I don't think that's exactly what Lucas has in mind.

"That pretty blush is back in your cheeks, Dakota," Lucas says, pitching his voice low, making me swoon all over. "Care to tell me what you're thinking about?"

My face burns hotter as I try to regain control over myself. This guy just does something to me.

He chuckles, moving his desk closer until they touch. Our shoulders brush. I refuse to look at how close he is, my face burning up as I try to listen to the dull narrator's voice talk about some animal that has a head of a lion but a body of a— Honestly, I don't fucking know. Unless that TV starts showing giant pictures of dicks, I've totally lost interest.

Lucas's breath hits my skin, and I freeze right where I am. My muscles tense. All those things that boy and I did that summer, turn to Lucas and I doing them. My mind is a wonderful place to be. I've always thought so. The things my brain can conjure up to take me out of my everyday surroundings makes it my most precious commodity. When life was hard, my imagination kept me sane.

Lucas trails his fingertips over my thigh. My leg jumps in response. I'm barely breathing at all as he moves his hand higher and higher until his wrist brushes my stomach. My muscles tense underneath. My core ignites like an inferno just begging to be released. I haven't been this strung up in a while.

"Dakota, you..." He licks his lips and trails off as his fingers move over the seam of my shorts until he's cupping me. His breath comes out in a whoosh. "Jesus fuck, girl. You must be on fire."

He traces a trail up the inseam of my linen shorts until I squirm in the seat. The desk creaks, and he stops. The muscles in his arm flex. With his other hand, he pushes my notebook onto my lap until it rests against the desk and my thighs, completely blocking anyone's view of what he's doing. I've never been more thankful to be sitting in the back corner of a classroom.

His fingers start exploring, and I grip the edge of my desk. Much surer now, he works his finger up and down my inseam, pressing the doubled fabric to the side so it feels as if he's sliding right over my panties.

I know this is wrong, but I can't help myself. Lucas is eye candy on a whole other level. My brain also tries to tell me that he stood next to me earlier in the cafeteria, sticking up for me. But let's get real. That's not what this is. This is about release, plain and simple.

"How far will you go?" he whispers, more to himself than to me.

I buck into his fingers, and he grips the desk now, pressing his lips together to keep whatever sound he was about to invest in back.

"You think because it's dark in here, they won't hear you scream?"

I swallow, trying to tame the beating of my erratic heart. I lift my eyebrow. "I'd like to see you try."

Lust confiscates Lucas's features. "Now, you really shouldn't have said that." He snakes his hand up, moving underneath the waistband of my shorts, slipping past my panties, and cups my sex. His fingers deftly find my clit, and I bite my lip, moving my legs wider for him.

He starts in slow swirls. For a moment, I dart my eyes frantically around the room, making sure no one is paying any attention to us. The professor is no longer pretending to watch the movie either. She's dozing off in the corner of the room, and—

Lucas quickens the pace. My fingers are white knuckling the desk at this point as I try to rein everything in. He leans toward me, keeping his next words just from his lips to my ear. "You're so fucking wet. I want to drop to my knees right now, in front of everyone, until you're screaming my name. Do you think they'd mind?" When I don't answer him, he stops. I let out a breath and glare at him. He starts in lazy circles again, my body practically begging for it. "Answer me," he demands. "Do you think they'd mind?"

I nod because I don't trust my voice.

"There you go," he urges. He watches my profile, lips pouting. "I wonder what an unrestrained Dakota sounds like. Maybe I should wait."

He starts to pull his fingers away from me, but I let go of the desk and grab his wrist. I slide my hand down his, moving him along with it until I'm pushing his fingers back on me. He swirls his fingers again, rhythmic strokes that are threatening to make me explode right here, right now.

"Look at me," he purrs.

I close my eyes, press my lips together, and turn my head toward him. Removing all stimuli but Lucas and his fingers has me biting down on my lip. My eyelids flutter open. His eyes are everything. They're like dark spheres in the shadowy room. He's highlighted by shade-drawn windows, but it may as well only be the two of us in here.

He eyefucks me. They say everything his body wants to do as he rubs my clit into submission. Teasing it. Giving her everything she's been without lately. His nimble fingers work as he watches my every move. He sees every tightening of my shoulders, every noise of pleasure I want to make.

My body doesn't care that we're in a classroom. It doesn't care that there are witnesses right next to us who only have to turn their heads to see what's happening. She's greedy, and she wants *him*.

"You're beautiful," he whispers.

He tightens the circle around my clit, flicking the nub faster and faster. I plunge into the moment where there's no turning back. Whatever reckless decisions led to this, I'm about to orgasm in the middle of our mythology class.

The moment hits, and my eyes close. I throw my head back, practically biting the inside of my cheek raw, so I don't cry out. I'm suspended for a moment. The pleasure licking at me again and again in ruthless waves. Lucas touches my hand, and I open my eyes to find him staring, face softening as he watches me come down from the restrained high he forced me into.

My heart beats a dangerous rhythm as we stare at each other. Our eyes connect in disbelief and something much more carnal. If he's like me, he's wondering how we got this far. Each one of us pushing the other until I couldn't have made him stop even if I'd wanted to. I chased that orgasm down. I wanted it. In its aftermath is a lucid sort of confusion.

I'm supposed to hate him.

Lucas swallows. "Mine," he growls, squeezing my

forearm. I tilt my head at him, but he just moves back into our private bubble. "Next time that happens, I'm balls deep inside you, Wild Girl."

He pulls his hand out but doesn't move away. He stays where he is, his shoulder brushing mine. I peek over at his lap, and he's hard again. He doesn't touch it. He doesn't acknowledge it. He doesn't throw me over his shoulder and run for the nearest bathroom. It takes the rest of class and what looks like some supreme willpower, but eventually, Lucas is fit to see other people without them knowing how turned on he is when class ends.

The overhead lights flicker on like harsh spotlights, yet the spell hasn't broken. It's nowhere near disintegrating. We stay in our seats, the class emptying out. The teacher dawdles, picking up her things and waiting. When Lucas just gives her a blank stare, she shakes her head and exits the room.

In a nanosecond, he's leaning over me, kneeling on his chair with one hand on my desk and the other on the back of my seat. He lowers himself, and I watch as he descends, half fear and half lurid curiosity eating at me. I don't move. I can't move. He hovers his lips over mine. "You surprised me. No one surprises me." And then he kisses me. His hungry lips part my own. He thrusts his tongue inside, taking over. He moves his hand to the back of my head where he holds me to him, fingers keeping me firmly in place as he obliterates my precious mind.

I may never be able to fantasize again.

I kiss him back with the same fervor. It's raw and demanding, yet still practiced perfection. He kisses me and kisses me. Minutes pass. Eons. His lips collide with mine over and over until his phone vibrates in his pocket. He groans into my mouth, pulling away like it pains him.

I stare at him in shock, waiting for him to say something nasty. To tell me that this is all a joke. I half-expect the door to open and for Wyatt and Stone to pop through it, Stone with his haughty air and Wyatt with his laughter, telling me that they played me. They played me so good.

Instead, Lucas stays in his present position, his hand dropping down my neck to land on the back of my chair again. He sits back down, keeping his eyes on me until he takes his phone out and presses it to his ear. "Yeah." He lets out a breath as someone on the other side answers. "We're coming." He hangs up then, pulling his desk away from mine, so I can get up. The only thing is, I'm not sure I trust my legs to work right now. They might be Jell-O. Or pudding. Just waiting to wobble around and embarrass the shit out of me.

Lucas pulls his bag up his shoulder and then moves around to me. "I can see you freaking out," he says.

"I-I'm not," I protest even though I am. I so fucking am. My lips feel ten times their normal size, and all I can think about is that I want to be this obliterated every second of every day.

He pulls me against him. "Instead of freaking out, why don't we just see where this goes, Dakota Wilder? When I called you Wild Girl, I thought I was teasing, but now I'm wondering what else I can get you to do."

I want to say nothing, but in my head, I'm wondering the same thing. He put me in a trance. A sexed-up alternate reality.

He slides his hand down to tangle in mine. "I think this school just got a thousand percent better."

I huff out a laugh. I love this school, and even I think he's right.

When we meet Wyatt and Stone in the hallway, Lucas doesn't let go of my hand. In fact, he holds it tighter when I try to pull it away. Stone glares at it like he wants to set it on fire, but then he turns without a word and shoves the main doors open.

"Well, this oughtta be fun," Wyatt coos, a wicked grin on his face.

I can't help but watch Stone retreat with taut shoulders and a look like he could kill. I guess if I have to put up with his ornery ass, at least I have Lucas.

19

*W*e walk through the parking lot toward Wyatt's truck. When Lucas takes the truck keys out of his pocket, I snake them and run past him to the driver's side door. I don't know what's come over me, but I'm feeling positively giddy.

Actually, I know what it is. I've just had the best kiss of my whole entire fucking life. And I let Lucas Govern play with my clit. In school. In front of people. Undetected. How could I not be riding a fucking high?

"Whoa, whoa, Tits," Wyatt shouts as I unlock his truck and jump in the front seat. Several students nearby turn toward us and snicker at my nickname. I just shrug it off because anything is better than Blue's Clues. "What do you think you're doing?"

I lean out, giving him a wink. "We're talking treasure, right? There's only one place to do that."

"No, I mean, what the fuck are you doing in my truck?"

I settle back in the seat and push the button to start it, then rev the engine.

Wyatt pales. "No. No fucking way." Before I can lock the door to keep him out, he sprints forward, winging his door open and jumping up into the front seat with me. I let out a squeal and try to scramble away before he sits on me, but he doesn't let me get too far. He sits the seat back a little and then pulls me onto his lap. "You want to drive my truck? Then we're going country. You're doing it in my lap."

I force out a breath as my body melts against his. "I know how to drive a truck, you know."

"Your piece of shit? How can you even put those two trucks in the same sentence?"

I shift in his lap and gape at him. "That truck is a classic."

He smirks. "A classic?" He practically bites the word out like he doesn't approve. "Your truck might as well be a giant ass paperweight."

"That's because your friend is a giant ass douche."

"An ass douche?"

I narrow my gaze. "I meant more *giant ass* with

douche as the separate word, but ass douche works fine, too. It seems appropriate."

Wyatt shuts the door and then leans out the window to catcall Stone. "Hey, ass douche. I guess you're riding by yourself." Lucas gets into the truck beside us, and Stone gives us all the middle finger before getting into his car and slamming the door. His tiny tantrum just causes Wyatt to laugh louder. He gives his friend a salute. "Follow us."

Wyatt puts the car in drive. Instead of backing out of the parking spot, he drives over the landscaped divider in front of us, his arms caging me in. The few Saint Clary's students who are still heading to their vehicles at the end of the day give us a wide berth.

He wasn't wrong on one thing. His truck and mine are way different. His is a monster. I could've driven it. I've been driving my dad's truck since before I was legally allowed. However, I only recently got my license when I enrolled in college. I'm glad I did, considering what happened to Dad. At first, I only did it because of Marilyn, but it turns out it was a good idea for a whole different reason.

Lucas reaches over, sliding his fingers over mine on the seat. I turn toward him, and he greets me with a smile. I start to get off Wyatt as he pulls out of the school, but Wyatt pins me to him with a strong arm around my waist. "Don't even think about it," he warns. "This is the toll for thinking you could drive my truck."

Lucas snickers. "You just want a sexy girl on your lap."

"Am I that transparent?"

"Always," Lucas says.

My face flushes, and I press my lips together. I'm not used to guys saying those things to me. Insults, I can handle. Being called a freak. Even the whispers about incest I took without batting an eye. I guess townspeople tend to think lots of weird things when families stick to themselves.

"What's a matter?" Wyatt asks, clearly enjoying himself. "Never sat on a guy's lap before?"

I restrain myself from rolling my eyes. "I was actually just thinking how nice it was to be sitting up here instead of staring you down before you ran me off the road."

Wyatt stiffens. "I didn't—"

The rumble of his chest vibrates my back.

Lucas hides a smile. "Don't worry. Stone already made him pay for that."

"Fuck off, Govern." He's quiet for a moment. "Tits knows I didn't try to run her over." He pulls me back again, his hand catching my hip and staying there while he steers one-handed. "She's just changing the subject because she doesn't want us to know that she's never sat on a guy's lap before."

Now that he brings it up... I sift through my memories. Of the little experience I have with boys, um, no. There was no lap sitting.

"Don't pick on her," Lucas says, his fingers stroking mine on the seat.

"I'm not," Wyatt says innocently before his playful nature kicks in again. "I'm introducing her to amazing things. Do you know how many girls would kill to be sitting on this lap? Now Dakota can say she's done it. Don't forget that Google review afterward. I want everyone to know how amazing it is."

I shake my head. "You sure think a lot of yourself."

Wyatt takes his cowboy hat off, sitting it on the middle of the seat over mine and Lucas's entwined hands. "Just showing you that though Lucas's moody, brooding bullshit is a turn-on at first, it'll get old. You might just want a nice, casual ride in the sack. No strings. No attachments. Just a good fuck." He rolls his hips exaggeratingly, like he's taken notes from a Chippendale dancer. I grab the steering wheel in front of me, so he doesn't knock me into it, but also to plant myself back into reality because Jesus hell. He has that move down.

"Wyatt," Lucas warns.

He shrugs behind me, and I can tell he's loving this. "Just sayin'."

Though he sounds casual, there's a thickening in his jeans. They don't call me Blue's Clues for nothing. I know what that means.

I shift on his lap, and Wyatt stops breathing. It's just to fuck with him at first. To let him know that I know he's getting something out of this too, even though he tries to act like he's a heartbreaker. A user. Hey, I'm not saying anything about no-strings attached sex. That's basically what my first few encounters were, and all it did was make me hungry for experience.

Like Lucas.

Oh shit. My cheeks heat when I realize I've actually added Lucas to my sexual experiences list. It wasn't even a conscious decision. It just kind of happened as I let my body take over for once, and I'm so glad I did.

I squirm again, this time because of the images my head conjured up of Lucas and I in the classroom. "Christ," Wyatt grinds out, expelling a breath. "Stop moving. If Stone sees me hard as a rock when I get out of this truck, his head is going to explode."

I stare daggers into the windshield as my body

instantly cools. "Stone doesn't have a say in anything that happens in my life. Fuck him and his father. Throw in his mother while you're at it."

The cab fills with a weighted silence before Wyatt finally breaks it. "Um, are you going to tell me where we're going?"

"We're headed the right way," I say. Now that we're on the way there, I don't know if I feel right about this. A Jacobs has never been invited onto my family's property for a reason. What if I give them information and they just drop me?

I gaze at Lucas to find his jaw feathering as he stares ahead. He's pulled his hand back, and I'm pretty sure I was too preoccupied with seething over the mention of Stone that I didn't feel it when he had. I miss the feeling of his hand in mine though. As crazy as it sounds, it felt right, and now I'm wondering *why* he took it away. Is this just a ruse to get what they want out of me?

I groan inwardly. It would be easy to dismiss what happened between Lucas and I if he hadn't kissed me like that afterward. Like we were both suffocating and the only person who could give us life was the other. My life has been sheltered, but that—*that* is what always kept me going. All the books I read can't be wrong. There are experiences like that out there.

We drive past the Leaving Clary sign. I lean forward, and I definitely feel Wyatt's hard-on against me now. He places his hand around me again and drags me back against it. Neither of us say anything, but my body goes haywire. I bet Wyatt would be a good fuck. Nice and casual, sure, but mind-blowing at the same time. There's an aura about him that screams he'll never settle down. From head-to-toe, he gives off that vibe of sex on a stick and nothing more. Wyatt Longhorn isn't looking for anything more than just rough, dirty, sheet-twisting sex.

Both men appeal to me in different ways. Lucas because there might be something there. Wyatt because my experiences are only just beginning and experimental. What he's offering sounds like what my fantasies are made of.

"Shit, right here," I call out, pointing at my family's house. Wyatt has to slam on the brakes and turn the wheel hard. Sand kicks up, leaving a cloud of brown that takes forever to settle.

When it does, the differences between Jacobs Manor and the rustic Wilder cabin are obvious. The house has been neglected at best, abandoned at worst. When I say my father has no interests other than the treasure, I mean it. It's not just something I say to show his devotion to finding his family's legacy, it's one hundred percent true.

From the street, it looks like a shack. At times, it was. At times, we didn't even have running water or a toilet that would fully work. My father would grab buckets in the nearby stream, and I would take showers with them. One initial, ice-cold water bucket to lather up and then one to rinse off the shampoo/conditioner and soap.

In commercials, I'd see these models on TV talking about how to tame their curly hair, and I'd long for it. Just something to make me feel a little normal. None of the women looked like they were taking ice-cold showers with rusty buckets. In fact, my shampoo and conditioner come from the dollar store, and I use them sparingly.

However, the two times I've taken a shower in Jacobs Manor has already made my hair feel ten thousand times better.

"Where the fuck are we?"

Lucas smacks Wyatt.

"We," I say, throwing his door open and quickly shutting it again when Stone pulls in to shield us from the deluge of dirt his tires kicked up. "...are at my house."

"This piece of shit?"

"Jesus, Wyatt. Shut the fuck up," Lucas snarls.

He's not wrong, but I feel it all the same. The shame. Growing up, I tried not to let other people's words get to me, but when they had a hint of truth, it was hard not to. I often wondered why the hell Marilyn would even look at my dad. Not when she had Lance. I rationalized it because I knew how much of a dick he was and that my father was just plain awesome, but now that I've seen the other side, I think I'd be willing to put up with a lot just to have consistent running water.

Though, Marilyn came in at the right time. She didn't have to deal with all the house issues I had to. We haven't had plumbing issues in years.

When the cloud of dust settles, I push the truck door open again and climb off Wyatt's lap to jump to the ground. The four of us meet in front of the cars. I stare at the house for a moment, thinking of my dad. When I peek at the guys, they're all wearing various levels of distaste. Confusion. Shock. Sneers.

No one outside my father, Marilyn, and I—and of course my grandfather who built it—have ever been inside this house. I know it's nothing like Stone's place. It has the workings of a madman inside. I used to try to keep up with all the paperwork he had, organize it somehow, but he seemed to like it strewn about where he could pick it up at a moment's notice and work on something on a whim. I just tried to keep it contained to one pile each on every flat surface.

When Marilyn first came, she cleaned the place from top to bottom, but as time went on, she just gave up too. My dad's stuck in his ways.

I clear my throat, letting the memories hit me. They go back in time, getting more familiar but harder to bear. It reminds me of just how alone I am right now.

Walking forward, I take out my own keys and unlock the front door. It isn't as if it's keeping anybody out. You could just put a hole in the side of the house to get in if you wanted to, but crime in Clary is practically nonexistent. The door creaks as it falls open, and I lead them into the big room that's the kitchen, dining, and living area, filled with shabby furniture and open shelving that shows every out-of-place item.

I swallow a lump in my throat. We're miles away from Stone's place. Not just in distance, but in quality of living.

I turn abruptly to face them, hoping to take their attention off the mess. "My father has years of research in this house. I can show you where it is, but—"

"This is a big step for you," Stone says, voice low. Not like he's trying to beat me to the punch line of my own sentence, but like he's acknowledging that this shit is sacred to my family. It won't give away the greatest secrets, but it gives a lot.

I nod, thankful that he at least gets it on a surface level. "This is a leap of faith, and I'm imploring you to let it stay here. To not publicize what you find," I say, staring at Stone whose discerning gaze keeps darting around the room. "This is years and years of my family's work, and I'd rather it *stay* in the family."

He focuses back on me. "You have my word."

"Mine, too," Lucas agrees.

"Really, Tits?" Wyatt asks. He gives me a smirk. "Who am I going to tell?"

Their assurances only give me a slight reprieve from my hesitation. When I lead them down the hallway, my feet feel like cement blocks trying to wade through mud, and I half-wonder if my father is sending me messages not to do what I'm about to. He would kill me. He would disown me.

But I have to find him. And it's not just the creepy as fuck note that has me positive that if I find the treasure, I'll find my dad. It's because if I know anything about Clark Wilder, it's that he wouldn't dare die until he found the treasure. Or, he would've died trying.

I nudge my father's study door open with my shoe

and come to a halt. Wyatt's chest bumps against me, and I step into the study with a gasp.

There's shit everywhere. The desk is upended. All of the cupboards have been torn down. Paper litters the floor with my father's distinct handwriting scribbled everywhere. The lamp is smashed on the floor, glass shards sparkle against the small rays of sun that peek in through the window.

It's been ransacked. In fact, it looks just like when these assholes went through my shit looking for stuff.

I'm an idiot. Of course, they've already been here. Why wouldn't they try here first?

I turn, locking them all with a glare as my hands turn to fists. "You assholes!"

20

My nails bite into my palm as I stare daggers at them. I can't believe I even half trusted them. A quarter trusted them. I can't believe I would even soften to any of them at all. "I see you've already been here."

Stone matches my glare and gives it right back to me. "What?"

I spread my arms out wide. My face heats like I'm going to explode. "You've already been through the room. Did you find everything you so desperately wanted? The one clue that was worth this?" What a violation of privacy. My dad always said they couldn't be trusted. It's a damn good thing he hides his most precious treasure information. If they only tore up this room like they did with my dorm, then there's no way they found whatever they were looking for. "You can kiss my help goodbye."

I try to push between them, but Stone grabs me. He sure does love grabbing me a lot, doesn't he? He hauls me back to his chest, his breath hitting my ear. "Is this not what this room usually looks like?"

"Are you serious?" I grind out.

I turn my head to stare at him but he only blinks.

"Honestly, it's not that much different from the other parts of the house," Lucas says in a small voice, like he's worried I'll start swinging. I just might. My father and I had a hell of a lot of time on our hands, and one way we passed the time was to make sure I could hold my own if I ever needed to. No daughter of his was going to be someone's punching dummy.

He was wrong about that because sometimes words hurt more, especially when you have a muzzle on you.

"Look at this," Wyatt says. His sneakers crunch over the broken glass as he tiptoes toward the over-turned desk. He pulls out a map of Clary that's from the 1800s. On the blank side, STUPID GIRL is written in big, block letters just like the stylized note I got a few days ago.

This time, I don't shy away from Stone, I move back into him. His grip loosens, and instead of forcing me to be where I am, it's as if he's shielding me.

"Same type of note from the apartment," Lucas says in a hushed tone but with that same rich energy. It draws me to look at him. "We didn't do this, Dakota."

I press my lips together. I'm beginning to think they're right, but it's not as if I don't have reason to doubt them. "I guess you'll have to excuse me if I still have lingering trust issues. I know you were looking for something that night in my dorm room. You broke my door down. You went through my stuff."

Lucas's face flushes. Pink creeps up his neck and balloons over his cheeks. Wyatt and Stone are less inclined to feel remorse though. Wyatt shrugs, "You were the enemy."

I want to tell him I was never their enemy, but that's not technically true, is it? That's not how Dad brought me up. I hate these guys, I just don't know why it's so hard to hate them when he isn't here. I'm being torn in two different directions, and I'm not sure which path I should go down. Should I trust my gut or my father's?

Thoughts collide, crashing into one another, and I yank my hair down with the start of a splitting headache.

Stone leads me to Lucas in the corner of the room

who pins me to his side and starts running his hands over my hair. He even rubs my temples like he knows what's going on inside my head. This guy definitely plays the part of silent observer well if he knows about my headaches, hair-driven or not.

Wyatt and Stone pick their way through the mess. There's no rhyme or reason to my father's research they're finding even though they try to make sense of each paper they pick up. Stone's practically having a stroke with how messy and unorganized my father's writings are. He keeps twitching involuntarily.

Eventually, they get everything off the floor and in piles on the desk that they turn right side up again. I move to the kitchen to grab the broom and dustpan that are in the corner. When I come back, they're talking in hushed tones, so I stop just outside the room. "You think it was them?"

"Or your dad."

The last was from Wyatt. They were obviously talking about Lance and even from here, I'd know Lucas's voice, so I can rule him out.

"This wasn't my dad," Stone growls.

"Yeah, you say that a lot." A sigh filters through the room. "You have to tell her what's really going on."

"I tried, but she wouldn't listen. It's not my fault she's stubborn."

"Make her listen," Lucas demands, and the hairs on my arms prick.

"Just because you want to fuck her now," Stone deadpans.

I peek around the corner as several heavy footsteps sound. Stone and Lucas are in each other's faces, and Wyatt, with his wide-brimmed hat, pushes them apart.

"It's more than that and you know it," Lucas seethes. "You'd feel the same if it weren't for the fact that you're content being your father's little bitch."

Stone roars and moves forward. Wyatt shoves them away from each other again. "This is hardly helping. Save your pissing contest for later." He eyes them, studying their stances. He must like what he sees because he steps back. "I agree with Lucas. We have to help her see what's really going on. We aren't being fair. We dragged her into this, now look what's fucking happening."

Stone lets out a sound of frustration, turns, and pulls his fist back to punch the wall. I step through the doorway, stopping him in his tracks. A myriad of emotions play over his face until he pushes past me, storming from the room. A few seconds later, the front door slams.

"What's his problem?" I ask, pretending I didn't hear their conversation. I don't think any of what they just said to each other was for my benefit. Something else is going on with these notes, but I'm also not convinced it isn't Jacobs related.

"Explaining just one of his many problems would take forever," Wyatt says, sighing.

At first, I think he means it as a joke, but he doesn't laugh. I drop the dustpan on the floor and go to work sweeping. Lucas and Wyatt pick up the bigger pieces of the broken lamp and rearrange things in the room, so it doesn't look like a bomb went off. When they drag a broken cupboard outside, I wait until I hear the front door open and close, and then I run to the loose plank in the wall. I feel inside, and my fingers close around a set of keys. I let out a long sigh. My heart's been in my throat this whole time waiting to make sure that this was still here. The one piece needed to get to my father's most important papers. "Thank fuck," I whisper.

I slip the keys into my pocket and continue sweeping up every last bit of glass but end up getting a big pile of dust bunnies and dirt too. It's been ages since anyone has cleaned up in here. I quickly sweep everything into the dustpan and head to the kitchen to dump it in the trash.

It would be impossible to figure out if anyone took anything from here. My guess is they were looking for something specific and didn't find it. In that case, it's a damn good thing they didn't find the keys. Though, if they did, they wouldn't know the hiding place.

Or this could be something else entirely. Just another scare tactic like with my dorm and the letter I got in the mail.

I don't know what they're referring to in the last two notes though. The first said, GOOD GIRL. The second, STUPID GIRL. They're obviously referring to me, but what exactly are they referencing? A cold shiver runs through me. If they're picking apart my life, then they must be watching me too.

I'm so deep in thought about being watched that when the door slams behind Lucas, I jump out of my skin, a scream working its way up my throat. I stop it before I let the whole thing out, but Wyatt and Stone run back into the house as Lucas places his hands on my shoulders to calm me. "Christ," I breathe out when I'm no longer worried I'm going to scream bloody murder.

Stone gazes at the house and walks right back out. No doubt he thinks he's going to catch a disease just by being in here. Unless it's the poor disease, which isn't even a fucking thing, he's wrong.

"There's really not much we can do here right now," Lucas says. "You want to go back to the house?"

I glance around the room. I can feel my father everywhere. I'm not saying I had the best childhood. Obviously, that would be a lie. But I am saying that I miss him. Being here brings me that much closer to him too. It makes me feel like he's still alive out there somewhere, and that I have a chance to find him. I hope.

I nod, and Lucas steers me out of the house. I lean the broom against the countertop and exit, sifting in my pockets for the front door keys instead of the other. I'll have to hide the other set of keys in my room at Jacobs Manor somewhere in case whoever is looking for treasure shit comes there next. Then again, as they've already pointed out, we're much safer there than here. To think I thought about coming home when my dorm got trashed. Who knows what would've happened if whoever did this would've found me here alone.

The drive to Stone's house is much more solemn. Even Wyatt doesn't joke. There's no pulling me onto his lap as punishment that wasn't a punishment at all— for either of us—unless you count blue balls as one. Stone beats us there, pulling into his spot in the garage. Wyatt follows, parking in the other bay, and then we all get out.

"I don't know about you," Wyatt says, "but I don't feel like cooking." he lets the sentence hang in the air for a bit before he says, "Oh, that's right. None of you assholes cook at all." He playfully hits himself in the forehead. "I forgot who I was talking to."

"Just use the credit card to order some pizza," Stone says, ignoring Wyatt's jab.

"Yes, Master," Wyatt says. He starts walking like Quasimodo. "You know I only live to do your bidding."

When we get in the house through the garage door, Stone apologizes. "Sorry," he says. "I'm just stressed."

Wyatt claps him on the back. "I know, bro. Just keep the dickishness to a minimum before Dakota up and leaves us all."

Stone tracks his gaze to me, lingering there for a moment, before he retreats further into the house, turning down the glass-lined hallway.

Wyatt goes to a drawer in the kitchen and pulls out a credit card. "What do you like on your pizza, Tits?" He smirks to himself. He's really too proud of himself for that nickname.

Lucas speaks up. "Dakota had pizza for lunch."

"Oh right," Wyatt says. He grins. "That was fun, by the way. I loved seeing you stick up for yourself in front of those bitches."

"Weren't you just talking about shoving your dick in one of those bitches this morning?"

He shrugs. "Seemed like a good idea at the time. Turns out it was more fun watching Tits get revenge."

"That name really doesn't bother you?" Lucas asks.

I shrug. "I've heard worse."

He frowns, but Wyatt interrupts. "Have you ever had a calzone? It's like pizza but not."

"If it's not, then what is it?"

They explain to me the ins and outs of calzones, and it sounds like heaven.

Wyatt orders enough food for an army and then hangs up the phone.

"They really deliver out here?"

He winks. "We give them an extra incentive. It helps that the card is under Jacobs." He walks past me. "I don't think I need to explain to you the almost celebrity-like fervor that goes through the air at that name."

My jaw sets. He sure as hell doesn't.

With Wyatt and Stone gone, Lucas leads me to the couch in the living room. I wasn't sure anyone ever sat on this furniture. Like it's one of those pieces for show that I've seen on television before. That's obviously not the case when Lucas pulls me next to him, draping my legs over his lap. He works his fingers through my hair again, and I sigh.

With his other hand, he rubs at his face like he could sleep for days. "I know there are more important things to talk about, but...do you want to talk about what happened in Mythology earlier?"

He's right. There are definitely more imminent topics to discuss, but maybe not one that's as much fun. "If you want," I say casually like it's no big deal, but I doubt I'm hiding anything from him. While kissing him, I felt more exposed than I ever have.

His fingers trail over the line of my jaw and then back into my hair. "I just want to say that I'd like that to happen again. Maybe not that exact scenario, but now that my hands have been on you, I don't want to take them away."

My breath hitches. His brown-eyed stare takes me down roads I wasn't sure I'd get to. My only chance was getting out of Clary, and I wasn't sure that was in the cards for me. At my worst moments, I pictured myself as an old lady in my father's house, living in the walls he built up with no one.

I snap myself out of it. Lucas isn't offering a forever here. He's just offering more fun. "I'd like that, too."

Stone strides out into the living room with different clothes on. "If you're done making heart eyes at each other, we have more important things to discuss than you getting your dick wet."

I glare at him, and he matches me stare for stare as

he takes a seat on the couch across from us. "Save it, Jacobs," Lucas purrs.

Something's gotten wedged up Stone's ass though. He leans forward with his elbows on his knees, "Your house was a pigsty."

My stomach rolls. "Oh, sorry it offended you, your highness. Not all of us can afford a goddamn maid. All we had was your mother, and she was shit at it."

Stone charges to his feet. "Leave her out of this." He clenches his fists, his nostrils flaring. In the next moment, he regains control of himself like the outburst never happened. The man has more self-control than anyone I've ever met. He straightens his shoulders. "It's bad enough she was living in that filth."

Lucas sighs next to me.

"Maybe you should take that as a lesson learned. There's more to being a man than just having money. Your dad has all of it that he'll ever need, and your mom still left him for my dad."

Stone laughs. It's maniacal, nothing like the cultured laughs I've heard spill from his mouth before. "You're still under the mistaken impression that she wanted to be there." His blue-gray eyes twinkle with delight. "It was all a ruse, Dakota. She hated being there," he growls out. "And most of all, she hated your father."

I suck in a breath as air gets sucked from my lungs. The truth of what he's just said is in his cold, heartless eyes. Marilyn marrying my father was some sort of ploy? A sham?

My insides twist with second-hand pain for my father. He was always so happy when he looked at her. To think someone could've played him so badly makes me want to vomit. I stand on shaky legs. "You're despicable, Stone Jacobs. Stay away from me."

21

I stride from the room. My body thrums with hatred for him and everything he stands for.

So, that's what his problem was at my dad's house. The reason he couldn't stand to be in there. Marilyn.

Behind me, Lucas sighs. "You know we're never going to be able to get shit done unless you two can learn to be in the same fucking room as each other without acting like children," he growls at Stone.

In front of me, Wyatt turns the corner in nothing but a pair of sweatpants and his cowboy hat. His chiseled torso is backdropped by the setting sun behind him, leaving him in a haze of oranges and pinks. The whole scene is dreamlike. If only he had a pair of low-slung jeans, it'd be the perfect picture. A cowboy out on the ranch, performing his evening duties so the rest of the house could sleep.

Dear God, my imagination just takes me away sometimes, doesn't it?

Before I can slip past him in the hall, he places his arm out, barricading my exit. His blue eyes hold heat. "Where are you going? I thought we were talking."

I turn to face him, and he searches my face for clues. Whatever he sees there makes his brows pinch together. Back in the living room, harsh whispers are thrown back and forth. I smile without feeling, which I'm pretty sure makes me a psychopath. I can't help it if Stone brings out the worst in me. "Your douchey friend strikes again."

He flicks his gaze toward the living room then back at me. "Yeah well, he's *our* douche." He lowers his voice and leans down. I take a step back, but he follows me. We do this awkward dance until my back hits the wall and he's caged me in with the brim of his hat just barely skimming my forehead. He reaches up to pet my hair. There's no other word to describe what he's doing. He watches as his fingers skirt over my curls then returns his attention to me. "The line between love and hate is painted with ill intentions."

"Did you read that out of a Cracker Jack box?"

He smirks, shaking his head as he looks away. "I like you, Tits."

I force my chin in the air, pulling some self-confidence from somewhere within me. Or maybe I'm just channeling all the literary heroines I've read about in the past. What would Jane Austen make her characters do? "I felt your—" My gaze drops, signaling that I'm referring to his package when I was on his lap in the truck. I don't know why I think Elizabeth Bennet would've started off with that line. They weren't even allowed to be alone with a dude, but if she'd been forced to live in the twenty-first century, she would have.

Wyatt chuckles. "Oh, Tits. In this house, we use proper terms. You felt my cock against your ass? Is that what you're trying to say."

A fierce blush rises to my cheeks. It's been such an odd day. The incident at school. Lucas. My dad's house. Now this? I feel like I'm living two different lives. One where I'm being seduced by devils, and the other where the unthinkable is happening.

"Say it, Tits," Wyatt presses. "Be the Wild Girl Lucas thinks you are."

I smirk because it's funny he thinks I need to be taught. Dude, please. I've been reading romance books since I was twelve years old. Most of the time, my only entertainment was books. I place my hands on his chest and push. I keep going until he hits the opposite wall. I can tell Wyatt likes it. Like this is all a big game he means to keep playing until it bores him. I slip up onto my tiptoes. "I felt it," I say, my voice barely above a whisper. "Your cock growing beneath me every time I moved on your lap, poking my ass like if you could just. Slip. Through."

Wyatt's smile grows more appreciative. "You know it, baby. I'm a horny asshole. I don't care where the pussy comes from, I'm down."

Unfortunately, I think that's true in Wyatt's case. His humor has to be a shield from something.

Not that I should care.

"Well, now that we've got that settled," I say. I turn and start to move toward my room again.

Wyatt grabs my shirt, pulling me backward. I stumble into his chest, and he moves an arm around my middle. "Two things, Tits," he breathes. "One, I don't care how much of a dick Stone just was to you, we have a job, and we're getting it done. So, you're going to march your pert little ass back out to the living room so we can talk." His fingers dig into my side in a dominant way. It's not uncomfortable, it's...hot. Wyatt Longhorn knows how to play the alpha asshole, that's for sure. His hands linger there, and he forgets to keep talking.

That one-track mind of his is going to get him in trouble.

"What's number two?"

He moves my hair from around my shoulder and leans in, his lips just grazing my ear, making fire roar through me. The barest of touches fuels my lust like the first spark of dynamite or lick of heat. "Oh," he breathes. "I just wanted to tell you that when you said cock, my own responded." He presses his hips into me as proof. Just like when I was sitting in his lap, his hard cock sits firmly against my ass.

I swear I'm going to combust just by living here. "So, does that mean I own you?"

He freezes and pushes me away. His dark laughter rings behind me. He's very good at that. Flicking from normal to prick in an instant. All of them are. "No one's ever been able to claim that," he says, voice as sharp as jagged glass. He walks past me with a dismissive once-over. "I highly doubt it will be you."

He leaves me in the hallway and waltzes out into the living room. I could just turn around and head back to my room but there's no lock on the door and I'm afraid the caveman here would just throw me over his shoulder and drag me out. Part of me wants to try to see if he would, but the other part of me knows he's right. Whatever shit Stone and I have needs to be put away for the greater good. If he can't be a man and put it behind him, I'll have to do it.

The doorbell rings.

Plus, there's pizza. Who am I to say no to trying whatever this calzone thing is?

Wyatt whoops it up as he answers the door. I walk back into the main room and stand there awkwardly. Wyatt opens the door, and the pizza delivery guy strides in. He gives me a double-take, and my own heart sinks. I'm just like my father. I hate seeing people I know. Seeing people means being forced into socializing, and that's never been my strong suit. Mainly because Clary is filled with a bunch of gossip-mongering, hateful hypocrites.

I'm surprised this guy even remembers me.

"Is that you, Dakota?"

His gaze moves up and down, taking in my hair all the way down to my outfit. I feel exposed. Stone really did only pack a few articles of clothing. Not that there were many at all, but he left all my comfortable clothes. All the clothes that let me fade into the background. I guess no one fades into the background in a house like this though. "Hey, Matt..." I say, waving awkwardly.

He slips the pizza onto the island in the kitchen, eyes still round. "Damn, you look so different. I mean, I don't think I've ever seen you with your hair down before. I barely recognized you."

I blush. He won't stop looking at me, and I'm used to being a shadow. Matt and I went to high school together. I was no one then. Well, I was there to be made fun of, that was it. I'm surprised he didn't call me Blue's Clues like Todd. "So, you're working at a pizza place?"

He shakes his head. "Yeah, it's not much, but you have to find something to do around here." He rubs his face, his smile growing wide. "You know, we should catch up sometime. I haven't seen you since high school."

My brows furrow. Catch up? In order to catch up, we'd have to be caught up at some point in our lives and that never happened. I can't remember any definitive memories where Matt made fun of me, but he certainly wasn't a friend either. When I say I was a no one, I fucking mean it. I'm not just being dramatic. No one ever looked at me to see me.

Stone breaks our staring contest by stepping into our line of sight. He dwarfs Matt. They all do. It's like the Jacobs and their cronies are from different stock than the rest of the population. It's not just that they were born from an asshole tree and hit every branch on the way down, they're out of place in other ways too. "Wilder's going to have to pass."

"Oh, I'm sorry, man." Matt says. "I didn't realize she had a boyfriend."

"She doesn't," Lucas says, moving to stand next to his friend.

I clench my jaw and step forward, but Wyatt stops me. He grins down. "Ours, remember?"

"Oh, fuck off."

"Mmm. I love it when you talk dirty. I think I'm going to have to make you my pet project, Tits."

I growl at him, and he just laughs.

Behind us, Stone is telling Matt to get fucked. He throws money at him. It hits his chest and falls to the floor. Several twenty-dollar bills that Stone just pulled from his wallet stare at him from the ground. I cringe when Matt falls to his knees, grabbing it up. I don't blame Matt. I'd be doing the same thing if I didn't think I'd ever hear the end of it between these guys, and right now, our lives are irrevocably stuck together.

"Get the fuck out of here," Lucas says, charging to the door and throwing it open.

Matt doesn't look at me again. He stuffs the twenties in his pocket and takes off. As soon as he's stepped over the threshold, Lucas kicks the door shut and the guys return to normal as if they didn't just act like giant dicks. They head toward the pizza, Stone getting plates out for everybody, not even discussing what just happened.

My mouth drops open. "You guys are insane, you know that, right?"

They all gaze around at each other and just shrug. They give zero fucks about this. Zero fucks about whose lives they interfere with or who they make act like a fucking animal, scrambling around on the floor for the scraps they deem to throw like he's a peasant and they sit in a gold tower. Actually, they kind of do. Jacobs Manor might not be made of real gold, but it feels like it is. Everywhere you look, they're showing off their wealth. The house. The cars. Their clothes. No wonder why everyone is drawn to them at Saint Clary's. They're shiny, dressed up like new toys every single day. People say being wealthy doesn't matter, but that's all a crock of shit. Beauty always attracts the eye, and it doesn't even have to be from the person itself. It's from the expensive shit they surround themselves with.

Lucas hands me a plate with what I assume is my calzone. It looks like what Wyatt described earlier. Suddenly, I don't have an appetite though. Am I just being one of the adoring masses, falling to my feet with the scraps they decide to give me? Good food. A nice bed. An orgasm to pass the time, even if it was the most daring thing I'd ever done. For a few minutes, I wasn't Dakota Wilder, and that was nice.

But I am, aren't I? I'm just like Matt, picking up twenty-dollar bills from the floor.

I'll never be one of them.

"You okay?" Lucas asks, reaching out to touch my cheek.

I pull out of his reach. "Why did you guys just do that?"

A smirk starts to pull Lucas's lips up. "Because you're ours, Wild Girl. We're not going to sit back and listen when some asshole tries to hit on you. He was practically tenting his pants."

"Not that," I say through clenched teeth. "Treating him like a dog. Throwing money at him like he's no one. Practically making him bow at your feet. It's disgusting."

Stone drops his plate to the island, and it clatters. The sound makes me jump. Haven't they ever heard of paper plates for crying out loud? Within a moment, I'm not thinking of that anymore because Stone Jacobs is once again breathing my air, taking it all up for himself because that's what he does. He's selfish and greedy. He steps into my space, taking more and more from me without a care in the world. "No one told him he had

269

to lower himself to pick up the money. He did that on his own. You want a tip?"

"From someone like you? No fucking thank you."

He grins evilly. "If you don't want to be seen as a low-life subservient, don't cower at my feet."

"God, you think so much of yourself, don't you?"

"If I don't, who will?"

I open my mouth with another cutting barb at the tip of my tongue, but his response wasn't what I expected.

His smile smooths out, lingering somewhere between ringing so completely false that it almost tugs at my inner heart strings and holding so much truth that it's hard to decipher who he really is. "There you go, Dakota Wilder. That's the secret." His gray-blue eyes hook into mine, keeping me there for much longer than I want. He's giving me a window into his soul. When I peek inside, it's not all bad. It's fucked up, yes, but it isn't laced with cruelty like I imagined. "Now," he says, making sure his polo is sitting right across his shoulders. "We're going to eat and discuss. I will act civilized, and I'm asking you to do the same. I think there's something we can agree on. It's in both of our best interests to get the treasure. Working together is the only way we're going to do that, so...can we start?"

I breathe out a breath I'd been holding captive. If I

was in a book, this would be the moment I could tell them all to go to hell...or finally put our differences aside. The thing is, that's assuming this whole thing is going to end up as a happy ending, and in real life, there are just no guarantees that's ever going to happen. My life isn't destined for that prize at the end. No matter how much I've tried to make it happen, I've come to grips with the outcome. The only thing I can hope for is getting my father back, so that's what I'm going to focus on. "Let's do it."

22

The guys and I settle down in the pristine living room to eat our pizza. It seems wrong to eat in such a beautiful room. I'm almost afraid to touch the fabric for fear of getting stains on it.

However, the guys are less worried. They dig into the pizza like rabid animals. Even though Stone seems firmly like a knife and fork type of pizza eater, he eats it with his hands like a regular person. I'm almost impressed. It's like he's thrown caution to the wind.

Me? I steady my calzone on my lap. The first piece is delectable. I almost moan. So much cheese. So. Much. It's like heaven in my mouth.

As we eat, Lucas decides he's going to be the mediator, starting the conversation where we need to. I gaze at him while he eyes all of us and wonder if he's used to this role he's filling. I thought him silent before, and he kind of is. He doesn't speak much when one, he doesn't care about you, and two, when he doesn't have anything to say. It's refreshing after listening to the idiots in Clary talk all their lives. They never cared what kind of ignorance came out of their mouths.

"So," Lucas starts. "We need to plan our first trip into the mountains." Each of the guys eye me. If they're wondering if I know where to start, the answer is yes. I think. Though I could kick myself for keeping my distance from Dad in the last few weeks before he took his last trek into the mountains. If he was on a hot trail, I'm not sure I would actually know about it. The key in my pocket burns. I have to get to the safe sooner rather than later, and I still don't trust these guys to show them where it is or what's in there. "What do you need, Dakota?"

I swallow. When my dad went missing, I made trips into the mountains, but without the right gear. It was always tough. Whatever my dad had was with him. "I need the works," I tell them, shame heating my face. "Backpack. Tent. Boots. You name it, I need it. My dad's stuff went with him."

It's one of the reasons why I was never able to find him right after. I didn't have the proper equipment, and I sure as fuck didn't have the money to go buy it. I had to make do with Dickie's old stuff, but it was ancient and worn. Not really suitable for my needs. I couldn't even spend the night up in the mountains, which I know hindered my progress.

"We have most of the stuff you need, but we'll get you some boots," Stone promises. He even sounds decent about it. Not a hint of annoyance that he has to buy the poor girl things in order to take her into the mountains. "Also, I'll have someone go into your father's house and pack up all of his research. If it's okay with you," he tacks on. "I don't think it's safe there anymore."

"I agree," I say. "I can do it though."

Stone shakes his head. "We have more important things to do." He swallows thickly, eyeing his pizza. He sets his plate down on the coffee table and leans back, clutching his stomach. Wyatt glances over at him. "You feeling off?"

"No, I'm fine."

I eye my calzone and wonder if the heavy head I'm feeling isn't a headache coming on like I thought. The plate doubles then triples. There are three calzones which then merge back into one. I shut my eyes, and the world starts to tilt. "Guys, there's definitely..." My tongue thickens in my mouth. I press it against my teeth, trying to get it to work correctly.

Wyatt, who's been focusing more on eating than on the treasure conversation, slumps forward. He bangs his head on the coffee table and falls to the floor.

Shit. From the corner of my eye, I see Stone and Lucas attempt to go to him. Lucas stands, but he tumbles to the floor like he can't hold his weight. A haze filters over the room like heat waves distorting the landscape.

The last thing I remember is the calzone slipping to the floor. I don't even hear it hit because I'm out.

I WAKE WITH A POUNDING HEADACHE. I DON'T even want to open my eyes because when I do, it feels like someone is trying to shove a screwdriver into the back of my skull. I groan, trying to turn over, to stop whatever the hell is doing this to me. "Hey," a soft voice says. "It's okay. I've got something for you to take right here."

A hand caresses my head and pulls away.

"It's Lucas," he says. "It's okay."

"It's not okay," I mumble, thinking about what the fuck happened. We were drugged. We had to have been.

"You're right, it's not. But we're okay now. Can you

sit up? You need to drink this water, and I've got something for you to take for the pain."

I push my hands against the mattress, realizing I am in fact on a bed for the first time. They must have moved me. I don't get anywhere though. My limbs are still too weak.

"I got you," Lucas says. He hooks his hands under my arms and hauls me against the headboard. The quicksand feeling drags away from my head, filtering down through my body. I can open my eyes now and find Lucas sitting on a chair next to my bed. He picks up his phone. "I'm just going to text the guys to tell them you're awake."

"Am I the last one awake?"

He nods as his fingers fly over the keyboard. "We think it's because you weigh a lot less than the rest of us. Wyatt came out of it first."

I can see why. He's big and bulky. Not in a negative way, obviously. Most definitely in a hunky man sort of way.

Lucas smirks at me. "Pretty sure you didn't mean to say that out loud."

"Fuck. Did I?"

He nods.

"Let's just pretend that never happened."

He finally puts his phone down and grabs the

water, holding it to my lips. I take a few swallows before having the strength to actually hold my own cup. I down it, my mouth suddenly as dry as the desert, the water only quenching it so much. Lucas takes the empty glass from me. "I'm going to go grab you some more so you can take that pain reliever, okay? Just hold on."

He passes Wyatt in the hallway who waits for him to leave before he waltzes in. It's one of the only times I've seen him without his cowboy hat on. "You look like shit, Tits."

"I feel like shit," I grumble. It feels like I have the hangover from hell yet also still drunk at the same time. It's taking way too long for things to compute inside my head. Like I can see the words coming in, but I have to disseminate them one by one before drawing conclusions about what's being said. "What happened?"

Wyatt leans against the glass wall, dropping his head to the glass. He shakes his head. "It's my fault. I didn't fucking lock back up after the pizza guy came."

I narrow my gaze at him. "I don't—"

Lucas comes back in. "We'll get to that," he snaps, glaring at Wyatt who sighs, shoulders drooping.

"She asked, dude."

"Just let her wake up for a second because she's not going to understand anything until she does."

He's got a point there.

"Thanks," Lucas says smiling.

"Jesus. Fuck me," I say, wishing I could tell the difference between saying things out loud and saying them in my head.

Wyatt winks. "Just tell me when you're down, Tits. I'll rock your world."

"I already know your type, Wyatt. You'd tap it once then convince yourself you don't need it again, and then we'd be like lost little puppies in a cardboard box, never finding a way out."

Wyatt frowns. "Some of that made sense. Some of it didn't."

Lucas hands me two pills and the glass of water again. I take the pain reliever, then continue to drink until the glass is empty again.

After a couple of minutes, I sit up in bed. The swimming through quicksand feeling has rescinded, and I'm fairly sure I can talk without thinking I'm saying things in my head but saying them out loud instead.

"You should take a shower," Wyatt suggests. "It'll make you feel better. Let me know if you want to be lost little puppies." He lifts his brows seductively.

I smirk. "I can already tell I'm not going to live that one down."

"'Fraid not, Tits."

I shrug and swing my legs over the side of the bed. Lucas is right there. He helps me to my feet and stands right next to me to make sure I don't fall over. "Good?"

"Good," I tell him, thankful he's here to help. That they both are. I can't imagine what I would've done if I'd woken up all alone after something like that. I would've freaked the fuck out, I know that. "I think I can handle it from here."

Lucas's face pinches. "I'll check on you but come out to the living room when you're done."

I nod in agreement, and then the two of them leave. My feet feel like sledgehammers as I make my way into the bathroom. I start the shower and then strip. The rain showerhead thrums across my scalp in nice, even drops. It's divine. While standing there, I dissect what happened. Someone knocked us out. They put something in our food. The dorm room. My father's house. Now this. There's something more going on that those three assholes need to come clean about.

The simmering anger over the intrusion into our lives spurs me to move faster. I shut the showerhead off and ring out my hair. Stepping out of the shower, I quickly dry off before going into the room to find clothes to throw on. I settle for a pair of my pajamas. The dark night full of stars I spy through the glass ceiling in the bathroom tells me it's some time in the middle of the night. We must've been passed out for hours.

I walk out of my bedroom in a flimsy pair of cotton shorts and a tank top. I threw a bra on under the shirt because I decided my nipples were too visible. I wouldn't mind Lucas seeing that, but Wyatt's too much of a manwhore and Stone is just...well...a dick.

I pass through the hallway, feeling much better. The throbbing pain in my head is still there, but my brain and muscle functionality has pretty much returned to normal the longer I'm awake. The shower helped a lot too, just as Wyatt said.

Before I even get to the living room, Stone's raised voice carries toward me. It doesn't take long to figure out that he's not talking to Wyatt or Lucas, he's on the phone. "It was a mistake," he growls. When I emerge, his head snaps up to meet me. His irises are huge. His hair is disheveled like he's run his fingers through it ever since he woke up from being drugged. His face is pale, and if I didn't know the true Stone Jacobs, I'd feel sorry for the guy in front of me. He looks like he could use a hug.

Not from me. Definitely not from me.

"We're taking care of it," he snaps again. A beat of silence follows before he stands up straight, throwing his shoulders back like a soldier standing at attention. "No. No, of course not. Yes, Father."

Lucas comes up behind me, entwining our fingers. Stone's gaze drops to our joined hands, and his eyes flare with something like jealousy.

I must be really out of it because that can't be it. His father must be saying something on the other end of the line to cause that reaction. As I've already been told, whatever Stone's infatuation with me is can't happen. Not that I truly believe there's any sort of infatuation.

"We'll take care of it," Stone says, calmer now before hanging up the phone. He spins on his heel and throws the phone across the room. It crashes against the cupboards, glass splintering and denting the wood. He lets out an inhuman growl that makes me stiffen.

"Stone..." Wyatt starts.

"Give me a minute," he says in a voice like sandpaper being dragged over jagged stone. He takes several deep breaths, his fingers lost in his hair as he stares at the ground. Like he promised, within a couple of minutes, he gazes up again. His calm facade back into place. It's scary how quickly he can change his demeanor. It makes me wonder if I'm ever seeing the real Stone Jacobs, or if everything he wears is just a pretense.

He turns to the couch that he slumped against earlier and falls back on the cushions like he owns the place. Wyatt pats him on the back as he eyes Lucas and I. Lucas guides me over to the opposite couch, and we sit.

"How are you?" Stone asks, the gravelly texture in his voice gone. In its place is the even tone I'm used to hearing from him.

"I'm better," I say.

"You probably have a lot of questions."

"You could say that."

Stone leans forward, draping his hands over his thighs so his fingers dangle over his knees. "We were given a dose of Rohypnol that was ground up and put on our food. It was a high dosage which caused us all to pass out. The drug is most commonly referred to as the date-rape drug."

"Wait." I cock my head. "How the fuck do you know all this?"

"I called a scientist I'm friendly with as soon as I woke up. I had one of his lab assistants pick up a piece of the pizza and rush it to his lab. He tested it and told me, confirming my suspicions." He takes a breath. "We don't believe you were raped, but I will send you for a rape kit if you so desire."

"Wait. What?"

"Jesus Christ, Stone," Lucas snaps. He pulls on my arm to make me look at him. He sears me with his brown gaze. "You weren't disturbed at all. When Wyatt woke up, we were all in the same positions. You were fully clothed. Nothing out of place. There is absolutely no evidence that anything happened to you, even from the video feed." He motions toward the cameras in the room. "Stone just likes to be thorough, that's all. You *weren't* raped," Lucas promises.

My heart beats like crazy in my chest.

"Pretty sure I just said that," Stone argues. He takes another deep breath and lets it out. "Continuing," he says, agitation lacing his voice. "While we were out, whoever did this to us took pictures and sent them to my father. That seems to be their whole aim, just letting us know how easily they can get to us." He pauses for a moment, then with a straight face and little emotion says, "I'm very sorry."

I close my eyes. Is he a robot? Like, what is wrong with him? I was given roofies and photographed while I was incoherent. "Just tell me what's going on," I grind out. "All of it." As much as I want to be mad at them, some of this is my fault. I have a sneaking suspicion this is a lot more dangerous than I originally thought. They tried to warn me, and I dismissed it.

"I've been waiting for you to be ready to hear this," Stone says.

Lucas grips my fingers tighter. I lean forward, eyeing his friend and my family's natural enemy. "I'm ready."

"There *is* someone else after the treasure," Stone says, lifting a brow to stare at me. "And it's not a normal outfit. They're not tracking off our leads. They're not looking for what we know, so they can make inferences and go search for themselves." His Adam's apple bobs up and down. "They're exploiting my family. If we don't get them the treasure, they're going to kill us."

*T*eye Stone on the way to school from the backseat. All of us are functioning on very little sleep, yet he looks the most put together. There's just the tightening around his eyes that's proof of us staying up late into the night after being drugged so he could tell me the story of his family being threatened.

I wrestle with the idea of feeling sorry for him. Not his dad. He can go fuck himself. But Stone, who tries to be perfect at everything, yet has had this thing hanging over his head. He manipulated me. He blackmailed me. But what they've done to me is nothing like what's being done to them.

His mother is missing.

The last time he saw her was when they met up briefly after my father hiked up into the mountains never to be seen again. She left my house that day and hasn't been heard from since. He doesn't even know if she left on her own volition, or if she was abducted. It doesn't surprise me that I hadn't heard from her, but it does surprise me that Stone hasn't. Honestly, I don't know what to think. The only thing that's clear is that *something* happened to her after she left Clary.

So, yeah, this morning, I didn't fight any of them when they said we should all ride to school together. I may not have had the best childhood but at least I never had to worry about violence. About losing a family member.

They don't think my father's disappearance has anything to do with this asshole who's threatening the Jacobs. I came clean about the note that was left for me at school. The guys all looked at each other and agreed it was a good thing they made the registrar put at least one of them in every single one of my classes. Dampening my outrage at that deceit was hard, considering I'd just woken up from being drugged, but I did manage to get a few barbs in which were totally justified.

If we don't find the treasure—the treasure that's been missing for over a hundred years—these people, this insane asshole, is going to start killing the Jacobs and their known associates. That includes Lucas,

Wyatt, and now, me. Since Marilyn is missing, it only makes sense that they started with her, which is why I keep finding myself staring at Stone. I would never know his mother is missing just by looking at him. He wears his shields like armor, and I can give him props for that. I never mastered that level of indifference.

Wyatt is giving me a list of things to do as we turn into the school parking lot. "Don't act weird. Just act natural. We have no reason to believe anyone at the school is in on it. We're keeping appearances normal," he says, just like they told me last night. Apparently, Wyatt is their enforcer type guy. He secured the perimeter while the rest of us were still passed out, and then he finally pulled the security footage of the intruders entering the house dressed in all black with homemade ski masks who snapped pictures of us and left. Now, if only Stone had led with that instead of saying he didn't *think* I was raped. That would've been helpful.

"I got it," I say to Wyatt with more force than necessary. He's got me paranoid now. I keep looking at everyone heading toward campus wondering if they're out to get us.

"We'll always be around. After school, we're going to Leedsville to get you a cell phone and hiking boots and whatever else we need to plan our first big trek into the Superstitions."

"A cell phone? I don't—"

"You need a cell phone," Stone says, finalizing the argument with that no-fucks-given tone of voice.

My father hated cell phones. He hated phones all together. We never had one. If anyone wanted to talk to us, they could just stop by or send us a letter. Those same denials buzz at my lips. At the same time, though, I always envied everyone in school who had phones. With their pretty cases and fancy apps that played music or took pictures. In the end, I ended up despising them because I knew I was never going to get one unless I bought it myself. And even then, I'd have to hide it from Dad.

Lucas's discerning eyes are on me. It's hard to keep things from him. I swear he can read my mind, and I'm wondering if he's already putting things together, realizing just how odd my father really was. I've always defended him. Always. But I have to admit, this is one rule I never quite understood. It wasn't just the fact that we couldn't afford the phones or the service, it was more than that to him.

"It's for safety," Stone says, softening his tone. He's really making an effort to stifle his dickish ways this morning. Or maybe it's just that his facade has crumbled a bit, and I know what's going on now so there's no sense in keeping up the pretenses anyway. "We'll save our numbers inside it, so you can get a hold of us whenever you need to."

"Feel free to send me nudes, Tits," Wyatt says as he rakes his gaze over the crowd. His voice lacks all the normal teasing as he scopes out our surroundings.

Stone pulls into the only available front parking space left. Despite the parking lot being full, everyone seems to have reserved Stone's silver Audi a place of honor amongst the other cars. Students pass us, making their way up the stairs and in through the main doors. Some fiddle with their bags, some talk on their phones, and as much as I'd like to say I feel so apart from them because of what I've just found out, the truth is, I've always felt apart from them. I've been on the outside looking in my whole life, wondering what it's like for people to live normal lives. I've never had a normal life, and that still continues. It's just that now, there's danger added in. Real danger.

A cold chill shivers up my spine. Fear threatens to overtake me, something I've been struggling with since everything was explained to me last night. These people aren't just messing around. They drugged us just to prove a point. They've been able to get to me at school. They got into my dorm and my father's house.

Hell, they probably even took Marilyn. I don't think there's much they won't do.

Stone warned me last night that we weren't dealing with just run-of-the-mill criminals. These people aren't to be taken lightly. They have power. What they've done so far is just child's play.

When I asked who it was that was threatening them, Stone told me his father had gotten into a bad business deal with the wrong people.

That's the understatement of the century. Maybe I don't want a normal job if this is what happens.

The crazy part is, my father always knew the Jacobs were going to be the Wilders' downfall.

When we walk into school this morning, everything's changed. I'm flanked on either side by Wyatt and Lucas. Stone leading us like the king he thinks he is. People take notice, too, just like they've been taking notice of the new guys at school, but this time, they're taking notice of me too. Whispers rise. People talk with their friends behind palms, hiding their lips from us.

It's not the reception into school that I need. I'm already worried about monsters hiding behind corners, and now this is making me second-guess everyone. I liked it when everyone was so apparent in their hatred of me. At least it wasn't being hidden behind closed doors. It was out there for everyone to see. It certainly made it easier to see what you were up against.

Then again, I'm probably just being paranoid. Paranoia runs in my family, but also, that kind of happens when you're told you're involved in a plot that consists of a maniac who's vowed to start killing people if he doesn't get his way.

We walk past the school office, and the doors open right into Wyatt. We all stop as the secretary peeks her head out. "Oh dear. I'm so sorry, Mr. Longhorn. I was looking for Dakota, and I could've sworn..." She trails off, flushing at the mere sight of Wyatt. Not that I can blame her. Despite the shadows under his eyes, he's looking like quite the specimen this morning. It might be because I saw him pack a knife in a concealed holder in his jeans, but he's giving off an aura of dangerous cowboy that I'm not even going to pretend doesn't make him ten times hotter than normal.

"I'm right here," I say.

"Oh, yes," the secretary says, clearing her throat. "I knew I saw you." She smiles at me, and it's pleasant. "Another letter came for you." Her face pinches like she wants to ask me if I'm sure they have nothing to do with my dad's disappearance like she did the first time, but she wisely keeps the question to herself.

She holds the letter out, and Stone plucks it from her fingers. "Thank you."

"That's for, Miss—" she starts to say.

"Oh, I know," Stone states, using that level tone of his. "It's okay. Dakota and I are good friends. Aren't we Dakota?"

I glower at him. "The best of friends."

"Oh," the secretary says, her eyes widening along with her smile. She gives me an enthusiastic grin which makes me wonder how much she watches. She's probably seen my outcast status like many people here have. She seems like the type that would root for the underdog.

"Thank you for giving it to me," I say, tearing the letter from Stone's grip.

"Do you know who sent it?" Stone asks the secretary, ignoring me.

The secretary shrugs. "It came through the mail room, so I'm assuming the regular mail."

"Thank you," he says, his good boy smile plastered all over his face. As a unit, we start to walk away. He lowers his voice as we all move toward mine and Stone's first class. "Is this how the previous letter was sent to you?"

I nod, confirming his theory.

"Anyone else think it's weird she's getting it at the

school and not at her dorm? You do have mailboxes at the dorm, don't you?"

"Yes," I say, rolling my eyes. The dorms aren't much to look at or live in, but to act as if we don't get the basic necessities is just so pompous on his part. Not that I should be surprised.

We stop as a group outside History, and Wyatt turns to address us. "Listen, either those bastards knew we were going to ask Dakota for help because they were spying on us, or they just guessed it."

"Wait. You asked me for *help*?" I almost laugh. "That's not how it all went down."

Stone gives me his cold gaze. His blue-gray eyes are like steel, impenetrable and guarded. "I don't need your help."

"I mean, it sounds like you do. You kind of just said it."

"Enough you two," Wyatt scolds. "We'll talk about this later. Just get into class and don't kill each other." He gives us both a look and then he and Lucas take off to get to their classes.

Stone walks in first, looking every bit the part of college co-ed, if college co-eds wore nice, expensive clothes. He looks like he belongs in a yacht club, but in land-locked Arizona, that can't be right. Maybe a better analogy is that he looks like he's on a sports team when the team is told to dress up on game day, except, every day is game day in Stone's world.

He stops in front of his seat—that should've been mine—as I make my way to the back. "Move, Meghan," Stone says.

I stop in my tracks. I can't believe my ears. No one has ever spoken to Meghan that way, and trust me, I would know. I had the unfortunate pleasure to be in almost all her classes all throughout high school.

She's leaning toward him, smiling, but that quickly drops. "Excuse me."

"I said," he sighs, voice turning darker like he hates having to repeat himself, and she's being so basic by asking him. "Switch seats with Dakota. I need to sit next to her."

"Da-kota?" she says, breaking up my name like it's the only time she's ever dared say it, and she has to force her tongue to make the sounds. Funny how Blue's Clues rolls off her tongue so easily though.

With a grin, I move back to them, standing next to Stone. I may not like Stone all that much, but he's making my fantasies of pulling all these assholes down a couple of notches come to life.

"Looking good, Dakota," Todd says, giving me a wink.

I stare down at my clothes. They're just normal. A

pair of jean shorts with a red top. My hair is down, too, lying in controlled waves over my shoulders. Having conditioner for my hair has been a lifesaver. I no longer look like I stuck my finger in a socket before coming to school.

Stone walks toward Todd, leaning over his desk. "Say that to her again, and you'll be walking funny for a week."

"What the fuck is this?" Meghan hisses, like the whole world has gone topsy turvy. Honestly, it seems like it has.

Todd glares at Stone but doesn't say anything. Stone though, hovers over Meghan's desk until she starts squirming in her chair. At first, I think she's going to tough it out. Pretend like it doesn't bother her that all eyes are on her. I know that feeling. The flushed face. The beating heart. The fact that you know people are looking at you right now and not in a good way.

Finally, she gives in. "I like it better in the back anyway. Have fun smelling Mr. Burns' coffee breath, bitch," she says as she gets up.

"Now that wasn't very nice," Stone says. "I can't believe you would spread the rumor that Mr. Burns only has one testicle, Meghan."

At that moment, Mr. Burns strides in, coffee in hand. His gaze darts to Meghan. "I'll be seeing you after class, Miss Tanner. We can talk about appropriate topics of conversation at Saint Clary's."

She sits with a huff, and I turn back to the two desks. Todd's eyes gleam at me, and he looks all too comfortable with the prospect of sitting behind me in class. Instead, Stone takes that seat, nodding toward the seat I wanted the first day.

Well, look at that. I take a seat. *It looks like Stone Jacobs is good for something.*

24

*I*t turns out the letter I was handed is blank. Stone ends up taking it, and I let him. He has way more resources than I do on what to do with those types of things, so he can have at it.

On the way to Leedsville, the guys tell stories about Meghan and her friends. I can't help but smile. She's so fucking confused. She doesn't even know what to do with herself. The fact that the new, hot guys are hanging around me is throwing her off bigtime. She's so off her game that she even conceded to every attack they threw at her today.

I don't know if the guys got together to talk about it ahead of time, but with every class, they made her move her seat for me. By the end of the day, other people were laughing at her, and I'm sure there was more than one person in the room who was thinking the same thing as me: *Payback, bitch.* Ahh, it feels so good.

I watch the scenery whiz by as Stone brings the Audi up to speed on the highway. For a moment, I glimpse the small knoll I've been known to watch the highway from. I know, I know. It doesn't sound like a fun pastime, but it always was for me. I would make up stories for the different cars going by. I would follow their car for as far as the eye could see, telling myself that that car was on their way to the Grand Canyon. Or to California. Or to Vegas. It was a once-in-a-life-time trip that the whole family decided to take because their father was diagnosed with cancer, and this trip was his last wish.

Yes, I can be kind of morbid. And weird.

Every car had a different story, and that's what fascinated me so much. Each of us have a different story to tell. One we'll pass on to our loved ones. We're all different, and that's what I always wanted to get through the heads of the small-minded people who live here. My family hunts for treasure. So what? There are plenty of shows out there right now where people are doing the same thing. One of them was even about the gold hidden in the Superstition Mountains, but the Jacobs got that shit shut down really quick.

It was fine by us, we didn't like it either. That was one of the only times my father was happy that the Jacobs had that kind of pull, so they could demand it.

And now, here I am, heading up to Leedsville with three guys. Ever since we passed the Leaving Clary sign, my heart's been in my throat.

I've never left Clary before. Only just outside the small town to go to the mountains. Clary and the Superstitions are my home. I've made up a thousand different stories about going different places, but they were never true. My father didn't like to go out, but even when he did, I wasn't allowed to go with him.

My heart beats rapidly. I rub my palms down my shorts, and my foot starts tapping the floor of the car. Excitement and nerves burn through me like I'm made of the driest brush.

Wyatt is in the backseat with me. He does a double-take just as he finishes talking about how he made Meghan's whole table move in the lunchroom, even though we decided not to sit there anyway. We headed outside to sit by ourselves so we could talk about what supplies we were going to buy in Leedsville. The prospect of leaving Clary had thrilled me then. Now? I'm not so sure.

Wyatt knocks his knee into mine. "Are you okay?"

"Yeah," I say, planting a fake smile on my face. There's no way on this earth I'm telling them what's going through my head right now. I'm walking a tightrope with these guys. They were picking on Meghan today, but it could so easily be me tomorrow. Right?

I don't know. Maybe not.

I sit back in the seat and take a deep breath, closing my eyes. I want to open them. I want to take in the scenery. I want to be in the driver's seat of my life for once. I always chalked up Dad never letting me go anywhere to being a bit overprotective, but it's hard to fight those feelings. If he was overprotective, what was he trying to protect me from?

I guess I didn't even need to leave Clary to have something bad happen, but still. I'm rattled.

Wyatt puts his hand on mine. "Dakota?" Fuck. My real name? He must be worried about me.

I'm so screwed. Why can't I just fucking relax? Act like this isn't a big deal. Going to Leedsville? Sure. Easy. Done it a hundred times.

"Pull the car over," Wyatt instructs Stone.

"No," I shout. "I'm fine." My voice is high and tight, cracked with fissures so that anyone listening can clearly tell I'm not alright despite me saying otherwise.

Because they are listening, Stone pulls over.

I growl. "I'm fine."

Wyatt gives me a look. He knows I'm full of shit.

Fuck. So do I. I just need to get over it though.

Lucas turns around from the front seat. He takes one look at me and frowns. "You're white as a ghost."

"I don't know why," I say. I rub my arms to try to warm them. "Maybe I'm still tired. Or it's an effect from the drugs."

Stone turns in the seat now, too, and I'd rather claw his eyes out than have him see me like this. I close my eyes, pretending that if I can't see him, then he can't see me.

"Maybe I'll just get out and walk around for a bit," I say, throwing the door open. It opens up onto the sandy side of the road. Cacti of all different sizes dot the landscape. Seeing them instantly puts me at ease. That's normal. They're familiar.

I shut the door and stretch my limbs. I walk out across the dirt, my feet kicking up dust clouds as I go. Behind me, cars pass the Audi making a vroom, vroom noise. A door opens and closes, and I already know it's going to be Lucas who comes out to check on me. The peacemaker. The silent one who observes. Plus, I'm fairly certain Stone doesn't give a fuck and that Wyatt is on the fence about me. Well, he likes to make comments about my body, but that's about it. Who even knows if Wyatt is capable of having girls who are friends?

"Hey," Lucas says in a sure voice.

I kick the dirt in front of me, sending up a plume of brown.

"Wyatt says you're freaking out. Are you?"

"I'm fine," I say, stretching my lips into something I hope resembles a smile.

Lucas moves in front of me, dipping his head to look me in the face. I wish he wasn't so nice—and I really can't believe I'm saying that—but he makes me want to tell him stuff. I've never had someone who I could talk to before. Well, besides Dad, and I really couldn't have said anything to him. If I asked about going places, he just told me there was no reason I needed to go. He didn't get that I was so sick of living in my head or through books. He didn't get that I wanted something real.

That's why I don't understand why I'm freaking out right now. I want this. I've been wanting it for so long.

"A truth for a truth?" Lucas asks. He's posing it as a question, but he doesn't waste time waiting for my answer. "My parents died when I was young. I was in and out of homes until the Jacobs took me in. Five years ago, they adopted me. Sometimes, I have this weird thing that happens where I feel like I don't belong anywhere. I recognize that in you too. I think that's why I like you."

My brain gets hung up on the words, *I think that's why I like you*. No one has ever said that to me before. Ever. Not a boy, not a girl. Not a friend. Not my father or Dickie. Literally no one.

My walls start to crumble. I'm completely fucked with people like Lucas. How many guys are there like him in the world? He told me once that I might realize there were more people like me in the world, and maybe he was right. I've just never met someone like me because... Well, I've barely met anyone new.

"Your turn," he prods.

The earnestness in his gaze peels me open. I already know I'm going to talk. "It's dumb."

"Nothing you feel is dumb."

I groan up at the sky, watching the hawks fly overhead, circling their prey. It's kismet that Lucas and I have come to this moment. Like, maybe this is how we were supposed to end up all along. Him and his lost puppy, yet gorgeous features. His haphazard style of not looking like he cares, but also that he totally does.

His truth clicks a lot of his personality into place for me. Maybe if I give him my truth, he'd be able to help me. "So, I've never actually been out of Clary."

The words hang in the air like the humidity, clinging to us like weights. I wait for him to laugh. I wait for him to tell me that that makes me a loser. He doesn't. Instead, he says, "Wow. I had no idea, Dakota. None of us did. If we did, we would've..." He trails off. "I don't know. Tried to make it easier on you somehow. Is that why you're freaking out? Because you're leaving Clary?"

I gaze into his eyes. "I think it's a combination of being excited and worried. There's just a lot of shit in my head that my dad has said in the past, and even though I don't agree with it, it's still there. I guess I actually don't know what I'm feeling."

Lucas takes my shoulders, his thumbs rub circles into my skin. "One thing Stone has had to learn is that you are not responsible for your father's issues. Okay?" Before I can ask him what he means by that, he continues. "Now, I'd say leaving Clary for the first time is cause for celebration. We're going to get back in that car, we're going to turn the radio up and party, and maybe after we spend all of Lance Jacobs' money on supplies, we'll go out to eat to celebrate."

A smile tugs at my lips. Excitement burrows a hole in my stomach and opens, letting out butterflies that tickle my insides. He's right. It's not something to be afraid of. Sure, I can feel the fear, but that doesn't mean I have to let it stop me. If I let it stop me from doing these things, I might as well just resign myself to staying in Clary my whole life, and I've never wanted that. Ever. "Okay," I say, smiling.

Lucas gives me a quick shake then turns me around, pointing me back toward the car. Stone and Wyatt aren't even trying to hide the fact that they're curious about what's going on. I settle the nosedive my stomach makes and brush it off. It doesn't matter.

Lucas opens the backdoor for me, and I slide inside. He closes it after me and then gets in the passenger seat. "Let's go," he says, but his voice doesn't have the same amount of cheer it just did. He reaches over to turn on the radio, and his jaw feathers. He scrubs at his cheek like he has a festering wound there. When he turns to look at me, though, he winks, a broad grin tugging his lips that should be on display behind a glass case if it wasn't so fake.

It's the switch between anger and happiness, and they all wear it so damn well.

With the radio on and Wyatt deciding to serenade

us all the way into Leedsville, the rest of the ride is better. It also helps that I know where the fear is stemming from. I can deal with it as it breaches the surface, telling myself that living in my father's bubble was never the way to go. I always wanted much more than that, and now I'm finally getting it.

In reality, the car ride doesn't take that long at all. We pull into Leedsville fifteen minutes later which is much more modern and boasts a sleeker Welcome sign than Clary has ever thought of having.

I press against the glass as I watch the houses give way to modern buildings. A town only fifteen minutes away, and I've never been to it. I tell myself I'll unpack that later because I don't want to miss anything. Their downtown area is bigger than ours, and more people are out on the streets here than there ever is in Clary. "Jeez, if this is Leedsville, I can't imagine what Phoenix is like."

"Wait, what?" Wyatt asks. He pushes up the brim of his cowboy hat to get a better look at me.

Lucas turns in his seat, eyeballing his friend. "Don't."

Wyatt's eyes flash. He looks like he wants to say so much more, but he doesn't. I look back out the window, but Stone catches my gaze in the rearview mirror. His eyes are narrowed as he watches me, and I realize I've just given myself away.

I shake it off and narrow my gaze right back at him before turning away. The last thing I need is to hear Stone Jacobs' thoughts on me growing up so sheltered. Someone like him wouldn't get it.

25

We get out of the car at the sporting goods store, and Lucas entwines our fingers. I feel like a fish out of water next to all these people, and I guess I really am one. It doesn't matter how much I've experienced through books, being out with other people is both thrilling and daunting. Lucas's quiet strength helps though.

Wyatt and Stone take note of our joined hands but don't say anything. I'm glad for that because I don't want to give it up.

The automatic doors open before us as soon as we cross the parking lot and approach the sporting goods store. We step inside, and I stop. Wyatt runs into me from behind. He immediately grabs my hips, tugging me against him. "You can't just stop in the middle of the walkway, Tits."

"Sorry," I say in awe while I gaze around at everything. There are *things* everywhere. Shirts. Pants. Shoes. Kayaks. I'm in a sea of stuff. New stuff. Bright and shiny and just waiting to be purchased and taken home by their new owner.

Lucas tightens his hold on me, spurring me to move. "Boots, right?" Stone asks, voice thin.

I nod but as soon as we get into that section, I freeze again. My eye is immediately drawn to the price tags on everything. I don't know why I didn't think of it before but there's no way I can afford a pair of boots. I don't have any money. Zero money. And if I did, I probably wouldn't spend it on a pair of boots. Surely there's something less frivolous I could purchase with it. And I'm certainly not going to let Stone Jacobs buy me boots, right? He'll think he owns me even more than he already does.

"What's wrong?" Lucas asks. "You don't know your size?"

The fact that he asks that is even more humbling and humiliating. I've always worn my father's hand-me-downs and stuffed socks in the heel and in the foot to make it work. "No. Well, yes. That, too. But I—" I drop my voice to a whisper and lean toward him. "I don't actually have any money."

Apparently, I didn't do that great of a job of whispering because Stone steps in front of me. He pierces me with one of his stone-cold gazes, and it hits me then that I can't help but wonder if his parents named him Stone because he came out of the womb looking like this. Or maybe they were just preparing for the kid they wanted. The one with the heart of stone who would be just like them.

He takes my chin in his hands, making me look into the bottomless pit of his eyes. "*I* am buying you what you need. I will buy you the whole damn store if you want. Do you hear me?" He steps closer, making my neck arch back. "Anything. Everything."

My breath gets lost somewhere between my mouth and my lungs. It just disappears into a void until he steps back, then I gulp in air easily. The way he controls my body is disconcerting, and it makes me salty. "I don't need you to do that."

"Dakota Wilder." The look he gives me slices me to my core. It feels like he wants to say so much, but instead, he drops his stare to my shoes. "You want to walk up into the mountain with those? You want to follow the trails with the clothes you're wearing? Put aside the stupid pride bullshit for one second. You know you need those things. Get out of your damn head and let me do it for you."

Everything in me is telling me not to give in to him, but I really don't have a choice. I don't have the money. I probably never will have the money. What's most important now is that we find my father and the treasure. "Fine," I seethe.

"Follow me," he demands. We all do as he says because, well, he's Stone Jacobs. He stops in front of a bunch of shoe boxes that all look the same. "This is a good brand. Find the style and the fit you like, and we'll get those. And actually, get a couple of pairs. Lucas, come with me. We're looking at tents."

Lucas's hand tightens around mine as he gives Stone a perplexed look. "I thought you said—"

"Just fucking come with me," he growls out.

A woman who walks past us at that exact time places her hands over her son's ears, as the son gazes up at Stone wide-eyed. Stone has the decency to apologize in his most well-mannered good boy voice, and the woman smiles back. Stone just has that kind of look when he wants to. He can turn on the charm in an instant which makes him almost like a snake in the grass. Just biding his time.

I shake my head as I watch Stone and Lucas walk away in the opposite direction of the mother and son.

Their heads are together as they walk through the store like they own the place.

Wyatt gazes at my feet in my ratty pair of sneakers I've had for at least five years. I'm good to my things. I wash them when I get them dirty, but it's obvious they're old as shit. They're just clean, old as shit shoes that are out of style and fraying along the edges. "Do you know what size those are?"

I sit on a nearby bench and take them off, feeling the loss of Lucas next to me. I peel the tongue back and look but the label is faded. "Nope," I say. "And in any case, these have always been a bit too tight."

Wyatt's jaw ticks. He points at an employee and crooks his finger at him, beckoning him toward us. The guy comes right over, and Wyatt says, "We need her sized. Also, I need a cart."

"Excellent," the guy says. He's all smiles. "I can size her, and the carts are at the front of the store."

"I said I need a cart," Wyatt snaps.

The guy, who already dropped to his knees, preparing to put a metal contraption on my feet, glowers. "Of course," he says through clenched teeth. "I'll get you a cart when I'm through." He slides my foot on to the metal then makes me stand. "Looks like you're about a seven and a half. Depending on what you're getting, the sizes could run up or down, so just make sure to try everything on. After I'm done getting your cart," he says flatly. "I can get any size in the back that you need."

Wyatt nods at him, and when he walks away, he gleams at his back. I switch my gaze between the two. "You're such a jerk." My first experience in a store like this and it isn't going all that well.

Wyatt shrugs. "With the amount of money we're going to drop today, they should be handing us a fucking gold cart, Tits."

I shake my head and scour the line of hiking boots at the top of the brand Stone picked out. I pick out a pair I like and try on the seven and a half. I take them back to the seat with me and slip them on. I almost cream my underwear when my feet slide inside. They fit like a glove. And the cushion? It's like I'm walking on a cloud.

Wyatt chuckles. "If you like them, wait until you try on sneakers." I take the boot off to throw it back in the box, but Wyatt stops me. "Whoa, whoa. You're missing the most important part of trying on shoes."

"I'm not buying sneakers, too," I snap.

He narrows his gaze at me. "No partner of mine is walking around in frayed shoes that are too fucking tight for her, so yes, Tits, you're going to suck up your pride and accept the fact that you're getting new shoes."

"Stone—"

"I don't give a fuck about Stone. I'm buying you the shoes, okay? Me."

I gaze over at Wyatt, who dropped to his knees like the store clerk did and is now forcing my foot back into the boot. "You don't—"

"I know I don't have to," he says, sliding my heel into the boot and then moving his hand up my calf to set my foot back down on the ground. He stares up at me. "I want to."

We lock gazes. He and his sparkling blues that catch just under the brim of his hat. The way he's looking at me makes goosebumps dance over my skin. He blinks, almost like he's ensnared in my trap as much as I'm ensnared in his. His hand moves up over my knee and onto my thigh. He squeezes, and heat floods my core. Goddamn there's just something about Wyatt Longhorn on his knees in front of me with that cowboy hat on. I'm damn sure I've had a fantasy like this before.

"You need to realize something, Dakota," Wyatt says. "Everyone deserves nice things, but people like you deserve them most of all." He moves his palm up, his hands coarse against my skin. "So, if I want to buy you something, I will. You didn't see the look on your face when you tried these new boots on, but I did. And that's a moment worth having again and again."

My breath hitches as we stay entranced by one another's gazes. It isn't until the rickety sound of wheels hits us that Wyatt stands, his face morphing back to hard lines with the brim of his hat acting like a privacy fence. "Here's your cart," the employee says.

"Much obliged," Wyatt says, dipping his hat at him, and the worker seems a little taken aback. I am too, actually. He turns back to me. "Now, Tits," he says with a wink. "Put the other boot on and take a walk up and down here. You need to see how they feel when you're walking, not just sitting. You know how much walking we're going to be doing up there, and we need to protect those precious feet of yours."

I do as he says, slipping the other boot on and lacing them up before walking around. Unfortunately, Wyatt's right. They pinch my feet a little when I walk. "I need a bigger size," I grumble as I sit back down on the bench, bending over to untie the boots.

Wyatt looks up. He opens his mouth to tell the worker to get me the next size, but instead, he's on him in a flash. He pushes him against the rack of shoes and gets in his face. The display shakes, and some of the shoes tumble over. Once again, his hat is hiding most of his features from me, but the hard line of his jaw is unmistakable. "You looking at her rack?"

"N-no," the guy squeaks out, clearly scared out of his mind.

My stomach drops. "Wyatt," I whisper-yell as people pass by. They hurry down the aisle, but Wyatt doesn't give a fuck. He's not going to apologize like Stone did.

The brim of Wyatt's hat hits the guy in the fore-head. "Just because I call her Tits doesn't mean you get free looks, you understand me."

The guy swallows. "Yes, of course."

Wyatt steps back and shoves him toward a door that leads to the back. "Now get her a size eight in those shoes."

The guy hurries away, and I glare at Wyatt. "What was that about?" Embarrassment creeps up my cheeks. "You can't just treat people that way."

"I can and I will," Wyatt says, stepping up to me. "Those tits are off limits to others, and the way he was salivating over them..." A disgusted tremor rolls through him. He balls his fists at his sides and moves closer. He bends over, whispering right into my ear, making shivers run down my arms. He hovers there, and I close my eyes because I'm sure he notices the effect he has on me. "Just FYI, you can tell by the way he didn't fight back that he'd be a terrible lay. Remember that. Boys with bite will give you everything you need and everything you think you didn't but do. I'm sure Lucas is close to showing you, and he's a sleeper. Trust me."

By the time he steps away, my knees are shaking. I already know Lucas is a sleeper. That he's exactly what I want. I haven't been able to forget what happened in class even though there are more pressing concerns happening around me. However, my blood boils when Wyatt is near too. He acts like an ass and then licks my wounds afterward until I just want to spread my legs to see what he can do down there when he's like this everywhere else. I don't doubt he's everything and more in the bedroom.

I've read about guys like him. I just thought they were all fictional.

I go to stand, but he bites down on my earlobe. A spark of momentary pain hits. He sucks it away until I have to sit down again, my knees too weak to hold me upright. I nearly miss the bench, and Wyatt chuckles as he makes sure I land on the solid steel.

Thankfully, a new worker comes out of the back with my size eights. Wyatt smirks as he takes the box from him and helps me slip them on. These are much better. I end up grabbing that pair and another of a different kind while Wyatt throws two bags of hiking socks in the cart along with some athletic socks. We stop at the sneakers next, and I bite my lip over all the different colors and styles. I always just wore what my father brought me home from the second-hand store. I never got to pick out anything myself, so standing here is like being a kid in a candy store. Speaking of, I've never been the kid in the candy store either, but I can imagine it so that's all that matters.

I'm deciding between two pairs when Wyatt puts them both in the cart. I start to argue with him, but he just walks away, and I have to run to catch up with his long strides. We head toward the clothing section next. At least this I can help with. I know my sizes in clothes based on my father's shopping experience. I remember the growth spurt I went through in middle school. He had to buy me new hand-me-downs every three months and wasn't happy.

Wyatt shows me some women's hiking pants, and I smile. I've never had pants specifically for hiking. Even though I know my size, he makes me try them on. He waits outside the fitting rooms as I change out of my old jean shorts with the rips in the hem and try the hiking pants on. While I'm pulling the new material over my hips, I find I'm actually having a good time shopping with Wyatt.

On the other hand, of course I am. How could I not be? I'm about to get a bunch of brand new stuff. This good mood must be a shopper's high which will probably dissipate as soon as we leave.

I check the pants out in the mirror and decide they fit well enough. Before I can get changed back into my shorts, Wyatt says, "You better be planning on showing me those pants, Tits."

I cock my head. "I'm a grown woman. I don't need to show you."

Instead of coming back with something sarcastic or even worse, more demands, he says, "Please?"

My shoulders slump. Any other argument and I could've ignored it, but not this one. I begrudgingly open the door and step out. He leans on the cart we have and then twirls his finger in a circle, indicating for me to turn around. By the time I'm facing him again, he shakes his head. "They're a hair too big. Here." He holds up the same pants but in a different size.

"These are fine, Wyatt."

"Actually, he's right." I turn to find Stone and Lucas walking toward us. "Those are too big. When you buy something new, they'll relax over time. The first few times you wear them, they'll be fine, but then they'll be slipping past your ass while we're trying to hike up the Superstitions, and we can't have that. Can we, Wilder?"

I take the pants from Wyatt and slip back into the fitting room. Before I can come out with them on for their inspection again, more tops and pants are thrown over the top of the fitting room door. "Try these on, Wilder."

I groan, but I take them anyway. There's nothing wrong with my clothes. In fact, I'd have more clothes if Stone had grabbed everything from my dorm, but he didn't.

My mind gives me all those excuses, but the truth is, when I try the first shirt on, I just stare at my reflection in the mirror inside that tiny dressing room for ages. My hair is wild like normal, but my eyes seem brighter. Standing there in new clothes is like wearing different shields of armor, a luxury I've never had before.

Maybe I let everyone pick on me at school because what they said was true. I was wearing someone else's clothes. We were poor. My dad was kind of out there, and I'm sure I had my moments where I seemed out there, too. I didn't have experiences like everyone else.

"Dakota?" Wyatt calls through the door.

"Yeah," I say, and for a moment, I forget to put my solid exterior back in place because my voice cracks.

I groan again and wipe at my eyes, but movement at my feet makes me step away. Wyatt, sans cowboy hat comes squirming in underneath my fitting room door. He stands to his full height in front of me while I fight back tears. Goddammit. I think I actually do like shopping with Wyatt Longhorn.

A small smile flickers across his face. "I'd cry too if I saw the real me for the first time."

His words drop anchor into the pit of my stomach. The *real* me. Without someone else's clothes that already lived through their lifetime. Without someone else's shoes that have already walked someone else's miles. Me. Just me.

I don't realize the tears have actually tracked over my cheeks until Wyatt pulls me to him. He presses my head against his shirt, and I just know I'm leaving splotchy wet marks over his t-shirt. His breaths flutter the hair at the top of my head, and I close my eyes, oddly comfortable in his arms.

He must feel it too because after a moment, he loosens his hold, and it's then that he's really hugging me, arms falling before pulling me closer.

We stay that way for too long.

26

J come back out a few minutes after making Wyatt leave the room so I can change back into my regular clothes. I've put myself together now, but when I glance over at the cart, it's full of clothes. I frown at it, but Stone of all people gives me a threatening look that makes me keep my mouth shut. At first, I don't think they're all for me but when we look for other items we need, I notice the sizes they're pulling off the racks and realize they've literally stocked up on brand new clothes for me. Not just hiking and treasure hunting clothes either. Normal clothes.

I hate to admit Wyatt was right though. The clothes I'm wearing feel cheap. They're not quite my size. They're hanging off me, and there are dull parts or stains I've never been able to get out despite the fact that I do my own laundry and am very diligent about making sure every item of clothing I have is clean. If I couldn't have new, at least I could be tidy.

When they check out, I feel like their doll. After Wyatt and Stone fight over who's going to pay for the sneakers, the cashier ends up ringing everything up on one bill, and even though I have a minor heart attack at the price, the guys don't even balk.

We head out of the parking lot with a trunk full of new shit. Nervous butterflies flutter in my stomach as Stone picks the perfect restaurant to go to, and the day keeps filling with new firsts. I've never been to a restaurant before. It's kind of like going to the school cafeteria but better. The waitress is super nice, which probably has everything to do with the fact that she's serving three hot guys and well, me, but that doesn't count. She even has the audacity to ask if I'm their sister. The guys laugh, and Wyatt points out I actually *am* Stone's stepsister.

I cringe. I think very un-stepsister like things about him a lot. Other times, I hate him so much I can totally see how we could be stepsiblings.

I accidentally on purpose read a romance book about stepsiblings before. Woo-ee. It was so raunchy. My blood was boiling by the end. It's the idea that the whole relationship is on the border of being wrong that makes it so damn sexy. When Stone turned out to be my stepbrother, I put the brakes on that fantasy because he's Stone Jacobs, and despite how good looking he is, being an asshole brings the hot points down.

Honestly, I wish that was the case. Sometimes I wonder if it makes him that much hotter.

When we're back home, the guys help bring my bags to my room, including a small one that holds my new phone that I have no idea how to use. They drop my things and leave, Lucas the only one lingering for a little while until he senses I want to be alone. When he leaves me to myself, I dump the new purchases out on the bed and lie down in the pile, a huge smile on my face. I thought that I would be embarrassed that Stone paid for these clothes, but somehow, I'm not. I don't want to think about it too much in case my brain decides to change its mind, so instead, I spend the next hour trying on all the clothes. However, they did it, the guys knew my perfect sizes, and I'm sitting on an awesome new wardrobe.

I keep on a pair of shorts and a tank top and head out of my room. I wander, first checking Lucas's room and finding it empty. When I walk toward the other part of the house, I find Stone outside, sitting on the half-moon bed with a plastic container at his side. He brings out a handful of paperwork and sifts through it, his brows pulling down. He must be looking at my dad's stuff.

The sun is going down when I slip through the glass doors, my bare feet hitting the stone walkway. The heat from the sun still lingers in the warm stone, but now that the sun is disappearing behind the mountains, it's bearable to hang out outside. I head toward Stone, and he glances up as I approach. His gaze travels down my new clothes, but he doesn't remark on them. "Is that my dad's?" I ask, pointing to the wad of crumpled up papers in his hand.

He nods. "You were right. There's so much."

I gaze at all the papers he's holding in front of him. He's sitting upright on the half-moon bed, his legs outstretched and crossed at the ankles. He moves the paperwork that's strewn around him, and I take the opportunity to sit on the edge to look it over with him.

I've been through all this paperwork at least once. Some of the stuff I haven't seen in years, though, and some of this stuff isn't nearly as relevant as we wished it would be.

"How did he even find anything in all this?" Stone asks, sighing. "They brought over ten plastic containers. This is just the first one."

I sense his frustration, and it reminds me of

listening to my dad over the years. He always felt like he had all the pieces to find the exact location of the treasure, but he just hadn't put them together in the right places yet. I smile. "My dad used to say that searching for treasure was seventy-five percent research, twenty-five percent actually hiking the Superstitions."

Stone crinkles his nose. His family doesn't agree with that sentiment because they've gone all over the Superstitions with their technology. Mapping everything. Searching. Everyone knows what they do because it's broadcasted on the news and podcasts. My father just loved to hear about the new thing they were trying so he could laugh at it, and I have to bite my tongue before I do the same thing.

He sighs. "I just don't know how we're going to find it."

I turn my gaze toward Stone. It's the first time I've heard him sound anything less than uber confident. It's disconcerting, actually. I reach over, placing my hand on his. "We'll find it," I tell him, speaking to the boy who looks lost and scared over what's going to happen to his family. I know about those same feelings where family is concerned. I'm sure we'll find the treasure because we need to. I keep holding out hope that the note I was given is true. The guys are less convinced, but I'm not going to let go of that. Just like Stone won't let go of finding his mother.

Stone stares at my hand on him, and my cheeks heat. I slip it off him, not knowing why the hell I even did that, but he stops me. He drops the papers in his hand and covers my hand with his, holding me there. Our gazes connect, transferring a pulse of electricity between us. It's like a homing beacon calling to me.

He sits back, relaxing into a reclining position as he eyes me. Without thinking, I move forward, crawling up the crescent bed close to him. It's like I'm caught in his orbit again. When he moves, I do. His gaze trails down my body, hitting all the places where this outfit hugs me instead of swallows me. His stomach rises with a breath, his shirt riding up to show off that peak of taut abs he's sporting underneath. Maybe it's the thought of that sexy stepbrother romance I'd just been thinking about, but I'm suddenly so taken by him. Enough that I have to look away. "Thank you for the clothes," I say.

His jaw locks. "I was brought up to take care of people I—" he cuts off. "They suit you."

I cock my head at him, wondering what he was going to say. The thought lingers between us still, making me bolder. I like thinking I can get through his defenses. I like thinking that even though Stone is an asshole, I can help him not to be, too. Maybe I'm just pushing it, seeing how far I can take him. It's like playing with the devil and people do that every day just for fun.

"What are you doing?" Stone asks as I swing my legs over his hips, straddling him. Instead of forcing me off, he clutches my hips with a bruising grip. His eyes show that he's grappling with a decision. He simultaneously wants to throw me off and bring me close. I know it because I feel the same way too.

I shrug. It comes out coyly, but I only did it because I couldn't think of anything to say. I don't know why I'm doing this. He calls to my body, and for once, I'm letting it act on its own volition.

He moves his hands up my arms, grazing my bare skin. A muscle jumps underneath his touch, like every part of my body is ready to get closer to him.

"Can I ask you a question?" Stone asks, fixing his gaze on me. Like usual, he doesn't wait for me to say yes. "What was it like growing up the way you did?"

I close my eyes and swallow. "I don't want to talk about that."

"I'll reward you," he says, shifting on the cushion.

I peek at him. "What kind of reward?"

He lifts his hips, his hard cock brushing between my thighs. "You'll see."

I gasp. It's the moment in the classroom with Lucas all over again. I must be sick because I want to see where this goes. I couldn't get off Stone if I wanted to. I'm too intrigued.

"How come your dad never took you out of Clary?"

His right hand moves upward, and I can barely breathe. It's wrong, right? But I can see the track he's making, and I just know he's about to touch my breast, and I want it. I want it so badly. I hold my breath. "He said Clary had everything I needed."

His hand closes around my waiting skin, and I fall forward into his grip, holding back a moan.

"But he barely took you around Clary either. How come?" His thumb traces over my nipple. I can't talk. I can't think about anything else, but then he stops. "Dakota?"

I let out a breath. "He said it was safer for us if I stayed home."

His thumb continues to move until my nipple strains against my shirt. At the same time, he moves his other hand up my body. "He used to get you everything, didn't he? Clothes. Food. You never went with him?" His other hand reaches my opposite breast.

"Everything," I say, my panties dampening.

"What about school?"

"What about it?" I ask, moving into his touch. As long as I keep answering his questions, he keeps going.

"Did he want you to go?"

He pinches my right nipple, and I let out a small cry I can't hold back. Stone switches his grip on my tit, stroking my nipple. "He always threatened to home-school me, but he never did. It was the one thing I could keep for myself."

"And you went despite everyone treating you like trash?"

"It never mattered," I say. I've completely lost the plot. Was this me trying to show Stone I had some control over him? I think that's what it was supposed to be, but it's so exactly the opposite that it's frightening. He's absolutely in control, working me over.

He wets his lips. "Do you know some women can come just from nipple play?"

I shake my head. "Not me."

"Is that so?" he asks, raising an eyebrow.

"I need clit stimulation."

His jaw ticks. "Is that how Lucas got you off in the classroom?" I freeze, and Stone smirks. "We tell each other everything. We're like brothers."

"Must be nice," I say, pretending like that doesn't bother me. I guess it shouldn't. I'm not trying to hide what happened with Lucas. I wouldn't try to hide this either. Whatever this is. I tell myself that this is wrong on so many levels. I don't even like Stone. He's my fucking stepbrother. Lack of socializing must've made me insane because that just makes me wetter.

I blame books.

Stone doesn't respond to my taunt. "So, you already know what you like, huh? I bet I could find something different." He pinches both of my nipples, and I grind my jaw together to keep from crying out again. "How many guys have you been with?"

"Stone," I say in warning, realizing we're taking this entirely too far.

He drops his hands to my hips and arches into me as he drags me over his erection. "How many?"

"One," I say, my core throbbing now. "Multiple times but just one."

"What did Daddy think of that?"

I scoff. "My dad would've murdered the guy. We were in the mountains on an excursion. We snuck out of our tents."

"Mmm, naughty. Did he make you come?"

I nodded, knowing it wasn't really him. I'm pretty sure I blew that guy's mind when we were together. Yes, it was like an exploration of how everything fits, but I'd been pleasuring myself for years before he showed up. I knew what I liked. I didn't just let him have control. If I had, I never would've orgasmed. Instead, I rode him, and it was only a miracle that had me coming before him. Both of us were virgins, and he came so quickly the first time it was almost laughable. I was prepared for that though. I showed him right where to touch me, so that when I finally climbed on, I was already headed in that direction, all I needed was a little push, and he only needed two pumps more.

"Now you're making me jealous," Stone says, groaning as he moves me over his cock again.

It feels too good. Too tempting. "Things like that aren't supposed to make my stepbrother jealous."

He growls, sending a vibration through me. He takes my hand and places it on his cock. "Would a step-brother be this fucking hard? Would a stepbrother want to tear your clothes off and fuck you until you screamed his name? Would a stepbrother fuck you so good you'd keep coming back?"

I squeeze his dick in answer, and he grunts, thrusting into my hand.

"Fuck," he says, doing it again and again. He's about to lose control when he rolls me off him. Instead of following like I expect, he gets up. He runs his hands through his hair. "Game over," he grinds out.

He walks away, his shorts straining. I smirk at him

retreating. He can use words like "game", but I know that's not what that was. It was far from it.

I lie back on the half-moon seat, sucking in air, my body electric. Usually, I'd sneak my hands under the hem of my waistband and rub my clit until I come, but that seems like a tragedy right now. It's not like having his or Lucas's hands on me. It would be a letdown, so I don't even bother. I stare up at the sky, watching the stars until my body thrums lower. I'm still wired tight, but I don't feel like I'm going to die if I don't come anymore.

When Stone doesn't show back up, I toss my father's papers back into the plastic container and retreat to my room. The guys bought me a new book bag, so I transfer my school things over while looking through the assignments I need to do before tomorrow. There's a short one, so I decide to settle down and finish that one to keep my mind off how huge Stone Jacobs' cock is.

Because of course the biggest dick around has to have the biggest dick. It's only natural.

27

The assignment takes me longer than I thought. By the time I'm done, I get ready for bed and lie down, slipping under the comfortable sheets. I gaze into the open closet. I put away all the clothes they purchased for me earlier. Here, in this room, I feel normal.

Normal's such a boring word. Or at least I used to think it was. But, in reality, it's nice to be normal. To not have to worry about little things. Like, if I interrupt my father while he's studying his papers, is he going to get pissed at me? The man would be at his desk all day, foregoing food just as long as he got more time reading the same shit over and over again. I never knew what was going to set him off. I never knew where our food was going to come from when the cupboards ran dry. Reminding him, sometimes, sent him into a spiral.

He always had more important things to focus on.

I should be exhausted since yesterday was such a clusterfuck, but I can't get my mind to wind down. It's Stone's fault, playing that game with me. I cringe at some of the things I told him, wondering if I should've kept my mouth shut.

I still don't trust Stone fully. I don't know much about him other than he's an asshole and that he's supposed to be my family's natural enemy. The thing is, he didn't feel that way today. Not at all. With a few swipes of his credit card, he'd given me more things than my father ever had...or could. Physical shit isn't everything, but there's a truth they don't tell you. It makes things so much fucking easier.

My mind keeps spiraling, so I get up, throwing the sheets off me. The thin pajamas I brought from home suddenly don't seem as cool as they once did. I want to karate chop myself in the throat. What happens when all of this is over? When we don't find the treasure and Stone and his friends dump me, all I'll have is a few clothes, some shoes, and a...longing for that brief moment in my life when I felt like a princess.

Yep. There it is. That's why I can't think straight. Whenever this ends, I'm going to be dropped right back at Saint Clary's—or worse, just Clary's—with only memories of being a part of something.

I grind my jaw as I turn left down the hall. My evil brain is telling me these awful things, but the truth is, haven't these past couple of days only given me the incentive to go out there and want to have more? These guys have opened up a whole different world to me. A world where there is no struggle. No people calling me names.

Just because this life is easier, that doesn't mean I have to think badly of my father and the way he brought me up. It tells me I can live differently, just like I always wanted.

I find myself outside of Lucas's room. I only vaguely remember Stone telling me where each of their rooms were when he brought me here the first day. I haven't been in any of theirs, but I'm hoping he's here now. He, out of all of them, gets it. He won't judge me for the thoughts bouncing around inside my brain.

The shades are down in his room already, so I don't know if he's asleep or if he's in there at all, but I knock anyway, my heart in my throat. "Yeah?" he calls out.

"It's Dakota," I say.

Within three seconds, he's pulling the door open, and then we just stare at one another for a moment. His hair is wild around his head. The lights are on in his room, so I know he wasn't sleeping. His room is a mirror of mine. There's barely anything in it, just the few simple yet tasteful pieces of furniture that match my own. A towel lies on the ground at our feet, and steam billows from the bathroom. He kicks the towel to the side. "Are you okay?"

Embarrassment creeps up my cheeks. I've literally never had anyone to talk to except for my dad and Dickie, and neither one of them were big on talking about feelings. I poured my feelings into the souls of books and they spoke back to me. I found the same thoughts and emotions I had murmured in words and phrases. It didn't matter that the characters weren't real. It let me know that I wasn't some freak like I'd been told all of my life.

"Hey," Lucas says, stepping closer.

My lips buzz, remembering his kiss. It was straight out of a fairy tale or chapter twelve of a romance novel. I'd never been so thoroughly kissed in all my life, but I knew what it was when I felt it because of the books I'd read. Those kinds of kisses don't come but once in a lifetime, but now that I'm standing right in front of him, I'm freezing up. I don't know what to say. Or what to do. I'm still in a cell of my own making.

Or was that my father's making? It's so hard to tell sometimes.

Lucas grabs my hand and leads me to the bed. The movement shakes my thoughts up, and I realized I've come to him in the middle of the night but haven't said shit. My social skills are definitely lacking. "So, today was...weird."

"Just weird?"

I take a deep breath, picking at a spot on his sheet while he puts a pillow behind his back, so he's propped up against the headboard. "Exciting and scary and humiliating," I say, finishing my thoughts. If I'm going to talk to him, I may as well go all out.

Lucas frowns. "The last thing you should feel is humiliated, but I can't fault you for it. I remember how I felt when I first met Stone and his father. I didn't have anything either and everything they did for me seemed like something I needed to pay back. It was a long time before I accepted the fact that gifts among friends are just that: Gifts. There's no payback necessary. No one's holding it over your head, wishing you would pay up already."

"I'm hardly friends with Stone," I say, a sudden longing hitting me in the chest. The picture Lucas paints for me is so tempting.

"No, you're more than that," Lucas says. When I give him a funny look, he sighs. "You're tied together by this treasure. Now you're tied together by what's going on. You guys couldn't escape the trajectory of your lives if you tried. Stone knows it, too. He always has."

That reminds me of something Lance Jacobs said. He told Stone to fuck me to get me out of his system. I peek up at Lucas. "Do Stone and his father get along?'

A crease forms between Lucas's brows. He runs his hands through his hair, looking away briefly. "That's a tough question, and I don't think I can answer it. Only Stone knows exactly how he feels about his father. I wouldn't want to put words in his mouth." He gives me a look like he's not trying to avoid my question, and I get that. "So, what is it that's bothering you?"

"I don't know," I say, lying down on the foot of his bed. "Anything and everything. I'm just overwhelmed, I guess. Everything is just so— I'm just not used to it," I say begrudgingly. "I'm not used to having people around. I'm not used to having new things. Hell, I'm not even used to being outside Clary." I groan at the ceiling. "It all just sounds so pathetic."

Lucas crawls forward, caging me to the bed. My heart immediately reacts, thumping against my ribs. He speaks, his lips so close to mine. "Don't do that to yourself. Nothing that's happened is your fault. Nothing."

"It's hard not to see the differences." I tell him,

scared to even breathe for fear of breaking whatever this is.

He frowns down at me. "You're looking at it wrong, Wild Girl. Think about all the similarities."

I screw up my face as I try to think. "Hmm. We're all human."

The corner of his mouth tips up. "There's that, but there are others, too. We've all become intoxicated by the same thing." He lets his words hang in the air before he says, "The treasure."

I chuckle while the tightness in my throat eases. For a second, I thought he was going to say me.

"I also happen to know that you and I are both amazing kissers. That you and Wyatt both wear your hearts on your sleeves, and that you and Stone might be more alike than you think."

"Mmm," I say, pretending to think about what he's said. "Why don't we go back to the part where you said we're both amazing kissers."

"You agree with me then?" he asks, posing his body over mine so we line up perfectly.

"Wholeheartedly," I say before I tip my head up and capture his lips with mine. Before, he dominated, taking complete control. This time, it's my turn. I slide my hand behind his neck, pulling him down over me, nipping at his lower lip. My fingers tangle in his hair as I deepen the kiss, but Lucas doesn't let me stay in the driver's seat for long.

"I told you you were ours, Wild Girl. And now I'm going to prove it."

I'm so lost in his kiss that his words barely register before he kisses a line down my throat, tugging the neck of my shirt down to place bruising kisses across my collar bone.

My body immediately responds. It's why I came here anyway, knowing that my time with Lucas would lead to this. I'm not ashamed of what my body wants. I never have been.

His hands creep up my sides before they flirt with my bra. I suck in a breath, hoping I can maneuver getting the damn thing off before he looks at it. My father picked this piece of clothing out just like he picked everything I wore, and this is about as dumpy as you can get.

He palms my breasts as he lowers his head, kissing a trail up my abdomen where he's pulled my shirt up with his wandering hands. He keeps moving up and up until he's so dangerously close to my bra line that nerves kick in.

"Wait," I say.

Lucas immediately pulls away, taking his hands

away from my breasts. "What?" he asks. "Do you want me to stop?"

"No, it's..." My cheeks heat.

"Don't tell me you're shy," he says teasingly. "I know you're not, Wild Girl. Do I need to bring up what happened in Mythology?"

"It's not that, it's—" I swallow. I might as well just tell him because I've already made a big deal about it. "It's my bra," I say finally.

He gets it right away. Locking gazes with me, he makes sure he has my full attention before saying, "I don't care what you wear, Dakota. I never did." He grips the hem of my shirt in his hands. "Can I?"

I nod, my throat growing thick. He lifts my shirt and keeps going. I lean up, holding my hands over my head as he slips it off.

I know it's the ugliest bra he's probably ever seen. There's no lace. There's no color. It's just white, and an off white at that with years of staining and some of it not even mine.

"I don't care what you're wearing," he says, moving the cup of my bra down so he can caress my nipple underneath. He does the same to the other until he closes his hot mouth over it. I buck underneath him, and he groans. "Jesus, Dakota." He reaches behind my back, unclasping the hooks until he pulls the bra up and off, throwing it to the floor. "Is this what you wanted to happen when you came in here?"

"Yes," I breathe.

"Stone got you hot earlier. He told me," Lucas says, flicking his tongue over my nipple.

I swallow. I guess Stone was right when they said they told each other everything. "Actually, I think it was the book I was reading."

"Liar," he growls. "You don't have any books here."

Damn. I'm caught. I lift his chin to meet my gaze. "Even if he started it, it's going to be your name I scream."

His wild eyes turn molten before me. "I'm going to hold you to that, Wild Girl."

He kisses his way down my body until he gets to the hem of my sleep shorts. He hooks his fingers around the elastic band and yanks them down, panties and all. He discards them and doesn't leave me time to think. He pins my knees to the bed, kneeling between my legs.

I've fantasized about this before while touching myself. I've imagined what the flat side of a tongue would feel like, lapping at me. His gaze meets mine before his tongue darts out, rolling over my clit. My hips come off the bed along with a low moan that emanates right from my core.

He keeps my gaze, flattening his tongue as he laps at me. His eyes are hooded as he yanks my hips against him. I cry out, unable to help myself as Lucas loses himself in pleasuring me.

My heart ricochets inside my chest. My breaths come in short pants as I watch him work.

He pulls away. "Mmm," he mumbles, licking his lips, and there's something so erotic about seeing him taste my juices on him. He lifts his hooded gaze. "Tell me that you're ours." I thrust my hips up and reach my hands into his hair, but he pulls back, giving me a devilish grin. "You already know it, Wild Girl. Just say it. Say you're ours. I'll make it worthwhile. You already know I will."

I let my head fall back down to the bed. Lucas's breath coats my pussy, teasing the pleasure he's already gifted me with and promising me even more if I just obey.

He plays his hands up and down my thighs. "You taste so good, Dakota. Are you going to deny me another taste?"

I squirm on the bed. It's stupid to hold this back. I'm already lost to them even though I don't want to admit it to myself. "I'm yours," I say, tipping my hips up again. "Just tongue fuck me, please."

Lucas lurches forward, sucking on my clit until I

cry out. A fiery sensation courses through me until he lets it go. "Say you're ours."

My fingers curl into the sheets. "Fuck, Lucas." I shift my hands to his hair again, pulling his lips to my clit. "I'm all of yours."

Lucas yanks me against him in a bruising kiss, his tongue lashing out expertly, flicking over my clit, lapping, and sucking in a rhythm that takes me high in no time at all. I breathe out in frenzied gasps and cries that surprise even me.

"You promised me you'd scream my name," Lucas reminds me.

No reminder needed. I hold him there, rocking into him in time with his movements. "Fuck," I gasp out. I already know it's coming, and it's coming quick. "Yes," I cry. A guttural moan pours from the back of Lucas's throat until it vibrates all the way through me. He sucks my clit again, and I explode. Literal fireworks spark behind my eyes. "Lucas!" He releases my clit while my body squeezes in quick succession, and short cries continue to break past my lips. He places a chaste kiss on my pussy and more shivers rack my body. "Jesus," I say, my body coming down from the biggest orgasm I've ever had.

"I can't believe I missed that reaction in class," he

says, resting his head against my abdomen. "You were definitely holding back."

"I think if you make me come that hard again, I'd be willing to do that with you almost anywhere."

"I'm going to hold you to that," Lucas says.

He lifts off me, and I lie back on the bed, staring at the ceiling. I don't even know what to do with myself. I've had some pretty intense orgasms before at my own hands, but nothing like that. Nothing with someone who I'm starting to have feelings for.

My stare follows Lucas as he goes into the bathroom. All I know right now is that I'm so fucked. That shit is addicting.

28

*L*ucas wouldn't let me leave his bed last night. At first, sleeping in the same bed with someone wasn't all that comfortable, but we got into a position with his arms around me, and coupled with the plush mattress, I fell into an easy sleep.

The next morning, I woke with Lucas's hard-on cupped between my ass cheeks. Thinking he was awake, I moved back into him but judging by the unmoving body behind me, it was clear he was still sleeping.

Last night had just been a taste of what Lucas could do. He'd known all the right buttons to push. The dirty talk on top of all the physical stuff was just icing on the cake. And despite all that, he hadn't asked for anything in return either, even knowing I would've given it to him. He could've asked for anything, and I would've willingly let him mold my body into a pretzel if it suited him.

I turn in his arms, pressing my fingertips against his chest and drawing them down over his navel where my fingers brush over his boxers that hide his stiff cock. Removing the covers from us, I drag my lips down his chest and abs, darting my tongue out every once in a while to kiss his salty skin.

I can't help myself. I pull the band of his boxers out and over his morning wood. His cock swells, veins cutting through his silky skin like coarse rope. I lick him from base to head. He immediately stirs, his fingers diving into my hair, squeezing at the base of my neck. "Fucking Christ, Dakota." His shocked words give way to his need for dominance. He places his hands on the top of my head. "Open that beautiful mouth of yours." I do as he demands, and he thrusts inside, filling me, hitting the back of my throat. I relax my throat muscles, taking him all in again and again. "Fuck," he growls as he uses my mouth as a hole to fuck.

I grip his base, hollowing out my cheeks as he continues to thrust. Hungry noises come from the back of my throat as my pussy slickens at his reckless abandon. I meet his gaze, his hard eyes taking in my submissive position as he continues to dominate me with almost punishing strokes.

My pussy throbs, flooding as a trickle of arousal drips down my thigh. I moan with him deep inside. "You like that, Dakota? My little Wild Girl."

My body makes empty thrusts of its own as my sex tightens. *Fuck, fuck.* I realize wildly that I think I'm going to come even though I haven't even been touched.

Lucas thrusts in deeper as I moan, forcing my lips around him as hard as I can. His noises continue to heat me up and turn me inside out. "Fuck Dakota, I'm going to come in your mouth. I'm almost there."

He hits a spot in the back of my throat, and my body responds, my toes curling as I throttle forward into a mild orgasm. It's obvious when I do, my eyes popping wide and a choked sound of ecstasy pours out of me even when my lips and tongue are otherwise engaged. Lucas's wild gaze screams approval as he jerks in my mouth, his cum spilling over my tongue as I take it all.

When he pulls away from me, I lie back on the bed, heart beating like a stampede of cattle. I don't know what thought to latch onto first. The fact that he just fucked my mouth like I was his, or the fact that I loved every fucking second of it.

He tangles his fingers in mine. "I'd apologize for being rough, but I think you enjoyed it."

I groan, not able to make words yet as I wonder if what just happened is actually physically possible. I mean, I know it is because it just fucking happened, but holy shit. I run through the scene in my head again, and sure enough, I came from giving head.

Lucas's cell phone alarm goes off, piercing the air, and I jump. "Shit," he says, quickly silencing it while my heart rate climbs to an even higher point.

I start to chuckle and then I full on laugh. My limbs are jelly. My mouth is tight and sore, but so fucking worth it.

"I was trying to find the right time to tell you that I like to be in charge," he says as he strokes the inside of my palms with his fingers. "You surprised me this morning."

I breathe out, my fingertips still buzzing. "I think I'm okay with it."

My admission does funny things to the look he gives me. He eyes my body like he'd be more than happy to see how far he could push me but then the door to his room opens. "Hey, do you know where Dakota—?" Stone stops. He drops his gaze down my body with an animalistic sort of stare down.

My immediate response is to cover up, but I push that thought aside. I have nothing to hide in front of them. They share everything anyway, right?

I stand, making Stone move back a step momentarily. "You found me," I say.

He swallows. "I hope part of that just fucked look had something to do with us last night."

I pretend to think about it. "Actually, I'm pretty sure I lost the ability to think with Lucas's cock rammed down my throat."

Lucas chuckles behind me. "You're pushing the beast, Wild Girl."

I find my pajamas and bra on the floor and carry them out as I slip around Stone. Well, attempt to, anyway. He moves in front of me until my nipple just barely grazes his arm. Goosebumps erupt all over me, but Stone keeps his gaze on my face. "We need to discuss something before we head to campus."

I run my hands over my curls, moving them to my other shoulder. "Can I shower first? Or do you want to have this conversation while I'm naked?"

He nods, his heavy gaze making me walk slower as I move from Lucas's room back into my own. Once there, I lower the blinds and lean against the door, my heart racing. Am I pushing the beast? I'm just trying to get under his skin like he gets under mine. Or maybe I am trying to show him what he could've had last night if he didn't dump me on my ass.

Either way, I strut into my bathroom with a skip in my step. When I get inside, I find a new shampoo bottle. I pick it up and read the label. It's for curly hair. A genuine smile pulls my lips apart. I don't know which guy thought of this. As much as I'd love to say it wasn't Stone, that's probably not true. We may have a deep-seated hatred for each other, but if my time with him tells me anything, it's that Stone looks at the finer details. When he feels like it.

I shower with the new shampoo and conditioner, loving how silky it makes my usually wild hair. There are more products on the bathroom sink, too, and I use every single one of them as I try to come up with the perfect combination to tame my hair. Because of that, I take a little longer in the bathroom than I usually do, but when I'm done, even I'm amazed at my head of curls. They're shiny and beautiful, not coarse and stringy like usual. I can even run my hands through them without it tying up into knots and pulling out almost half my hair.

With a smile, I dress in a pair of new shorts and a tank. I go back into my bathroom to check my reflection in the mirror, and I can't hardly believe it. My face is glowing, most likely from the sex. My hair is tame, and my clothes are new and fit me like a glove.

I stride from the room with my backpack on my shoulders like I fucking own the place because it feels like I fucking do. This must be how girls like Meghan feel all the time. Confident. Secure. Who knew what a set of new clothes and doing my hair could do for me? And the dick, of course. I can't forget the dick. It's absolutely insane.

My confidence level shoots up even more when I find Wyatt in the kitchen. He does a double-take that makes me blush. "Jesus, Tits. I knew you were beautiful, but you're down right captivating today."

"Please," I say, rolling my eyes, knowing he's so full of shit. This is what he does with girls, but I also can't help but take the compliment for what it is. A hot guy telling a girl who's been nothing all her life that she's looking good.

His shoulders slump after a moment. "Ugh, wonderful. We're going to be getting into a fight today. I can just tell."

My face scrunches up.

"Don't believe me? You'll see." He waltzes toward me, taking every instance to run his heated gaze over me. "I know what guys think. You have easy prey written all over you. They think you have self-esteem issues if they even remember you at all. Some guys are too fucking dumb to look beyond what's in front of them to see what's really going on. You, Dakota Wilder, have always been a hot piece of ass. It didn't matter if you had dirt brushed over your cheeks or your shirts had holes in them or that your hair looked like it was running you. Shitheads, though? Asshole shitheads who will only look surface deep are about to swarm you with their pathetic, tiny dicks. Judging by the way you screamed Lucas's name last night, he's not going to like that. And Stone? He's always wanted to throttle anyone who ever looked at you. Even us." He trails off. "Me?"

"You?" I ask, prompting him.

He grins, tipping his cowboy hat down so he shields part of his face. "I like fighting, so I'll be more than happy to oblige any fucker who thinks he can get close to you today."

We stand there staring at each other for a little while before he returns to the kitchen and starts to make something on the stove. I finally convince my feet to move when Lucas sounds behind me. "Oh fuck."

"That's what I said," Wyatt pipes up as he grabs something out of the cupboards.

"Like we don't have enough to worry about."

I just smile and laugh. Everyone should have a Wyatt and Lucas around when they get a makeover. It's good for the soul.

Lucas comes up behind me, his arm stretching around my middle. "Not that I'm complaining one bit," he teases, his hot breath caressing my ear.

I feel like a million dollars today. My shoes fit perfectly, so no more tired, aching feet. No more wishing I could fade away into the background. I realize with a start that these guys have a lot to do with that. They came out of nowhere, pulling me into the real world, helping me slay dragons like fucking Meghan, putting her in her place for once.

Lucas dips to kiss the soft spot behind my ear, and my knees go weak. If it wasn't for Wyatt at that moment dropping a plate onto the kitchen island that he says he made just for me, I might have even dropped all the way to the floor, hopefully taking Lucas with me. Instead, I move forward, recognizing right away that he's made me French toast, but it isn't the bland way we used to eat it. It's coated in what smells like cinnamon icing.

"Someday, a girl's going to lasso your heart, Wyatt Longhorn. When she does, she's going to be one lucky lady," I say, salivating over his breakfast.

Wyatt chuckles darkly, but he doesn't say anything

in return. The smell of his breakfast makes me dive right in, and it tastes just as good as it looks.

"I take it Stone and I are still fending for ourselves?"

"It's still midweek, isn't it? And before you say anything about Tits getting food, it's because she has a pussy and you don't."

"What if I had her pussy, does that count?"

"No, it means I ain't making you shit during the weekend either, you bastard."

Lucas grins over at me, and my heart melts into a puddle. I swear there's currently icing dripping from my lips, but he doesn't seem to care.

Footsteps mark their way into the room. My back heats as Stone comes up behind me. He drops a stapled stack of papers in front of me. I eye it, reading the first few lines. I swallow the food in my mouth as Stone says, "This is a contract I had drawn up for you. I want you to read through it and see what you think, but in a nutshell, it says that whatever you tell us about the Superstition Mountain treasure stays between us. The information will only be used in conjunction with working with you as part of our team. And that myself, Wyatt, and Lucas will do everything in our power to conceal your family's years of research and knowledge from any other parties."

I turn in my chair after briefly running my gaze over the words on the first page which affirm what he's just said. Yes, it's all legalese, but I think he's right. "You're serious?"

"One hundred percent," he says, sliding his cold blue-gray gaze to mine. "You always had my word. Now you can have it in writing, complete with a clause that says if we default on any part of this contract, you can sue me for a hefty sum of money."

"It's not about money," I say, still sizing him up, almost disbelieving that we're having this conversation.

"I know," he growls. "It's so much more than that, but I had to offer you something sizable in return so you can be assured that we're all on your side. This is a contract between teammates with one common goal."

I lick my lips, tasting the sugary sweet of the icing still there. "Thank you," I tell him. "I'll read it over today and have an answer for you by the end of the day."

"If you want, I'll pay for your own lawyer—a disinterested third party—that you can discuss it with, but I assure you everything in that contract is legal and binding."

"That won't be necessary," I tell him, feeling a little breathless.

He nods at me and walks away, going to the

cupboards to retrieve a bowl and an oatmeal packet. I watch as he works methodically, like he's been doing this very thing his whole life. I bet I'm an anomaly to him. He dealt with me as he knew how, through lawyers and contracts. No matter how different it is from how I would deal with something, I can't help but think that what he's just done is monumental, showing his true colors.

Judging by the way Wyatt and Lucas are watching him too, I know I'm right. Stone Jacobs just relinquished control for once.

29

Instead of focusing on school, I read through Stone's contract. With each clause I decipher, I know he's trying. Actually, this is probably the best gift he could give me.

When we returned home from my dad's house a couple of days ago, I hid the key to the safe behind the nightstand in my room, taping it to the back where no one could easily find it. It's been years since I've even seen the safe, but I know what's in it. Dad used to say, "Everything you might forget, it's in there." Maybe he was preparing me for the time he wouldn't be here all along.

The last class I have for the day ends, and I don't even realize. Wyatt saunters up to me while everyone quietly shuffles out of the room. I try to hide the contract quickly, but it's no use. "He surprised you, didn't he?"

I nod. There's no use hiding anything from these guys anymore. It's sad, but I know these guys more than anyone else. My dad's gone and Dickie's a friend, but he could never be a friend I could lean on.

"He has a tendency to do that, by the way. You'll see," Wyatt says. "You're a part of us now, whether you sign that contract or not. That's just a formality to make you feel safe, but I know my best friends. There's no way they would let anything you know slip out. I can promise you that."

His words reaffirm everything for me, but I can't let him get away with that. "You going soft on me, cowboy?"

A hint of a smile teases his lips. "Don't be calling me out like that, Tits. I have a reputation to uphold."

I smirk and shake my head, peeking at the contract again. "I guess sometimes I just wish my dad were around, you know?"

He doesn't say anything for several seconds, but when he does talk, his voice is cold. "Actually, I don't know," Wyatt says. "Don't go getting all pissy, but I'm about to lay down a truth you may not be ready to hear."

My stomach drops. I switch my gaze to his, already

bracing myself for impact. It's as if I'm sitting in the front seat of a rollercoaster and I know I'm about to go downhill, but it's not as if I can stop it.

"Your dad didn't do right by you, Dakota. From what I've seen and heard, he was a hermit who dressed you like him, kept you to himself, and made you his little assistant from birth. That was no way to grow up."

I glare at him, sending him the iciest, piercing gaze I can muster before I get out of my chair and march away. "You ever heard the word poor before, Wyatt? It might be foreign to you."

He growls behind me, pulling me back into the classroom where it's just the two of us instead of the hallway where people are still lingering. "I get poor. What I don't get is him spending every last penny on finding the fucking treasure when he couldn't even buy you a decent pair of sneakers. You slum it in clothes that don't even fit you, and yet you just stand here, acting like he's the best father in the world."

"Stop," I say.

He slams the door to the classroom, caging me in on the other side. "Or what?" he asks, his eyebrow hitched practically into his hairline. "Or else you might have to think some hard truths yourself? There was money to search for the treasure, but no money for you.

361

Did you ever go hungry, Dakota? From the way you maneuvered around the cafeteria before you moved in with us, I think you have. I saw the scheme in your eyes. What else did he deprive you of, huh? I saw that fucking house you grew up in. Fuck," Wyatt says, slamming his fist on the other side of the door. "My heart fucking broke. Why do you think Stone could barely stay in it?"

I swallow, my heart jumping out of my chest. "My dad did what he could."

"Bullshit," Wyatt grinds out. The force of his words hit me full on in the face. I'm at the point in the ride where my stomach is in my throat and I can hardly breathe from screaming so much. "He abused you, and you don't even get it."

"He never touched me," I growl.

"There are different ways to be abused. How about neglect? How about emotional abuse? How many times did you stay alone in that house while your dad went out, huh?"

My mind reels. His words take me back in time, but I refuse to believe anything he's saying. I can't. I just can't. "You weren't there. You don't know."

"You're right, I wasn't. I wasn't always there. But I saw the scared girl in the mountains sometimes. The one that jumped as soon as her dad said something.

The one that ate his words up like they were the gold we were all searching for."

I close my eyes. I wish Wyatt away, but he keeps moving closer. He's in my space, his chest only a hair's breadth away from my own.

"You're twenty, and you've never even been outside of Clary, Dakota." His voice shakes. "Your dad's lucky he's gone because if he ever comes back, I'm going to kick his ass."

"Fuck you," I spit, shoving him off me finally.

He doesn't relent though. He gets right back in my face. "Get mad. You should be. He stole your life from you."

"No," I scream through clenched teeth.

"He did," Wyatt says much more calmly now, backing me right into the door again. He cups my face. "I saw you when you tried on those boots. A girl who never had not only new shoes, but shoes that actually fit. Ask me how that happened, Dakota?"

"He got them second-hand," I say, voice shaking. It wasn't his fault.

"And there were never shoes *your* size? I'm calling bullshit again. I don't believe it. There's a difference between being poor and neglect, and I don't think your dad ever cared whether you had shoes that fit, and I think somehow in your head, you just went with it. You made up excuses because it was easier to think there weren't shoes your size instead of realizing your daddy just didn't care enough to buy you ones that fit. That's what I think."

He drops his head to mine, and I suck in a breath. My body is vibrating. I'm at war with myself. "Why do you care?"

He takes a while to answer, his blue eyes darting to different areas of my face before he says, "I'm not sure yet."

As soon as the last word leaves his mouth, he moves forward. He claims my lips, pressing into them with a hunger that takes me off guard. He doesn't ravish me. He doesn't kiss me until we're breathless for more. He just leaves his lips on mine in a transfer between two souls, who in that moment, are connected outside of reality.

As quick as it started, he pulls away. He reaches for the handle, opening the door and marching away. He leaves me there, my mind in a merry-go-round of emotions. I stay leaning against the door until Lucas comes looking for me. He puts his arm around my shoulders and leads me from the room. He doesn't say anything, but I already know. They tell each other everything.

I told myself I had to go to the computer lab to

finally work on that English paper I lost when my laptop was stolen, but after everything that's happened, I find myself being led to the silver Audi in the parking lot where Wyatt is nowhere to be seen. It's just Stone, sitting in the driver's seat with sunglasses on. They unnerve me because I can't see anything he's thinking. When he sees me get close, he just looks out the front windshield, one hand on the wheel and the other on the gear clutch, waiting.

Lucas pulls the passenger side door open for me, but I shake my head. "I'll sit in the back."

No one speaks on the way back to Jacobs Manor. No one explains where Wyatt went even though we all left this morning in the same car, so I have no idea how he's even going to get home. When they pull into the driveway, I get out first, slinking to my room. I'm not in the mood to be around anyone tonight. At least for a little while. Besides, it's better off that I'm not. I have to make a decision about this contract.

When I hole myself in my room, Lucas knocks on the door, but I don't answer him. He's such a gentleman that he doesn't even force his way in. He knows I need my space right now. Because of the contract and because of what Wyatt said to me.

I spend too much time staring at the ceiling, sifting through my childhood memories to see if what Wyatt said has any merit. Then, I decide that I'm the only one who gets to decide what happened to me. He can't talk me into having daddy issues. Why would anyone want to do that?

On the other hand, some of his comments make sense. Dad never asked me my sizes. I thought it was because we both didn't know. But he could've taken me to the stores to figure it out just like we did yesterday. Like Wyatt said, it's highly unlikely there was never any clothing my size, even in the second-hand shops.

But he's a guy, right? What would he care about styles and sizes and—

I scream into my pillow, punching the bed. My dad is the only person I have. He's been my only person. I can't just sit here and think poorly of him. I'm trying to find him for Christ's sake. I need to. As soon as I do, this will all blow away. They'll see what kind of father he really is.

Even though I've practically memorized the contract, I read through it again, trying to think of different ways it can be interpreted, but it actually can't. It's ironclad, just like Stone Jacobs said it would be. He's offering me a lifeline here. I'm more of a fairy tale girl, so I'd rather something like this be signed in blood, but I guess black ink will do. When we sign this, we'll be bonded in more ways than one.

After a couple of hours, I leave my room to find Lucas and Stone outside by the pool. They've ordered subs which are still wrapped on the patio table. Lucas is doing laps in the pool, but as soon as he sees me emerge, he pulls himself out in all of his bare-chested glory. I try not to stare. If I'm going to be working with these guys for the duration of this contract, then I have to get used to being around them like this. Plus, I have a feeling I can see Lucas shirtless any time I want now, and that gives me a tremendous shot of adrenaline.

He pulls a towel off a patio chair and starts wiping his chest down with it. A crease forms in his brow as he watches me, and I almost feel sorry for shutting him out. Being around people is something I have to get used to. I'm not used to having anyone around. Going to college and living in the dorms was a major adjustment. I've been doing nothing but navigating different waters since I matriculated into Saint Clary's, but now there's Wyatt, Stone, and Lucas, too.

"We got subs," Stone offers, sliding his sunglasses off and setting them on the table. He eyes the contract in my hand, but he doesn't say anything. It feels like we're miles away from where we were yesterday when he had his hands on me. "We didn't know what you liked, so we bought a bit of everything."

It definitely looks like they bought a tray big

enough for a huge party. I've had lunch meat before, but I've never had them on sub rolls. Just plain old white bread for me and Dad, and lots of times, we didn't even have mayonnaise or anything like that to put on it. I suppose by Wyatt's standards, that means I was neglected.

I'm itching to ask where he is, but I can't quite bring myself to do it. I shouldn't want to know. In fact, I'm a little terrified at seeing him next because I don't want to get in a fight again, I certainly don't want him to keep pushing me.

"What do you suggest?" I ask Stone.

He almost reels back. Almost. He catches himself so he only looks slightly flummoxed. Still, I take pride in knowing I've surprised him again. He picks up one of the sandwiches and hands it to me. "This is what I like. Do you want to try it?"

I nod, peeling the wrapper down. I don't even check what's in the sandwich before biting down. I figure I'd rather not know in case the looks of it deters me from eating. I chew, and at first, it's really good. I smile and give Stone a thumbs up but in the next moment, I chomp down on something hot. As fuck. My eyes widen, and I start to choke. I can't help but spit out the taste that's in my mouth and even then, my tongue is on fucking fire.

Stone chuckles in front of me. I want to hurl his dumb sandwich at him, but I keep coughing. Lucas hurries over to the outdoor sink, pouring me a drink of water and then bringing it over so I can down it. When I finally regain my composure, I ask, "What in the hell was that?"

Stone takes the sub from me, chuckling. "They're called peppers."

"Dear God. They're fucking awful."

He hands me another sub, telling me it's tamer, and then laughs as he takes a huge bite out of the sub I gave back to him.

I grumble at him, this time opening up the sub he gave me to see what's in it, so I don't have a repeat of what just happened. Instead, I'm happy to see that there's ham, cheese, lettuce, and mayonnaise on this one. Plain Jane. I guess that's the way I like it.

"You could've started her out with a little less heat," Lucas says, rolling his eyes as he sits next to me.

I hungrily eat the sub in my hands. One, because it tastes good, but two, because it helps tame the fire that's still raging inside my mouth.

"I'll keep that in mind for next time," Stone says. "I forget that she hasn't..." He trails off, peeking at me like he doesn't want to say the wrong thing which is a brand new look for him. Usually, he doesn't give a fuck.

"...you know, tried stuff before," he says, all politically correct as if he hasn't been the biggest douche to me before.

Stone's phone rings, and he brings it out. He frowns down at it then stands, shoving the chair back. "Fuck," he roars.

Lucas's hands flex on the glass table. "What?"

"It's Wyatt. Goddammit. I knew I shouldn't have let him go off by himself." Stone eyes me then Lucas. "We have to go get him."

"Shit," Lucas says. "Is he—?"

"Yep."

Lucas runs his hands through his hair. He takes a sub, then helps me wrap mine up. "Come on, Wild Girl. We have to go save Wyatt."

e've been speeding down desert roads for forty-five minutes, my heart in my throat. I'm sitting in the back of the Audi with a fierce grip on the two seats in front of me. Lucas and Stone don't talk. Stone's intense concentration on the road is both terrifying yet oddly satisfying since he's driving like a crazy person, and Lucas has a death grip on the handle above the car door, leaning forward like he could make the car go even faster if he tried.

The scenery blurs by so fast, I couldn't enjoy it even if I tried. We hit the limits of a city. The welcome sign whirs past before I can even think to see where we are. My mouth drops as the lights from houses, street posts, and other cars, light up the horizon like twinkling stars. I thought I had to look up to see that much light, but I was wrong. In a way, the city lights are just as beautiful. So much life. So much activity.

A car honks at us as Stone cuts him off. His jaw feathers like it's a personal affront. It's dark out now, which is another reason why the city lights are so bright, but it also lets a hint of fear creep in. I don't know where we are. I don't know where we're going, and I certainly don't understand why Wyatt needs saving.

Eventually, Stone slows the car, veering toward a highway exit. The tires squeal as he makes the turn, merging onto a different highway. A couple of miles down the road, he slows again, and I blink to make sure I'm seeing correctly. Chain-link fences loom into view. Barbwire tops bow out over the road. The straight line of fencing goes on for as far as street lamps light up the side of the road.

"Where the hell are we?" I ask, but in the next instant, the answer looms into view in the form of a sign. My gaze catches on the word prison. "Why is Wyatt here?"

Without answering, Stone drives up to a guard station. The guard comes out with a gun, sighing when he sees Stone, who immediately holds up his hand. "I know. I'm getting him out now."

"Man, you know we can't keep doing this."

"I didn't realize he was that bad again," Stone says to the guy holding a gun. *A fucking gun.* I mean, my dad had a gun that we took into the mountains with us, but that was for shooting poisonous snakes. This gun is for... Well, I guess to keep the people who are inside staying inside, which is a good thing. I can't keep my eyes off it as Stone drives into an inner perimeter. A parking lot opens up that's surrounded by another round of gates and fences with a thick, high wall. We can't even see the prison proper yet. Not that I want to. Nerves skate over my body. This place is terrifying. This is only my second time out of Clary, and I'm at a prison. I never thought I'd see the day.

Stone leans forward, gazing out the window. He picks up speed when a shadow in the corner moves. The bright lights shining down from above, cast Wyatt's imprint on the pavement in four different directions. When he sees us coming, he plops down on his ass.

Stone parks the car. "I'll get him," he huffs.

He exits the car, shoves his hands into his pockets, and strides up to Wyatt. I lean forward while I watch Stone and Wyatt talk. "What's going on?" I ask.

"Wyatt has a past," Lucas says softly, sighing as he watches the scene. It's obvious Wyatt is shit-faced. Stone pulls him to his feet and the cowboy nearly takes them both down when he struggles to stay upright. "We all do."

"But prison?" I ask, wondering what the hell has happened in Wyatt's past that he would end up here. Of all places. I don't know much about the outside world. Obviously. But this place doesn't seem like some ordinary jail either.

"Yeah," Lucas says on an exhale. "Here. Always here."

Stone has to almost carry Wyatt to the car. Lucas hops out, moving to the backseat to open the door for them. As carefully as they can, they help Wyatt into the back who has no problem sprawling out. His head starts out on my shoulder then falls because he lacks the strength to keep it upright. It finally ends in my lap. I take his cowboy hat off carefully and then stroke my fingers through his matted, dark hair.

"Do you want me to sit in the back with him?" Lucas asks.

At that, Wyatt grips me tight, pulling himself into a more comfortable position. I shake my head. "No, I'm good."

Lucas shuts the back door and then jogs around the rear of the car to get in the front again. When Stone gets in, he puts the car into gear and we're on the move once again. He lifts his fingers from the steering wheel to wave at the guard whose hard frown lines are impossible to miss.

Stone lets out a breath. "They're not going to let this keep happening. My last name only goes so far."

Wyatt turns onto his back, his hand moving out and falling against the backseat near my head. I have to slide out of its trajectory before it hits me. "I fucked up," he grumbles.

"Huh?"

Lucas turns around from the backseat. "Don't mind him. He blabbers when he's shitfaced."

I nod, and he drops his gaze to my steadying strokes through Wyatt's hair. Without his cowboy hat, he looks younger. His face holds a more youthful expression, or perhaps that's because he doesn't have the strength to keep the hard glint in his eyes he usually carries.

I'm not over what he said earlier, but this guy, the one in front of me right now, is obviously broken. At least in this moment.

"She probably won't talk to me again," he says on a sigh.

Stone's heavy gaze meets mine in the mirror, and it's then that I realize Wyatt is talking about me. His words are slurred, almost as if he's talking in his sleep. I guess this would be more aptly described as talking while passed the fuck out. "How did he even get the alcohol?" I ask the guys.

Lucas shrugs. "How does Wyatt ever do anything? When he sets his mind to something, he just gets it done. He probably took an Uber all the way here and made the driver stop at a convenience store off one of the exits."

I think back through our conversation earlier at school. Something isn't adding up. I'm not sure what I said or did that would've caused him to do this. He's the one who yelled at me, after all.

"Girls are bitches, man," he grumbles.

A growl works its way up my throat, but Lucas turns to put his hand on my knee. He shakes his head. "That's not about you," he whispers. Louder, he says. "We know, man. Everything's good."

"She killed my father."

Horror rips through me, and I gasp.

Those words were quieter than the others, but I'm sure I heard him right. I try to twist them into saying something completely different but when I lift my gaze and see Stone staring back at me, I know there's no way I heard it wrong. Someone killed Wyatt's father.

"We know, man," Lucas says.

I keep running my hand through his hair. He sighs into me, finally curling up until soft snores signal that he's sleeping it off. I guess there's the reason why Wyatt has issues with women? Whoever this "she" is fucked him up.

I lie my head back and close my eyes, wondering what horrors Wyatt has had to go through and just how far in his past these things happened.

We could drop a pin in the car and hear it hit. That's how silent the car ride back to Jacobs Manor is. When we get there, Stone and Lucas get Wyatt to his feet. He's combative at first, even taking a swing at both of them. He's too drunk to do any real damage, and it allows Stone to wrap him up, leading him toward the house.

I lag behind, watching the whole thing as they take Wyatt to his room and close the door behind them. I stand in the hallway for a little while. I hear the pipes start to run water and then a string of curses travels through the walls as Wyatt pitches a fit.

Fingering the brim of Wyatt's hat, I take it into my room with me. I set it on the nightstand and then strip, putting my PJ's on, so I can slip into bed. Despite wishing sleep would come, my mind keeps wandering to Wyatt and what he said to me at school and how the night ended. I'm upset still, but I also long to know what makes that boy tick. All of them, actually.

I'm easy to figure out. Poor girl with barely any

history. I mean, how much history can you have if you've barely ever left the house let alone the small town you live in? I've only started to gather a history since meeting the guys.

Here I thought I was on this grand adventure ever since I was a little girl, but now I know mine is just starting.

Halfway through the night, my door opens, and Wyatt steps in. He's dressed in nothing but a pair of long pants that dip well below his belly button. He tiptoes through the room to grab his hat, but when he looks at me, he realizes I'm watching.

He stops, his shoulders sagging. "I'm sorry about earlier."

I move back to get a better look at him, bringing my knees to my chest. "Which part?"

"The part where I yelled at you."

How did these guys enter my life and end up turning the whole thing upside down? I don't even know if I should be mad at him anymore. Maybe I should be mad at my dad, but even that seems kind of fruitless considering he's not even here...and maybe he won't ever be coming back.

"It's okay," I say, even though it's not. Even though those aren't the right words at all, but I'm not equipped to know the right words. My experience with people is so limited that I'm not sure what's what and how I should be reacting to anything. It's sad when you can't even trust yourself.

Even though I don't say more, I think Wyatt knows those words were just empty. Just something people say. His gaze drifts to his hat and then back again. "Can I lie next to you?"

I move back, practically plastering myself to the wall, but who am I to deny Wyatt? Not after the night he's had. He moves into place, staying on top of the covers.

"I was talking to Lucas about his magic fingers when he told me you were the one in the backseat with me. That was kind of awkward."

I grin at him, thinking it funny he thought I was Lucas, but in the same token, I could see Lucas taking care of him too, running his hands through his hair just like I had.

"It helped ease some of the thoughts in my head," he says, and for the first time, his vulnerability shines like a spotlight.

I bite my lower lip. "I can do it again, if you want."

Wyatt shuffles closer, still sporting his innocent

face. I move up, placing my pillow up under my rib cage, so I can lie in an elevated position. Wyatt closes his eyes, and I hesitate at first. This seems far too intimate now. Not like before when I knew he needed it but also that he probably wasn't ever going to remember. He'll remember it this time. He wants it.

With a breath held in my chest, I work my fingers through his thick, dark hair. He lets out a breath that I swear is more like a sigh or a kitten's purr. I skim my fingers all the way to the back of his head and then start again. After several minutes, Wyatt turns to his side, facing away from me. I lie my head against my arm, shifting into a more comfortable position while still running my hands through his hair.

On my second pass through, though, my fingers run over a bump. They still for a moment, but keep going, running over that same spot until I realize it's more like a raised ridge that's about four to five inches long along the crown of his head. I frown as my fingers run over it time and time again.

What happened to you Wyatt Longhorn?

This will be one of the few times I don't make up some fantastical story in my head because I'm pretty sure the real story is beyond anything I can imagine.

31

*M*y hand shifts on its own, making me stir from sleep. The bed depresses, and I blink awake to find Wyatt's back to me. There are freckles sprinkled over his cut form, and I resist the urge to reach out and touch his taut skin.

He stands, pulling his pants up. I almost got a glimpse of the curve of his ass. Instead, his tapered waist is all the view I'm getting. I shift down the bed, and he stills. There's a pinch in my neck from how I fell asleep. Making him comfortable had been my number one priority, but I hadn't expected him to stay in my room all night.

He looks toward his hat, then grabs it up, holding it south of his belly button as he turns toward me. He shrugs with a playful grin on his face before glancing down. "I woke up next to a beautiful woman."

My face colors as I realize what he's saying. It's like when I woke Lucas up. He was already hard and waiting for me. This isn't the same scenario though. My core still heats with his words, but the last thing I need to do is to fall into bed with Wyatt, especially not with all the unsaid words between us.

"I think I had the best sleep I've had in a while," he says, a yawn splitting his lips apart. He looks away, holding his free hand to his mouth and shakes his head like he's coming out of a coma.

"It must have been the alcohol," I tease.

"I think it had to do with something way different than that." A hint of color hits his cheeks. "I'm gonna go now, Dakota. Thank you," he says, rushing the words out like he's almost embarrassed to say them. He leaves, the door clicking into place behind him. I spread out on the bed. It isn't a tiny bed at all. Way bigger than the sofa I'd been sleeping on my whole life, but when you share it with a big cowboy, it feels smaller.

I check the time on the small alarm clock in the room. My eyes bug out of my head when I see it's well past the time we all should've been at class. I drag myself from bed, take a quick shower, but not too quick as to forego my new hair routine. That would be blasphemous. Once I get it styled, I put on a new outfit and slip from the room.

The smell of bacon wafts through the air. I'm confused until I move into the kitchen to see Stone and Lucas shoulder to shoulder, trying to cook. They're whisper arguing about something, and when I step a certain way, the floor creaks. They turn quickly and then both sag in relief. "We thought you were Wyatt."

"Sorry to disappoint."

"No," Lucas says quickly. "We were just trying to make him breakfast."

Stone scrolls through his cell phone. "Why does the recipe say *between* ten and fifteen minutes? Why can't they just say it takes this long, flip once at the halfway mark, and then boom, you got yourself some good bacon?"

I chuckle to myself, and Stone gazes at me, arching a brow. "Do you think you can do better?"

"We only had bacon on Christmas or at Dickie's, so no, I'm not the girl you want to cook for you."

Footsteps sound behind me, and Wyatt sighs. "Nooo, what are you doing?" He pushes forward, standing in front of the stove until the boys move. "I swear you do this just so I'll come in and save your asses."

Stone pockets his phone. "We were trying to be nice."

"Go be nice at the bar where Dakota's fine ass is."

"Hey, I thought I was Tits."

He grins at me over his shoulder and winks. "After last night, I have a lot of different nicknames for you."

"Magic hands?"

Stone stiffens at my words, and Wyatt cracks up. "Calm your horses. I didn't fuck her."

Stone takes a sobering breath. Once he's under control again, he says, "I don't care."

Even I recognize the lie when it flies from his mouth, I just don't know why he does care.

"Good because if I did fuck her, the whole house would know." Wyatt turns to wink at me again, and I can't help but roll my eyes. Despite the night he had, he seems to be full of it this morning.

Lucas laughs. "Even Dakota is calling BS on your bullshit."

I watch the scene in front of me with new eyes. It's like wiping the rain from a windshield. I see how they interact with each other. Lucas and Stone trying to help Wyatt while Wyatt puts on airs that he doesn't need help while secretly wanting help. They're like a family. A disjointed one, sure. Not your typical parents and siblings, but hell, my father and I were never the typical family unit either. Everything about us was abnormal.

Wyatt finishes the breakfast, and even though we should be hurrying to make it to at least some of our classes today, we settle in like it's the weekend. We take the plates and the food out to the patio like the morning after I first arrived. The guys talk easily, telling stories about other times when Wyatt was drunk off his ass and how they had to drag him home. Then, the stories expand to Lucas, and then even Stone. Stone's story surprises me the most. I didn't think he ever gave up control willingly. To get drunk, you have to give up the biggest control of all, yourself.

Despite the good-natured jabs, Stone immediately changes the subject when it veers toward him. He might as well be a warden from that prison last night for all he lets get free.

When we finish, I pick up the plates, even at Stone's disapproval, and move them to the kitchen. When I come back out, the contract is sitting in front of me. I'm not sure which one of them saved it last night, but they're all eyeing me expectantly.

Even more so than yesterday, I feel comfortable signing this document. There's just one thing bugging me. One thing that's not directly stated in the contract, but I want it to be.

"What do you think?" Stone asks. "Are you all in?"

I worry over my lip. My stomach dips low, surprising me with the feelings of how momentous this is. I went from being by myself, sticking to the shadows, to being front and center of three gorgeous men. Our plan revolves around me, and it gives me both a high and an overwhelming feeling that I'll never be able to measure up. What my family knows about the treasure didn't come from me.

My father always said I'd put my stamp in history when it came to the treasure, all I had to do was wait.

Me? I just thought that Dad would find it. He worked so damn hard on it that if anyone deserved to put their mark in history regarding the treasure, it was him.

Maybe it is my time now though.

I gaze up at Stone. I understand what's riding on this for him. Sometimes, I can see the panic in his eyes. The feeling that he doesn't have a hold of the reigns like he would prefer. "Is it just the four of us?" I ask.

Stone cocks his head. "What do you mean?"

"All this talk in here about never letting slip what my family knows, I want to make sure it's just the four of us."

He narrows his gaze, and it's not just him. Stone

and Wyatt look confused as well. "Dakota, you're going to have to be more specific."

"When we're talking about sharing information, how far does it go? Does that extend to your dad?"

I don't care if he is Stone's father, I don't like Lance Jacobs. Call it that gut feeling. Intuition. My father always said I should follow it, and I will. Spending time with Lance won't even change the way I feel, not like it has with these guys.

"My father would like the information, yes." His jaw clenches as he swallows. "If you're asking if the information can stay between us four... You, me, Wyatt, and Lucas, then we'll do that. My father is the reason we're in this shit anyway." My fingers buzz as he takes a pen and moves the contract in front of him. On the last page, he starts writing, then makes four underlines. "I added a new clause. If we all initial the new clause, it will be binding. If you want to make sure, I'll give you the number to a law—"

I hold my hand up to stop him. I trust him. God help me, but I fucking trust Stone Jacobs. "I believe you."

His eyes spark with emotion. He turns the contract to me and hands over the pen. I read his new clause, which states that the parties the contract refers to are the four signing parties, and that no other party shall be privy to any information shared within the group or even contained within the contract. "You're not going to tell your dad about this?"

"I'm saving my friends and the people who were pulled into this. That's it. I'm not here to save my father's ass for his poor business decisions."

A cold sweat breaks out across my forehead. There's still part fear, a long-held belief that there's no way I should be signing a contract with a Jacobs, but there's also encouragement too.

I sign my name on the first line and date it. Then, I initial in the spot Stone left for me.

Stone indicates that I give the papers to Lucas who signs it without reading it before passing it to Wyatt who does the same. When Stone gets it, he smiles. It isn't huge. It doesn't reflect on a happy occasion, it's just a look of solidarity between us all. He signs the paperwork with the most pristine handwriting you've ever seen, each letter almost choreographed to come out perfectly. The rest of our signatures look like kindergartners got a hold of it while his is one for the record books. When he finishes, he caps the pen and sets it next to the contract. "I'll get this filed and give everyone copies."

"Thank you," I say, my voice deep with meaning. It's just a piece of paper with three lousy signatures and one masterpiece on it but it means so much to me. More than I ever could articulate right now.

Maybe it's because those papers are a physical manifestation of what's been going on in real life. In real life, these guys have wormed their way into my every day. I'm well aware I'm past the point that if they left tomorrow, that I'd be stranded. Not just because of the lack of money, but because in such a short amount of time, they've made me feel more comfortable in my own skin than I've ever been in my previous twenty years of life.

I'm finally accepted.

I swallow the emotion down, refusing to let them see how much I'm affected by this. I don't think they could understand. They've always had each other. They can't possibly realize what it's like to be me. Obviously, with Wyatt's stunt last night, I realize they might all come with their own sets of baggage, but this is mine. And I can keep it close to my heart if I want to.

"I want to head up into the mountains on Saturday," Stone says. "I don't care if we don't even have a destination, I just feel useless down here. I want us going through those papers of your father's every night. I want that shit categorized and filed into something that makes sense. School is a priority, but these assholes aren't going to let us sit back." He leans back in his chair with eyes like ice. "They're dangerous, and if we don't start moving, I have a feeling we won't like their response."

"But they can't possibly think we'll be able to find the treasure just like that when it's been missing for over a hundred years, Stone," I say, trying to reason with him.

"I'm guessing they think if the motivation is strong enough, we will."

I never liked Marilyn all that much, but she's still Stone's mother. He must be worried sick about her. The worst part is the not knowing. I understand that more than anyone. She could be at their whim. Or she could've just left, deciding to spend time by herself after my father went missing. We don't know, but I have a feeling Stone thinks the worst.

If he's right, I feel sorry for her.

"I might have something else," I say, my voice pitching low. My father and I always talked about the safe in whispers, even though it was always just us. Dad was paranoid on the best of days. The guys move forward, resting their elbows on the table as they lock gazes with me. My stomach clenches. I'm about to tell these guys something my father never wanted out. He only ever wanted it for Wilder's eyes only, but the circumstances have changed. If he wouldn't let me use what we have to help save the guys in front of me, surely, he wouldn't mind if I used it to help save me. I'm just as much in this as they are. "My father kept his most important documents somewhere else. I know where," I say right away because I can just see the question on the tip of Stone's tongue. "I'll show you," I tell them, but I point to the contract, my heart seeping a little for what I'm doing to my father right now. "This is in full effect."

"You have our word."

When I look around the table, I don't even need to hear them say it to know it's true. We're in this together. From here on out, we deal with everything as a collective, not a single unit among others. And I'm almost frightened by the calm that comes over me when I realize that's what's happening. I'm no longer the freak, Dakota Wilder. Well, I still may be a freak, but I'm Dakota Wilder with her trio of guys, and we're going to search for the treasure until we find it.

We don't have another choice.

We sit in the car in front of the house my grandfather built. I haven't made a move to get out yet, so I guess that's why everyone in the vehicle with me hasn't moved either. They're all waiting on my cue. They're not pushing me to do this. It's on my terms.

Guilt still churns in my stomach though. If it didn't, I'd be worried about me. The number of times I've had it drilled into my head that these were Wilder secrets could probably amount to the gold we've been chasing.

Lucas squeezes my hand in the backseat. It's not a nudge, it's a motion to make sure I'm okay, but it does spur me into movement. I know what we need to do. It may not seem like it, but I'm doing this for my father. If he's still somewhere up in those mountains, I'm going to bring him home. Alive or dead. If he got mixed up in the same thing the Jacobs have, then I'm going to find him and bring him home from that, too.

I throw the door open, and it releases the floodgates for everyone else's movement too. They follow me out of the car and toward the garage. I use my key to open the rickety door and stick my hand just inside, searching for the shovel handle. My fingers pass through spiderwebs as I go, but I finally find the handle and pull it out, shutting and locking the garage once I have it.

Nodding, I take them around the back of the house, and we start walking. Our land is about as dry as the desert. Very few tufts of vegetation sprout out here and there, but it's mostly a walk through hard-packed dirt, the ground cracked because of the arid climate. "My family has owned this land for centuries," I say offhandedly. "My great great great great—honestly, I've forgotten how far back it goes—but he was around when they built Clary. When the gold rush happened, we were here. He bought this land." The truth is, we own acres upon acres. I used to play outside for ages when I was a kid, exploring all kinds of things. My father never minded as long as I didn't go off our property, which gave me a bunch of leeway. Once we're a ways back from the road, I point out a decaying structure that's skinned right down to the timbers. "That was the original house."

The guys let me talk as we traverse the walk to the safe. Wyatt takes the shovel from me, though, and I miss having it to keep my hands busy.

"Who built the house you grew up in?" Lucas asks.

"My granddad. When they put the road through, it only made sense to have the house near the road, so they abandoned the family house which was falling down anyway and built that one. Can you believe the Wilders used to be well off?" I chuckle to myself. My family has sunk every penny we ever earned into finding the treasure.

"I've heard the story a million times, but you know I've never heard it from a Wilder," Wyatt says. "You mind tellin' it?"

I know the story inside and out. It was my bedtime story for many years. This story made me think anything was possible. The story that sounded like it jumped right out of a book, a fairy tale come to life. The thing about fairy tales is, they end happily. My family has been waiting around for our happy for a hundred years.

"The story is," I say, unable to help the smile that tugs at my lips. It's no wonder that I grew up loving to read. I wanted to immerse myself in stories wherever I was. Not just the one I was living, but others, too. "My great great great you know," I tease. "He not only stumbled across the richest gold vein in the Superstitions, but one day while he was mining it, he decided to explore the caves nearby. He twisted this way and that through the tunnels of rock as he traversed the dark stone tunnels until he came across a set of dusty old sacks. People find a lot of shit up in the Superstitions, so he just nudged them aside with his foot, but when he did, he heard the tinkling of metal."

I stop, remembering the way my father used to get overly animated as he told me the story. It always amazed me that these stories were told to generations and generations of Wilder's. The same words passed down over the years. "Thinking it was a competitor's mining tools on his claim, he ripped the drawstring bag open. When he did, the bag practically disintegrated in his hands, and what poured out was the most beautiful array of colors he'd ever seen. In the light of the waning candle, the glittering jewels lit up the cave, splashing it in an array of colors that was just like a true-to-life rainbow in the center of a mountain."

A smile pulls at Lucas's lips. Wyatt kicks at a plant, causing dust to plume in front of us, and Stone just listens silently.

"Well, my great great great you know Granddad almost had a heart attack. He opened up all the bags, gleaming at the treasure before his eyes. There was gold, silver, and jewels. The prettiest jewelry one could ever imagine. He put everything right back where it was before he packed up his gear and went home. For ages, he acted like nothing happened. You know how secretive mining can be. He never told anyone about the vein he was on, and he sure as hell wasn't going to tell anyone that he stumbled upon a treasure the likes no one had ever seen before. Secretly, he did his homework, wondering what in the world he'd come across. When his sons were old enough, he started taking them to the cave, showing them not only how to mine the gold, but the treasure he'd found years ago."

"It happened like that," I say, "Every Wilder passing it on to their children. Did you know I'm the only Wilder child in history who isn't a male? Dad said that never mattered though because I have a heart of gold and the smarts, too."

Lucas leans over and presses a kiss to my cheek. "He's right, you know." He beams at me, then asks, "How did the secret get out?"

My blood curdles. "When my great great great you know grandfather had his fiftieth wedding anniversary with his wife, he wanted to get her something really nice. To show her how much he loved her. So, he asked his eldest son to grab the prettiest piece of jewelry he could from the mountain treasure. When he gave it to her, he told his wife they'd earned it mining, but in reality, it was from the deposit they'd found. The one he'd never uttered a word about before. It's as if he knew what was about to happen." I grind my teeth together. "Once she started wearing the ring around town, the other miners got jealous. They thought he'd struck it rich up there. Clary was like it is today. No one was making much money, so he was always very careful. He let it slip one time to get his wife something nice. Just one time."

The end of this story never ceased to make me madder than hell and more determined than ever to find the treasure. It's like I've been wanting to stick it to the people of Clary my whole life. Stick it to people like Stone Jacobs.

"Next time the son went into their cave, he was followed. A guy from town laid in wait, searched the caves while Wilder was mining. He found the treasure alright. He tried to take it out, right in front of my ancestor's eyes. They got in a fight, and my great great whatever granddad was killed. The loudmouth thief left the body and the treasure there, but when he got back to Clary, he started spilling the beans. It got back to the patriarch of the Wilders that his son was dead. He was so fuming mad, he went into the center of town where a bunch of townspeople were mounting horses to get to the treasure, and he shot that thieving son of a bitch dead for what he'd done." I gulp. "Unfortunately, he had a heart attack right there in the center of town. It destroyed my family."

I clear my throat to stifle some of the emotion threatening to burst out. It's a terrible story any way you look at it, but when you think that it's your own history. The same genes that ran through them run through me, I can't help but feel it more. "When word got back to the family that not only the dad was dead but his brother, too, the youngest son told his mom what they'd found. They vowed never to talk about it again. Most of the clues out there come from that thieving asshole's mouth when he told the townspeople where it was located. That's why it's all jumbled up and convoluted."

Creases cut into Wyatt's forehead. "Then how come your family hasn't found it yet?"

"The younger son never went back. He left family clues as to where it was, including telling the story I just did. Some say his family dying made him a little nuts, so his clues were more like riddles. They've been handed down for generations. But the thing is, the markers they said were there either haven't been found yet or have been eroded by history. Every generation since has tried to find the treasure. My dad said it's the Wilder's loudest call and our greatest downfall." He wasn't kidding.

Lucas shakes his head, staring down at the packed, red-tinted earth beneath our feet. I look up, shielding my eyes from the sun as I survey where we are. I'd gotten lost in the story and hadn't been paying attention for a while. I spot the tree in the distance and head that way. I often asked Dad if we should move the safe, but as you might expect, he didn't trust a whole lot of people. Even a bank. My family has deep-seated trust issues that go back to that guy trying to steal what was ours. We've been distrusting ever since. I always imagined it got worse with every generation, which was why my father is the way he is. A paranoid recluse.

He was okay if the secret died between us. I asked him what would happen to the treasure if something happened and we were killed together. He told me it would stay in those caves where it belonged. In my dad's mind, no one was bringing out that treasure but a Wilder. He was okay with our secrets lying to waste in the desert if something happened to our bloodline.

A curdling chill runs up my spine. I can't tell you how many times I've wondered if I'm the last Wilder alive. That's a pressure I can't even begin to describe. A lot of weight pressing down on these shoulders, that's for sure. My father even made me promise I'd have kids someday. Insurance, he called it. Just in case we never found it that we gave another generation of Wilders a chance.

Thinking back on some of the things I've believed all my life, it sounds fucking crazy.

Either way, I'm in our acres of acres of land with a shovel in my hand, so obviously I don't think it's that crazy.

Before we get there, I peer around like my father used to do a thousand times as we approached the hiding spot. We live so far outside the city and we're so far back from the road that I thought he was just being his paranoid self, but now that these secrets are mine to guard, I feel the same amount of pressure to keep them hidden. The coast looks clear. In this spot, you could see people coming from far away in all directions.

I head to the tree and lean the shovel against it, then I prop my hands on my hips and face the guys. "What's in this safe has never been shown to anyone outside the Wilder family."

"We're here for you," Lucas says.

I give him a small smile. "That's cute, but I just want to say one thing. If you double-cross me, not only will I sue you for that huge amount Stone put in that contract, but I'll also hunt you down and personally castrate all three of you with the biggest smile you've ever seen on my face while I do it. I will enjoy it. I will do it slowly, painfully. I will—"

"Christ, am I supposed to be turned on at this point?" Wyatt asks.

I glare at him.

He holds his hands up. "I get it. If I talk, no cock."

I go to say something smart, but I'm pushed against the tree, Stone's hard gaze on me. His chest heaves as he presses against the length of my body. Before I know it, he's on me. His lips claim mine, forcing my mouth open with a swoop of his tongue. He pushes and pushes, diving in and out, mesmerizing my lips until they're buzzing, feeling like they've been at war and bruised, but also like they enjoyed the fuck out of it. When he pulls away, he says, "I know what you're doing for us. I intend to never make you regret this for the rest of your life, Dakota Wilder."

I stand there stupidly. While he's promising me things I never thought to ask for, my mind takes a much dirtier path. He steps away, and my body immediately screams for him. I want to tell it to stop overreacting, but the truth is, I felt that kiss all the way to my soul.

With Stone, the intensity of my feelings are scary.

It's either I hate him so much I hope he drowns in a two-inch puddle. Or I want to run off into the sunset on his arm with a life growing inside me. There's no happy medium.

I press my fingers to my lips, the ghost of his touch still there. He'll be imprinted on me always now.

Fuck.

Stone picks up the shovel. "Just point me where."

I guess at this point, it would be inappropriate to point where I want him most. And that has nothing to do with digging in the dirt.

33

*B*efore I can point out the spot within three paces of the tree where the safe is buried five feet under the earth, the ground underneath my feet rumbles at the same time an explosion roars its way through the landscape. I whip around in time to see a fireball rise up from where my family's house would be.

"What the fuck?" I stagger back as the impact of what's happened hits me. Rubble from the explosion falls back down to the earth.

My house. My father's house. My memories. I run forward, needing to see it for myself. The guys call out behind me, but I don't stop. My feet kick up dirt all around me as I run as fast as I can back toward the house. Flames flicker just over the little knoll, reaching up toward the sun as if we needed another source of heat in this godforsaken place.

Hands capture me from behind, and I struggle to get out of them. Up ahead, an ATV roars over the little knoll, catches air, and lands in a plume of dust. Two more ATV's follow while Stone loosens his grip on me. We start to move backwards until Wyatt and Lucas flank us.

My flight response kicks in but there's nowhere for us to go. All there is are miles and miles of the same terrain. There's no place to take cover. Nothing to hide in or behind. Whoever these guys are would find us in a heartbeat.

"Fuck," Lucas growls. He stands next to me, his shoulder heaving against mine as the ATV's surround us.

I almost fall flat on my ass when I recognize Lance Jacobs. The dust plume hides his face for a moment but when he gets out, I growl on instinct.

"Thanks, son," Lance says, smiling at Stone.

I turn toward Stone, my stomach bottoming out. A physical pain hits me in the chest. His mouth drops, but I'm not falling for it. What was that kiss for anyway? Just something to distract me?

They've used me.

Other men dressed in suits get out of ATV's, all

driven by people I wouldn't think these rich bastards would even give the time of day. The separation between them is apparent. Three of the guys, including Lance, look like they just stepped out of the country club while their drivers sport tattoos peeking out of rolled-up sleeves and shorts that hang low on their asses, boxers peeking through. Thugs, basically. If it weren't for the smiles on all the rich guys' faces, I'd think we were in some sort of hostage situation.

"I told you we would get to the bottom of everything," Lance says, smiling at the guy who drove his ATV. The guy doesn't grin back. In fact, he looks scary as fuck. He has flame tattoos peeking out of his shirt collar, a five o'clock shadow that adds to his danger factor, and a presence that chills me to my bones.

And I thought Stone Jacobs had a look. This one is danger personified. That little niggle of intuition shivers up my spine. He may look years younger than Lance Jacobs. He may look like he belongs in juvenile detention with the earrings adorning his ears rather than driving an ATV for a rich dude, but he's the biggest threat in this scenario. I can feel it.

Lance Jacobs is his bitch.

"Dad," Stone says, gritting his teeth.

Lance shakes his head. "I let you play out this little scenario for too long."

A rumble comes from Stone's chest, but it cuts off as the other two thugs produce guns from somewhere on them. They hold them down next to their thighs, but just the fact that they have them makes fear skitter through me. I take a step back and hit Lucas's hard body.

Lance smirks as he looks around. The line in his jaw feathers, but he laughs it off. "It's good to have backup," he shrugs. "But the guns won't be necessary. Dakota Wilder is going to tell us where her father's important papers are, aren't you, Dakota?"

I clamp down on my jaw as the two gunmen lift their guns, aiming them right at me. My stomach bottoms out, and a cold shiver leaves me standing there, isolated. Wyatt pushes forward, profanities spilling into the air as he moves in front of me. One of the guys moves, aiming the gun toward him, and fires.

The sound is deafening, cutting through everything, and silencing us in a single heartbeat. The crack ricochets through me, and I gasp. Lucas puts his arm around Wyatt's waist like a protective band, still holding him back. I almost fall to the ground in relief to see them both standing there. *Jesus. He shot at him!* Wyatt, instead of slinking back into place, looks like he wants to throttle the guy for daring to pull the trigger, but he lets Lucas hold him back.

"Now that we have your attention," the leader says.

No kidding. Whoever these guys are, they mean business.

The leader gleams at me, a sparkle in his eye like he gets off on doing this. He bows. "Dakota. I hope you've gotten my letters."

My gaze darts around the men in front of me. The other two rich snobs have twin looks of scared shitless with an armor of puffed-up chests, telling me they want to think they're in control, but they're really not. If Lance wasn't such a good actor, he'd look the same. These wealthy fucks are in way over their heads. They know boardrooms and business deals, but these other three, there's something way more sinister about them. They're not afraid to shed blood.

"That was you?" I ask, trying to bide us time until we figure out what to do. What the hell am I saying, I'm trying to bide myself time. Stone double-crossed me. My gut wrenches, but I focus back on what we're dealing with now. There's no way on God's green earth I'm telling these hoodlums the exact location of my father's safe.

"I know I'm not the best poet, but I hear girls like letters." He gleams at me, the earrings in his ears catching on the Arizona sun and sparkling. A sickening feeling rolls over me like a riptide.

I shrug. "I'm not like most girls."

He chuckles, and it somehow sounds more menacing than his regular voice which definitely has the creep factor anyway. "I've been watching you," he says, moving closer. He shakes his head as if he almost doesn't believe what he's going to say next. "I like you."

Stone and Lucas close ranks around me as the guy approaches. I wish I could push Stone away, send him sprawling to his knees where he belongs. After everything he said. After everything he promised.

"Settle down, boys," the thug says derisively. "I'm not going to hurt Dakota. We won't hurt anyone as long as we get to leave here with what we want."

"And what's that?" I ask, already knowing that what they want, I'm not willing to give them.

The guy is close enough that I can smell his aftershave. His hair is shaved down to a buzzcut. He'd look almost military if he also didn't look as rough around the edges as he could get. He's the type who's hiding a few knives—and probably guns—and knows how to use them. In fact, he might actually be good looking if he wasn't so scary. When he grins, I expect his incisors to be shaved down to fangs, but they aren't. He shows me a perfect set of white teeth.

He lifts his hand. Tattoos start there and run up the length of his chiseled arm, disappearing under the sleeve of his shirt and reappearing in flames just above his collar. They reach up his neck, and as he moves, they look alive, flexing with his skin. I shy away as his fingers graze my face, but that only makes him smile wider, so I stand my ground. He brushes his fingers over my cheek. Wyatt curses again, colorful language filling the air around us until he leaps for the guy. One of the leader's goons intercepts, holding his gun right in Wyatt's face.

Fuck. The guy wouldn't accidentally miss if he pulled the trigger this close, and these guys don't look like they give more than one warning shot.

"It's fine," I say, hoping to calm Wyatt, but even I hear the waver in my voice. I'm practically shaking all over, adrenaline coursing through me with a healthy dose of unease picking at me. Five minutes ago, I was praising the fact that Wyatt, Stone, and Lucas had come into my life. But I wasn't in danger before them, was I? Now look what they dragged me into.

Maybe a boring life is better than a fear-filled one.

"That's right," the guy says, voice suspiciously soft. "It's fine. Now, I just need you to show me wherever this thing is that I need."

"What thing?"

He grins, and this time, he bares his teeth. "Are you

expecting me to believe you guys are just out here for a walk...with a shovel?"

"You never know what you might want to dig up," I say, my hands turning to fists at my sides. My father's words echo through me. *No one but a Wilder deserves to find the treasure. No one but a Wilder.*

"Don't play me, Dakota," the guy says, trailing his knuckles down my cheeks once again. His voice is laced with irritation this time. The veins on his neck stick out as his jaw tightens. He's slowly losing patience, and we definitely don't want that.

Think, think...

"She needs incentive, boss," one of his goons says.

Tattooed guy in front of me cocks his head. "Do you need incentive?"

"Need incentive for what? I don't even know what you're talking about."

"Dad," Stone growls, shooting a look toward his father.

"Shut up," Lance spits. He watches the situation with a devilish grin, eyes gleaming.

The rich fuckers have congregated behind the thugs now. This is what Stone meant when he said his father was in over his head, I'm sure of it. What he failed to explain was that his father was also trying to help them at the same time too. I guess that's what people like the Jacobs are all about. Saving their own asses.

Wow, I'm so fucking naive. I might as well be holding a sign that says, *Use me because I'm fucking oblivious.*

The leader nods, and my stomach clenches. The thug next to Wyatt moves forward. Anticipating his move, Wyatt ducks in under the butt of his gun and slams his shoulder into the guy's midsection. The goon growls, an angry red spreading over his cheeks. They wrestle to the ground, each punching the other. Stone and Lucas move to help their friend, but the other guy with the gun pushes the barrel to my forehead. "Move and she dies."

The metal is warm, and I close my eyes, my heart in my throat. The guys freeze right where they are. My heart gallops in my chest as the two guys wrestling on the desert floor beat each other to a pulp. Wyatt moves with a barbaric intensity that curls my toes. He's like a monster, giving as good as he gets. The leader watches on in approval, not jumping in to stop the flying fists and kicks or trying to end it sooner than it should.

It isn't until Wyatt's opponent pulls out a knife that I freak out. "No!"

It's too late. He stabs Wyatt in the side. When Wyatt slumps forward, he throws his body off him and gets to his feet, dusting the dirt off his clothes. Wyatt moans like a wounded animal, holding his hand over his fresh wound. Blood seeps through his fingers, soaking his shirt. The circle grows and grows.

Panic sets in. I run over to Wyatt. "Shit. Shit. Are you okay?"

He grins, showing off blood-stained teeth. "Don't tell them where it is," he says through clenched teeth. "Don't do it."

The same guy he wrestled with yanks me back by the hair. Pain flares over my scalp. He wipes at his nose, blood smearing across his knuckles as I struggle against his hold.

"Hey, hey," the leader says, throwing the guy's hands off me. I stumble back, and he catches me. He roams his gaze over my head before running his hands down my curls. "I read somewhere that curls were a sign of an angelic nature."

"The Wilder girl is a savage," Lance barks from behind us.

The leader's face melts. A cruel smile tilts his lips before he turns, punching Lance in the face with a sickening crunch. "Where I come from, we treat women with respect."

My burning scalp would disagree.

Lance lifts his hand to hold over his mouth. Instead

of glaring at the guy who hit him, he glares at me, spitting blood out onto the floor between us.

The leader runs his hands over his buzzcut, cracking his neck as he turns back to me. "Before this gets too far, baby girl, you're going to have to give me the location of whatever you have hidden."

Since I don't have a better plan yet, everything in me tells me to deny, deny, deny. "I don't have anything hidden."

The same dark eyes that just turned on Lance freeze me in place. My heart pumps wildly, but I move my chin into the air in defiance. The information in that safe is all my family has. It's our legacy. I can't just give it to anyone.

"My interest in you only goes so far. You should remember that. But since you want to play this game, I'll play." He nods toward one of his friends who wastes no time kicking Lucas in the shin, dropping him to his knees. He reaches over and grabs Lucas's brown hair, shoving his face into the sand before holding the gun to his head. A shot goes off, and I scream. Blood-curdling fear rips through me. I step toward Lucas, but the leader grabs me by the waist, hauling me back into his arms. "That was a warning shot," he growls. "Don't play me, Dakota. Not many live to tell about it."

My heart jumpstarts back to life when Lucas

moves, grabbing his ear and hissing in a breath. I close my eyes, my breath coming in shallow gasps. Tears prick my eyes.

"Tell my friends where to dig."

My mind races. Am I willing to let us all die to keep my family's secrets? My father was. He told me he didn't care if we died, at least the information was only left for a Wilder.

Fuck.

"I get it," the guy purrs in my ear, still caging me to him. The vein in Stone's forehead looks like it's going to burst as he stands there, watching the guy manhandle me. "You're wondering if we're serious." He releases one arm around my middle, using it to reach behind him. He's so close I can feel his lips tug up, but I just stare at Stone. "I think you know someone named Dickie."

He thrusts his hand in front of me. I peer down at what's in his grasp. I gasp when a photo of a bloodied Dickie stares back at me. "What did you do to him?" I cry, sobs racking me now.

I reach for it, but he removes the picture before I can even trace over the outline of Dickie's bloodied body. I can't tell if he's dead or if he's just beat to shit.

"Apparently, your father told him he had some-thing more. Something he never shared with him. I hoped he had so we wouldn't have to make this about you, but you can thank Lance Jacobs that you got pulled into this." He moves even closer, his hot breath hitting my ear as he whispers. "He's a piece of scum, but he's good for some things."

"He's vile," I growl.

"And unfortunately, I don't even think you know the half of it, baby girl."

Goosebumps spread over my arms at his nickname. It makes me feel cheap, but even then, it's not as worse as Stone's betrayal. To think I'd begun to trust him.

"Get your hands off her," Stone demands, gritting the words through his teeth while he just stands there.

The leader smirks again, the movement plastered against my cheek. I can feel the prick of his earrings pressing into my skin and the scruff of his facial hair against my cheek. "You sound jealous, Baby Jacobs, but aren't you her stepbrother? That's some kinky shit right there." He chuckles like he doesn't not approve.

"Where's my mother?" Stone demands, ignoring the leader's jab.

"How should I know?" the guy answers, but even I don't believe the tone of his voice. It sounds like the punchline of a joke no one asked him to tell. "Pick up that shovel," he directs Stone. "Dakota here is going to tell you where to dig."

Stone crosses his arms over his chest. "No, she's not."

I glare at him, looking him up and down as he just stands there even though his words are defiant. His gray blue eyes are sharp as he glares at the guy holding me, but he's also quick to look at his father.

Lance roars, striding across the desert floor to curse in his son's face. Blood is smeared over his lips like some sort of gothic lipstick. His vitriol is chilling, even more so when you realize it's being directed at his own flesh and blood. Father and son equal each other in height and stature. They're an imposing duo standing right next to each other. The same narcissistic blood running through their veins.

What a great show. That's all I can think. The pair of them are two peas in a pod.

"I can't tell Jacobs where to dig..." I say coolly. "...because the information is in me." I shrug, which is hard to do, considering the guy still has a death grip on me. "Do you think I'm dumb enough to actually bring these assholes out here to give them my father's lifelong work?" I laugh into the air, letting everything I feel about the Jacobs right now come out. They're twisted and deviant. And I can't believe I fell for it.

Finally, the leader lets me go. I step away, rearranging my clothes back on myself just as I've seen

Stone do a hundred times before when he's trying to pull himself together. "My father wasn't an imbecile like Lance Jacobs would have you believe. He didn't write shit down. The important shit is in my head." Truth, actually. Only the Wilders know the one thing that could break the treasure hunt wide open. Sure, we've never been close enough to utilize the piece of information yet, but no one will find it without one of us. No one. "If you want it, you're just going to have to take me, but I wouldn't unless you think you can make me talk."

"People always talk," the leader says, grinning.

"How about someone with nothing to lose? You say you've been watching me? Then you see where I live. You see the fact that I have no fucking friends and that my father is missing, most likely dead. People talk because they're threatened with losing something. Well, good luck finding something to get me with, asshole."

The guy straight up laughs, eyes sparking. "I recognize you in me. I admit, you have spirit, Dakota Wilder. But you've already shown your hand. Your weaknesses are these three."

I give him a dead glare, my heart pumping inside me. "You can test that theory if you want but you'll be sorely disappointed." I glare at Stone because he's the only one I can muster up the strength to hate as much as I used to right now. "Let me ask you a question instead. What are you going to do with the information when you get it? Are you going to trek up into the mountains yourself to get the very same treasure that has eluded my family for the past hundred years? Are you going to hand the job over to the Jacobs?" I laugh, mimicking his menacing style, which really doesn't take all that much acting. It is funny to think that the Jacobs would ever find the treasure before me. "I assure you they're all talk and no skill. Lance, as you've already clearly figured out, is a waste of space. He may as well live out the rest of his days as an ATM."

"You little bitch."

Lance takes a menacing step toward me, but the leader lifts his hand, silencing the toxic fuck. "How can I trust that you'll do what you say you're going to?"

Hope builds inside me. I may be able to get out of this after all. "I guess the question is how much do you trust yourself to keep watching me?"

A vile smile peels his lips apart. The danger in his eyes bleeds through his very being. "The Jacobs underestimated you."

"Everyone does." It's not smart to make a deal with this guy, but right now, all I want is to bide myself some time and find out how to keep my family's legacy safe from assholes like these guys. And yeah, not dying would be cool too.

"The thing is, baby girl," the leader starts. "Where I'm from, when we strike deals, we give something up." Amusement flickers in his gaze.

Shit. I thought I almost had him. Nervous energy pours through me, but I've already come this far. What's the big deal about striking an even bigger deal with an even badder devil?

I swallow. "Like what?"

"A freedom, usually. An innocence. Or a thing, something that you love. It'll be tricky with you because you say you don't love anything." He turns in a circle, taking in the scenario. "I think you're full of shit on that, but I'm willing to let you play that little scenario out for now because it suits me."

"So?" I ask, lifting a brow, my head thundering.

He gives me a cocksure smile. "So, you'll give up a freedom."

He's intentionally being vague, and I want to tell him to get on with it already, but I'm assuming he likes this part the best. The part where he gets to dangle the marionette strings over us. He can do it all he wants as long as my family's legacy stays safe, and hopefully, the rest of us too. "You'll have to explain that one to me."

He pulls a gun from the waistband of his pants and

holds it in front of him. "You have to prove your willingness to team up with us. In doing so, you give up a little piece of yourself and place it in our hands where we'll keep it nice and safe...or don't," he says, shrugging. "It all depends on what you choose."

I stare at the black handgun swaying from his fingers. My father taught me how to shoot when we were in the mountains. After we would make camp, we used to set up target practice, listening to the gun fire echoing around us.

"We'll agree to leave you alone for now if you put a bullet in...Lance Jacobs."

I gaze over my shoulder to watch the color drain from Lance's face. "The fuck? That's not what we agreed to. I'll kill you for this. I'll—"

"Soon, Dakota," the leader says. "If I have to listen to the words coming out of his mouth for much longer, the deal is gone, and you'll wish you were dead."

"I've never—"

"Take the gun," he roars.

I take it, feeling the weight of it in my hands. I stumble with it on purpose. I don't want him to know I've used one of these before. Sometimes, it's best to hold all your cards close to the vest.

"Dakota," Stone says, voice unsure. He swallows, and the Adam's apple bobs in his throat.

His low tone pierces my gut, but I block it out. He brought his father here. I owe him nothing, and I owe his father even less than that. "It's the only way," I say, looking away. There's something in his eyes that could make me change my mind, and I'm not going to do that. This is what will save us all right now. Unless I've completely read the situation wrong.

"Dakota," Stone urges.

Lance prowls forward, gazing from me to the gun. "You little bitch."

I raise the barrel, aiming it square in his chest.

He still strides toward me, face angry. He doesn't think I'm going to do it. He calls me every twisted name in the book. Whore. Slut. Cunt. Freak.

I peek at Wyatt, who's still clutching his side. He's white as a sheet, cringing, blood still pooling over his fingers. Lucas's face is still smashed in the dirt. His keeper has a booted foot on the back of his neck, holding him there no matter how hard he struggles. While I watch, he nudges the barrel of the gun into Lucas's head.

Lance is almost to me now. I line up my shot and take the safety off. His eyes round for a fraction of a second, the disgusting words he's shouting at me die on his lips as I pull the trigger.

I had no other choice.

The gunfire doesn't echo like I remember. It pierces my ears for a brief moment before it's carried away on the wind.

Lance slumps to the ground. I watch his body hit, but nothing comes over me. Not remorse. Not anger. Not even satisfaction.

The leader steps into my view, holding his hand out for the gun. I hand it over, and he grins. "It'll be nice working with you, Dakota Wilder. I'm Cole." His grin stays as he pockets the gun, but then it slips from his face as he reaches to the collar of his shirt, yanking it down to reveal a dragon. Flames shoot from its open mouth, leaping up Cole's neck. "You're now the property of the Dragons. We'll be in touch."

Cole moves out of my line of sight, his two friends trailing him to the ATV's. But all I can focus on is Stone. He leans over his father's body as bright red blood spills from the hole I made.

Calm washes over me. I guess I really am a Wilder now.

Treasure above everything else.

About the Author

E. M. Moore is a USA Today Bestselling author of Contemporary and Paranormal Romance. She's drawn to write within the teen and college-aged years where her characters get knocked on their asses, torn inside out, and put back together again by their first loves. Whether it's in a fantastical setting where human guards protect the creatures of the night or a realistic high school backdrop where social cliques rule the halls, the emotions are the same. Dark. Twisty. Angsty. Raw.

When Erin's not writing, you can find her dreaming up vacations for her family, watching murder mystery shows, or dancing in her kitchen while she pretends to cook.

Printed in Great Britain
by Amazon